The sensation of being watched was uncomfortable

Annja had experienced such things before. Women generally did. Usually it was better to just ignore things like that, but Annja was aware that she no longer lived in a *usually* world.

A figure stood at the window, and he was staring at her. Gaunt and dressed in rags, the old man looked more like a scarecrow than a human being. A ragged beard clung to his pointed chin. His hat had flaps that covered his ears and gave his face a pinched look. His eyes were beady and sharp, mired in pits of wrinkles and prominent bone.

He lifted a hand covered in a glove with the fingers cut off. His dirty forefinger pointed directly at Annja, and even from across the room, she read his lips.

"Annja Creed."

A chill ghosted through her. How did the man know her name?

"Annja Creed," the old man said. "The world is going to end. Soon."

Titles in this series:

Destiny
Solomon's Jar
The Spider Stone
The Chosen
Forbidden City
The Lost Scrolls
God of Thunder
Secret of the Slaves
Warrior Spirit
Serpent's Kiss
Provenance
The Soul Stealer
Gabriel's Horn

ROGUE ANGEL™

Alex Archer

GABRIEL'S HORN

A GOLD EAGLE BOOK FROM

W✺RLDWIDE®

TORONTO • NEW YORK • LONDON
AMSTERDAM • PARIS • SYDNEY • HAMBURG
STOCKHOLM • ATHENS • TOKYO • MILAN
MADRID • WARSAW • BUDAPEST • AUCKLAND

First edition July 2008

ISBN-13: 978-0-373-62131-6
ISBN-10: 0-373-62131-0

GABRIEL'S HORN

Special thanks and acknowledgment to
Mel Odom for his contribution to this work.

Printed in U.S.A.

The
LEGEND

...THE ENGLISH COMMANDER TOOK
JOAN'S SWORD AND RAISED IT HIGH.

The broadsword, plain and unadorned,
gleamed in the firelight. He put the tip against
the ground and his foot at the center of the blade.
The broadsword shattered, fragments falling
into the mud. The crowd surged forward,
peasant and soldier, and snatched the shards
from the trampled mud. The commander tossed
the hilt deep into the crowd.
Smoke almost obscured Joan, but she continued
praying till the end, until finally the flames climbed
her body and she sagged against the restraints.

Joan of Arc died that fateful day in France,
but her legend and sword are reborn....

1

Prague, Czech Republic

"He's going to catch fire when the motorcycle hits the back of the overturned car?" Annja Creed asked in disbelief.

"Yeah. But the real trick is *when* he catches fire." Barney Yellowtail calmly surveyed the wrecked cars in the middle of the narrow street between a line of four-story buildings that had seen far better days.

"When?" Annja asked, still trying to grasp the whole idea.

"When is important," Barney continued. He was in his late forties, twenty years older than Annja, and had been a stuntman for almost thirty years. "If Roy catches on fire too late, we've hosed the gag."

Gags, Annja had learned, were what stunt people called the death-defying feats they did almost on a daily basis.

"And if you hose the gag," Annja said, "you have to do it over and risk Roy's life again."

Barney grinned. He claimed to be full-blood Choctaw Indian from Oklahoma and looked it. His face was dark and seamed, creased by a couple of scars under his left eye and under his right jawline. He wore rimless glasses that darkened in the bright sunlight, and a straw cowboy hat. His jeans and chambray work shirt were carefully pressed. His boots were hand-tooled brown-and-white leather that Annja thought were to die for.

Annja was five feet ten inches tall with chestnut hair and amber-green eyes. She had an athlete's build with smooth, rounded muscle. She wore khaki pants, hiking boots, a light-weight white cotton tank under a robin's-egg-blue blouse, wraparound blue sunglasses and an Australian Colly hat that she'd developed a fondness for to block the sun.

"That's not the worst part," Barney assured her.

"That's not the worst part?" Annja echoed.

"Naw," Barney replied, smiling wide enough to show a row of perfect teeth. "The worst part is that the director will be mad."

"Oh."

Barney looked at her as if sensing that she wasn't com-pletely convinced. "Mad directors mean slow checks. They also mean slow work. If you can't hit your marks on a gag, especially on a film that Spielberg's underwriting, your phone isn't going to ring very often."

Annja wondered if you had to be certifiable to be a stuntman.

"C'mon, Annja," Barney said. "I've read about you in the magazines, seen you on Letterman and kept up with what you're doing on *Chasing History's Monsters*. You know life isn't worth living without a little risk."

Annja knew her life hadn't exactly been risk free. Actually, especially lately, it seemed to go the other way. As a working archaeologist, she'd traveled to a number of dangerous places, and those places were starting to multiply dramatically as she became more recognized.

She thought about her job at *Chasing History's Monsters.* Most days she wasn't sure if it was a blessing or a curse. The syndicated show had high enough ratings that the producers could send Annja a number of places that she couldn't have afforded on her own.

The drawback was that the stories she was asked to cover—historical madmen, psychopaths, serial killers and even legendary monsters—were usually less than stellar. Fans of the show couldn't get enough of her, but some of the people in her field of archaeology had grown somewhat leery.

None of that, though, had come without risk.

"Okay," Annja admitted. "I'll give you that. But I've never set myself on fire."

"Roy's not going to set himself on fire," Barney said. "I'm going to do that for him."

"Oh."

"It's just that timing is critical." Barney stepped to one side as his cell phone rang. "Excuse me."

Annja nodded and surveyed the street. The film crew had barricaded three city blocks in Prague's Old Town. A few streets over, the Vltava River coursed slowly by and carried the river traffic to various destinations.

Prague was a new experience for Annja, and she was thoroughly enjoying it. Getting the job on the movie had been as unexpected as it was welcome. She'd done a bit of work with props before, but never on a motion picture of this magnitude.

Kill Me Deadly was a new spy romp that was part James Bond and part Jason Bourne. The hero even carried the same J.B. initials—Jet Bard.

Annja hadn't quite understood the plot because a lot of the

details were still under wraps. She was of the impression some of them were still being worked out, which was causing extra stress on the set.

Three cars occupied the middle of the street. Two of them were overturned. All of them were black from where they'd been burned. The stuntman was supposed to hit the upright car, catch on fire and turn into a human comet streaking across the sky.

When Annja had heard about the stunt and had received an invitation from Barney to attend, she'd thought about gracefully declining. Then she'd found she couldn't stay away.

Now her stomach knotted in anticipation. She'd gotten to know the young daredevil who was about to become a human fireball. He was a nice guy and she didn't like the idea that something bad might happen to him.

"Okay," Barney said as he stepped back to rejoin her. His gaze remained on the street while he adjusted his headset. "I'm going to need you to stay quiet for a moment, Annja."

"Sure." Annja gazed down the street anxiously.

Camera operators lined the street from various points of view. All of them remained out of each other's line of sight. The crews had worked on the setup for hours. Before that, they'd measured and mapped the distances on a model of the street and the cars.

According to the computer programs Barney and the other stunt people had run, everything would go fine. To Annja, it was a lot like exploring a dig site she'd read about. Even though she knew the background and the general layout, there were far too many surprises involved to guarantee everything was safe. Some of the early Egyptian-tomb explorers had quickly discovered that.

"On your go," Barney said softly. He held up an electronic control box in both hands. "I'm with you." He flicked a switch.

Immediately a half-dozen fires flamed to life within the pile of wrecked cars. They burned cheerily and black smoke twisted on the breeze.

"We've got fire in the hole, Roy," Barney declared.

The throb of the motorcycle's engine rumbled into Annja's ears. She watched with a mixture of dread and anticipation. Roy Fein was one of the top stuntmen in the game. Barney had said that a number of times over the past few days. She didn't know if he'd been trying to reassure her or himself.

"Steady," Barney said. "Okay, you're on track. Now increase your speed to seventy-eight miles per hour."

The exact speed had been a big concern, Annja knew. Too much and the impact angle would be wrong and the motorcycle might flip end over end. Too little and Roy would fall short of the air bag that waited at the other end of the jump.

The motorcycle roared into view. Roy Fein, dressed in dark blue racing leathers and a matching helmet, had raced around the corner. A car followed only inches behind him.

"You're on," Barney said. "Hit the Volkswagen and I'm going to light you up."

At that moment, the pursuit car slowed and slewed sideways. Actors inside the vehicle leaned out the windows and fired weapons.

"I got you, kid. I got you." Barney's voice was soft and reassuring. "Get that fire-suppression unit ready."

The motorcycle rider popped a slight wheelie just before he hit the Volkswagen. Effortlessly, the motorcycle climbed the specially altered vehicle.

"Now," Barney said. His finger flipped one of the switches on the electronics box.

Immediately, the motorcycle and rider were enveloped in flames. But something was wrong. Instead of arcing gracefully across the distance, the motorcycle went awry.

"Kick loose, kid!" Barney yelled. "Lose the bike!" He dropped the electronics box and ran toward the street.

Roy pushed free of the motorcycle and spread-eagled in the air like Superman. But he wasn't flying—he was falling. Flames twisted and whipped around his body. He threw his arms out and tried to adjust his fall as gravity took over and brought him back toward the pavement.

Annja ran after Barney, though she didn't know what she was going to do. There was no way she could help Roy. But she couldn't just stand there, either.

The motorcycle spun crazily, nowhere near the trajectory it was supposed to maintain to get near the air bag designed to break Roy's fall. Then it blew up.

The force slammed Annja to the ground. She tucked into a roll and came to her feet instinctively. Slightly disoriented, she glanced up to see where the flaming pieces of the motorcycle were coming down. She saw Barney was on his side. His face was twisted in agony as he reached toward a bloody gash soaking his shirt.

Annja went toward him. She yelled for help, but couldn't hear her own voice. She tried again. Her ears felt numb, then she realized she was deaf.

She dropped beside Barney and surveyed the wound. An irregular furrow ran along his ribs. She tried to tell him that he was going to be all right but knew that he couldn't hear her, either. She yanked his shirt from his pants and rolled the tails up to his wound, then leaned on the folds to put pressure on the wound in his side.

One of the other stunt coordinators joined Annja and

dropped to his knees. His mouth was moving. She knew he was shouting something. He was young, tall and gangly, and he was in shock.

Annja grabbed one of his hands and directed him to take hold of the makeshift pressure bandage she'd created. For a moment he froze. With authority, Annja caught his face in her palms. She met his eyes with hers and struggled to remember his name.

"Tony," she said. "It's Tony, right?" She couldn't hear herself.

"I can't hear you," he said.

Annja read his lips. "It's okay," she told him. "Your hearing will come back." She hoped that was true.

Sirens, muted and faraway sounding, reached her and gave her hope that her hearing hadn't been permanently destroyed.

Tony nodded, but he didn't look any less scared.

"He's hurt," Annja told Tony. "Hold the pressure on the wound. Like this." She guided his hands.

"Okay," he said. "I got it."

"I'm going to look for a first-aid kit," Annja shouted.

Tony nodded and held on to the rolled-up shirt.

Annja got up. Her legs were shaky. She felt her phone vibrate in her pants pocket. Still on the move, she took the phone out and glanced at the number. She'd been expecting a call from Garin Braden, but the call was from New York. It was from Doug Morrell, her producer on *Chasing History's Monsters*.

She switched the phone off and returned it to her pocket. With her hearing compromised, the last thing she needed was a phone call.

Burning debris from the motorcycle littered the immediate vicinity. Annja looked for Roy Fein's body, knowing that he might not have survived the fall and the flames. Fire-suppression teams worked the air bag's surface. White flame-retardant foam coated the bag and made it slippery.

Some of Annja's tension drained away when she realized Roy had made it to the air bag. Then she saw him moving. The distinctive motorcycle leathers bore scorch marks and charring, but he was standing on his own two feet.

All along the street, the set teams hustled to the site. Even with all the wreckage they'd seen and helped produce for the movies, the shooting teams weren't prepared for the damage they saw now.

Without warning, another detonation occurred and the three stunt cars erupted in flames.

The force of the explosion blew Annja from her feet and rolled her away. A wave of heat washed over her back. Stunned, she lay still for a moment and checked the sidewalk around her for shadows of falling debris.

A dark mass centered over her as if she lay under a solar eclipse. She pushed her right hand against the street and rolled to her left. She barely made out the twisted wreckage of a burning car falling toward her.

2

The clangor of the mass of flaming metal striking the street jarred Annja and filled her head with noise. She lay still and stared at the debris that had barely missed her.

In that same moment, she spotted movement on top of one of the nearby buildings.

Three men stood atop the building. One held a box that looked similar to the one Barney had used. He pointed at Annja and spoke to his companions.

Another man drew a pistol from under his jacket and pointed it in Annja's direction. She rolled to her feet and ran toward the building because it offered quick cover.

The third man slapped the second man's arm down and the bullet fired into the rooftop. The sharp crack of the report barely registered in Annja's hearing. She lost sight of the men as she ran into the alley.

When she spotted the skeletal fire escape tracking back and forth across the side of the building, she ran for it, leaped to catch hold of the lower rung and swung herself up like a gymnast. She raced through the ladders and landings as she pushed herself to reach the top.

The panorama of the red-tiled roofs that filled the city spread in all directions. The silvery shine of the river snaked through the heart of Prague.

Forcing herself to remain calm, Annja turned slowly. Thoughts of the pistol the man had been only too willing to use were foremost in her mind. She'd only been in Prague for a few days. She didn't know anyone there who wanted to kill her.

The keening wail of the sirens drew closer.

From the corner of her eye, she glimpsed the three men running across the next building. Annja launched herself in pursuit. She drove her legs hard and reached the building's edge in a dozen strides. By that time she was up to speed.

A narrow gulf nearly three stories deep loomed before her. She never slackened her effort. Her left foot landed on the building's edge and she propelled herself over the intervening distance.

Almost immediately she knew she hadn't jumped high enough. She had the distance covered easily, but she dropped too quickly. Desperate, she threw her arms out and slammed against the other building with enough force to knock the wind from her lungs.

Her fingers curled as she slid down, then caught the lip of the roof. She pushed her hiking boots against the stone wall and found purchase. When she climbed up, she started to run again.

The men she pursued remained a building ahead of her. Concentrating, she found her rhythm. She leaped the next alley, landed and didn't miss a stride. The distance between her and the three men was shrinking.

Ahead of her, the three men turned and looked back. The

man with the pistol stopped suddenly and whirled around with the weapon before him. A green tattoo of a curved sword covered the hollow of his throat.

A quick step to the side put Annja out of range of the first bullet. The second chopped into the roof where she'd been. By that time she had taken cover behind a chimney. She felt the vibrations of bullets squarely striking it.

Were the men going to continue to flee? Or were they going to come back to finish the job? Especially since she'd cut herself off from possible help.

You really need to stop and think some of these things through before you do them, she chided herself. The problem with that was there generally wasn't much time for thinking when something like this happened.

And information—any information—was better than no information. She wanted to know who the men were and why they'd tried to kill her.

She was sure they'd been there to kill her, not anyone connected with the movie.

Squatting down, her breath still coming smoothly in spite of her exertion, Annja reached for her sword. She felt it with her hand and drew it forth from the otherwhere.

The sword was a part of her life she was still struggling to understand. She set herself, arms bent at the elbow, balancing the sword straight up in front of her.

Her hearing was still muffled so Annja watched for moving shadows to either side of her. It was late enough in the afternoon that the shadows would be long, but they wouldn't be bent toward her since the men were south of her position. She also paid attention to the vibrations throbbing through the rooftop.

Three more rounds slammed into the chimney. Stone chips sprayed the rooftop. After a moment, Annja glanced around the chimney and saw the men fleeing. She sped after them with the sword in her hand.

After leaping to the next building, she made it to the fire escape before they could reach the ground. The man with the pistol leaned out from the second-floor landing and fired several shots.

Annja dodged back just in time for the shots to miss her. The bullets ripped along the low brick wall in front of her and tore through the air. She reversed her grip on the sword, stepped along the wall four paces and leaned out again.

The man stood farther down the stairs, almost to the ground.

As the man turned toward her and froze in his position, Annja whipped the sword at him. The keen blade caught the man high in the chest and knocked him over the railing. He dropped in a loose heap to the ground and writhed in pain.

He wasn't dead. She hadn't intended to kill him. Although she had killed while saving her life or the lives of others, the idea of doing that didn't sit well with her.

Annja started to climb down, but the other two men pulled out pistols. She ducked back again. Great, she thought. Everyone has a gun but me.

Bullets smacked against the building. She felt the vibrations more than she heard the harsh cracks of the gunshots.

She concentrated for just a moment, felt for the sword and pulled it through otherwhere again. On the ground, the man screamed in agony. The blade appeared in her hands blood free. Annja still didn't know how the sword did what it did, but she'd come to trust it and use it when necessary.

She shifted and moved to a new position. Then she looked over the roof's edge again. Below, the two healthy men had the third man between them in a fireman's carry. They ran toward the street. One of the men talked on a phone.

Annja started down the fire escape with the sword in her hand. She took the steps two and three at a time, boots thudding against the steps, almost spilling over the landings in her haste. At the second-floor landing she let her momentum get the best of her and vaulted over the side. She flipped and landed on her feet, her sword swept back and ready.

A dark sedan screeched to a stop near the three fleeing men. The rear door swung open. The two men carrying the third stared in awe at Annja. They passed their wounded comrade inside and climbed in after him.

Annja ran after them, thinking that she might be able to keep pace. She willed the sword away and reached for her phone. For a moment she kept up with the retreating vehicle and strained to make out the license plate.

The rear window sank down smoothly. The wicked mouth of a submachine pistol jutted out just as Annja closed in on an outdoor café packed with diners.

Annja couldn't risk innocent bystanders. The people at the café would never see the threat in time, much less be able to take evasive action. Frustrated, she stopped, then dived for cover as the submachine gun chattered to life. Bullets passed over her head and shattered the windows of the clothing store behind her.

Glass shards rattled down all around her. She kept her hands and arms wrapped around her head to protect her face. The deadly rain had stopped, and she made sure she wasn't bleeding from anything serious. When she looked up, the dark sedan was gone.

She punched the car's license plate number into her phone's memory and hoped the police would arrive soon.

3

Annja watched the Prague police detective and tried to read his lips. The man's mouth hardly moved, and the bushy mustache further disguised what he was saying.

"I'm sorry," she said. "You're going to have to speak up." Her own words barely penetrated the thick cotton in her ears. "I can't hear very well since the explosions."

The detective, whose name was Skromach, calmly started over. He looked like a patient man. Slight of stature, he exuded an air of competence. His salt-and-pepper hair needed the attention of a barber, but his suit was impeccable.

"You ran after the men, Miss Creed?" Skromach asked.

"Yes." Annja sat on the steps of a nearby building. An ambulance attendant treated a thin cut below her left eye and another along her jawline. Neither was bad enough to scar, but they would show for a while. She hoped Garin wasn't planning on taking her anywhere too elegant because she would look like a ragamuffin.

Skromach held his pen poised over his notepad. "Why would you do such a thing?"

"I didn't want the men who did this to get away."

The detective nodded. "You think they did this?"

Annja nodded at the burning pyre of cars the local fire department was dealing with. Water streamed from hoses. Gray steam clouds mixed with the black smoke.

"That wasn't supposed to happen," she said.

Skromach shrugged. "Perhaps it was an overzealous special-effects person."

"No," Annja said, feeling the need to defend Barney and his crew. "That blast was deliberately set."

"For the movie, yes?"

"No." Annja shook her head. The ambulance attendant, a no-nonsense woman, grabbed her chin and held her steady. "The special-effects crew is good. They wouldn't make that kind of mistake."

Skromach flipped back through his notes. Annja had seen him questioning movie people while she'd talked to Barney and Roy. Both of them were banged up but they were going to be fine.

"I see here that you're not a special-effects person," the police detective said.

"No," Annja said, realizing her hearing was beginning to clear.

Skromach nodded. "You're here as an archaeologist attached to the film?"

"Yes. But I'm only loosely attached. I'm taking care of the props."

"I see. Tell me about the props."

"They're Egyptian. Statues of Bast and Anubis."

"Were they pharaohs?"

"No. Gods. A god and goddess, to be exact. Bast is an ancient goddess worshiped since the Second Dynasty. About five thousand years, give or take. Anubis was the god of the underworld. Usually he's shown having the head of a jackal."

That seemed to catch Skromach's interest. "These statues are valuable?"

"Only to a collector. They aren't actually thousands of years old, but they are a few hundred."

"A few hundred years seems like a valuable thing. I collect stamps myself, and some of those are worth an incredible amount of money after only a short time."

"That's generally because they're issued with flaws. This—" Annja tried to find the words she wanted but failed "—wouldn't be like that."

"I see." Skromach didn't sound convinced.

"Someone hosed the gag," Annja said.

Skromach blinked. "Hosed the gag?"

"Sorry. The explosions were no accident," Annja said confidently.

"You're no authority," the detective replied.

Annja sighed. The conversation seemed determined to go in circles. "Check with Barney Yellowtail. He'll tell you the same thing."

"I expect that he would. Especially in light of the fact that he was responsible for the *gag,* as you put it."

Don't get angry, Annja told herself. He's just trying to do his job.

"If these statues are not so much valuable, why, then, are you shepherding them?" he asked.

"I'm *shepherding* all of the Egyptian artifacts in this movie," Annja replied. "Those two props are the more important ones. The director wants everything realistic."

Skromach scratched his long nose. "You were hired for your expertise?" he asked.

"Yes."

The detective smiled. "Perhaps also because of your own notoriety. You have a certain…reputation."

"I suppose."

"Come, come, Miss Creed. *Chasing History's Monsters* is very popular, they tell me. My wife is a fan." Skromach looked utterly disarming.

Annja knew to be on her guard. It's the quiet ones that always get you, she cautioned herself.

Skromach looked at his notes again. "Why did you chase the men?"

"Like I said, I didn't want them to get away."

"Such a thing is dangerous."

"Today has been dangerous," Annja countered.

"You could have been shot."

"I wasn't."

"You said there were three of them?"

"Yes."

"Men you had seen before?"

"I didn't say that," Annja told him. Finally finished with her chore, the ambulance attendant stepped away.

"Had you seen them before?" Skromach asked.

"No."

"Would you recognize them if you saw them again?"

"Yes."

"Perhaps, when you're able—say in a few minutes or so—you could come down to the police station and look at some photographs."

Inwardly, Annja groaned. She wasn't looking forward to

her date with Garin and didn't want to be stressed before she joined him.

"I've got plans for this evening," Annja replied.

Skromach checked his watch. "We're still hours from evening, Miss Creed. And I'd rather you came down voluntarily than me going to the trouble of making my invitation official."

"Why me?"

Skromach smiled. "Because you were the only one who chased those men."

"I gave you the license plate of the car they were in."

"Unfortunately, that car was stolen this morning. The owner is very distressed."

"Does the owner have any tattoos?" Annja asked.

Brows knitted, Skromach studied her. "Why do you ask?"

"One of the men had a sword tattooed on his neck." Annja touched her own neck in the place where the man's tattoo had been.

"Ah." Skromach wrote in his notebook. "You didn't mention this before."

"I just remembered," Annja said. "What about the car's owner?"

Skromach thought for a moment, then flipped back through his notebook. "I see no tattoos, sword or otherwise, mentioned." He looked up at her. "Perhaps I'll go see him. Just in case. In the meantime, I'd like to offer you a ride down to the police station."

Skromach was very good with surprises. He waited until he had Annja seated beside him in the back of the police car before he sprung his.

"So tell me, Miss Creed," he said. "What did you do with the sword?"

The car got under way. Annja fumbled for the seat belt to

cover her reaction. Her heart beat fast and her hands suddenly felt clammy. She tried to relax. No one could find the sword. Only she could call it forth, she reminded herself. When she had the seat belt fastened, she asked, "What sword?"

"Policemen working this case canvassed the street where you chased the men," the detective replied. "Witnesses said you threw a sword at one of the men and pierced him."

Annja held up her hands. "No sword."

Skromach scratched his jaw with a thumbnail. "They seemed most adamant, these witnesses. And there was a lot of blood at the scene."

"One of the men fell."

"The one with the sword tattoo?" Skromach touched his neck.

"I think so," Annja said.

"I see."

"Maybe the fall hurt the man and caused an injury."

"The witnesses said the man had to be carried off."

Annja waited. She wasn't very good at lying, but lying was better than trying to explain a supernatural sword.

"If you or your men can find a sword up there, then I must have had one," she replied. "Things got confusing very quickly."

"They usually do." Skromach shrugged. "We also had reports citing the number of men from two to eleven. Although how all those men fit into one car is beyond me. Eyewitnesses, as every policeman knows, are unreliable at best." He leaned back against the seat. "Besides, even if you did have a sword, you would only be guilty of self-defense."

"Yes."

"If those men were the ones who hosed the gag, as I believe you said."

"That's right," Annja replied. "That's what I said."

"Hopefully, we can find them."

Annja hoped so, too. Because if they didn't, she had the distinct impression the men might come looking for her again.

4

"Annja, you've got to listen to me. You're in Prague. That's almost Romania. They've got vampires in Romania. Therefore there are vampires in Prague."

Seated at the small metal desk she'd been shown to in the police station, Annja stared glumly at the page of photographs of known criminals operating in Prague. Actually she'd looked at so many pictures of criminals now that she believed Skromach had borrowed books from other countries.

After a while they all started to look the same. There were some who were old and some who were younger, but they all had earmarks of desperation or deviance. She wondered if her best friend, Bart McGilley, the NYPD detective, ever noticed how similar the criminals he chased looked.

She glanced at her watch. It was after five. Dinner was at eight.

Now I'm going to have to rush, she thought as she listened to Doug Morrell continue his tirade about vampires. She hadn't wanted to rush. This was a date. More than that, it was a date with Garin Braden, a man she knew she couldn't trust.

And how did you dress for something like that? It was a question that had been plaguing her for weeks. Ever since he'd told her that it was time for her to pay off on her promise to have dinner with him after he'd helped her out of a dangerous situation in India ages ago.

"I must have been brain-dead when I made that deal," she said to herself. At the time it hadn't seemed like a big deal. Now it felt as if she'd made a deal with the devil.

That was one thing she was certain of—Garin Braden didn't walk on the side of angels.

But what kind of conversation did she expect to have with someone who was seemingly immortal? It was intimidating and that was a feeling she rarely experienced.

"Doug," Annja interrupted. Her head throbbed from studying photographs and trying to deal with Skromach's suspicions about the sword.

The police detective had checked in a few times, usually to bring her something to drink and once to see if she wanted anything to eat. Despite the fact that he'd consigned her to this room and these photographs, he wasn't a bad guy.

Doug hadn't been thrown off his game. "Don't you see that this is important?"

Be patient, Annja reminded herself. She took a breath. Then she spoke slowly.

"There…are…no…vampires…in…Prague."

"There have to be."

"Doug," Annja sighed, "vampires don't exist."

"They hide," Doug said. "No one's as good at hiding as a vampire."

"Really?" Annja leaned back in the straight-backed chair and tried to get comfortable. She couldn't.

"I'm telling you there's a story about vampires in Prague," Doug whined.

"I'd rather do the one on King Wenceslas that I suggested."

Paper turned at Doug's end of the connection. "This is that sleeping-king thing, right?"

Annja felt encouraged that Doug had read her proposal. "The king in the mountain. Yes."

"Yeah, yeah, yeah," Doug said. "Sleeping king. King of the mountain. Same diff. Supposed to be called forth from the earth in times of great danger to the world. Did I leave anything out?"

"The legend of King Wenceslas coming back to fight evil is an important part of why I want to do the story. It's been woven into the King Arthur myth."

"He comes back from the dead?" Doug sounded excited.

"Yes."

"Why didn't you tell me that before?"

Annja took a breath. "I did. I sent research notes."

"You know I don't look at that stuff. This is television. All you need is a good beat line to make anything fly. I like the idea of him coming back from the dead," Doug said. "Kind of spooky, actually."

Annja looked around the small office and spotted a picture of Skromach with a woman about his age and three kids, two girls and a boy.

"Didn't they write a song about this guy?" Doug asked. "I seem to recall you saying something about a song."

"A Christmas carol." Annja focused. The story about King Wenceslas would be a good one.

"Yeah. 'Good King Wenceslas,' right?"

"Yes." Annja was even further amazed when Doug tried to remember the chorus.

He kept singing "Good King Wenceslas" until she couldn't take it anymore.

"Stop. That's not how it goes."

"Are you sure?"

"I'm positive." Annja looked at the mug shots. Those were preferable to dealing with Doug when he went obsessive-compulsive with her.

"Guy was supposed to be Santa Claus, wasn't he?" Doug asked.

"Not exactly. That's a connection a lot of people make."

"I have to admit, I like it."

Annja felt hopeful. "You do?"

"Yeah. So this King Wenceslas comes back from the dead? Correct me if I'm wrong."

"You're wrong," Annja said immediately. She had the worst feeling that she knew exactly where Doug was headed. "He's not supposed to be dead. Just sleeping."

"Hibernating," Doug said. "Kind of like a vampire."

"No."

"Comes back from the dead. Wants to wreak havoc on whatever villain is sucking the life out of the world. Kind of sounds vampirish to me."

"No," Annja repeated.

"I like it," Doug said. "I want this story."

"King Wenceslas wasn't a vampire."

"Maybe you just haven't dug deeply enough. Maybe his whole vampire nature is there waiting for you to discover it."

"It's not."

"I mean, can you imagine this?" Doug asked.

"No," Annja said. "I can't. Doug, Wenceslas was *not* a vampire."

"He could be."

"He is a saint."

"Cool," Doug exclaimed. "A vampire that's been sainted. You know what'll really sell this piece, though?"

Annja was afraid to ask.

"Picture this," Doug went on. "We show Wenceslas as a warrior knight. A big sword or ax. Horned helmet like the Vikings wore."

"The Vikings didn't wear horned helmets," Annja said. "That's just a perception created by Hollywood. It's wrong." But she knew Doug wasn't listening. He was lost in his own world.

"So we see this big knight with this gnarly weapon." Excitement thrummed in Doug's voice. "Big burly guy. Muscles out to here. And let's make the armor red. With a hood. So the Santa Claus connection comes through."

Annja didn't even try to interrupt. She'd been through sessions like this with Doug before. It was already too late.

"A red hood," Doug said. "Get it? Then the camera pans in and Wenceslas grins at us. Only instead of regular teeth… he's got *fangs!*"

Annja hung up. There were times when talking to Doug, though she counted him as a friend, were exhausting. She could always claim a dead battery later. She laid the phone beside her notebook computer.

While she was looking at the mug shots, she was also searching the archaeological sites for information about the green-scimitar tattoo. She felt certain there was something significant about the design.

So far there weren't any responses on the boards.

THE PHONE RANG a few minutes later. At first Annja was just going to let it go to voice mail. Then she noticed that the number was local to Prague. She scooped up the phone and answered.

"You're not at your hotel," a strong male voice accused.

The voice belonged to Garin Braden. Just like that, all the trepidation Annja had about the upcoming date slammed into her.

She took a deep breath in through her nose and let it out her mouth. This is a mistake, she told herself.

"I'm not," she said in a calm voice. Still, she felt her pulse beating faster than normal. She didn't like it. Garin was a dangerous man. If she'd had her preference, she'd have kept him as an enemy the way he'd been when they'd first met. He'd tried to kill her then.

"I thought this would be something special." Garin didn't sound disappointed; he sounded irritated. "I've gone to considerable lengths to make tonight happen."

Unable to sit in the chair any longer, Annja got up and paced the room. She rubbed the back of her neck and tried to relax. Her shoulders felt knotted and sore.

"Things didn't go exactly as planned at the movie set today," Annja said.

"You're only there as an adviser," Garin said in a pleasant baritone. At least, if he didn't sound as if he was ready to chew nails his voice would be pleasant, Annja thought.

"Leave the movie set and go to your hotel. I've got reservations," Garin said.

Was that a command? It definitely sounded like a command. And Annja didn't intend to be commanded. She had reservations herself, and they weren't at a restaurant.

5

"This isn't working out," Annja said.

"Prague was your idea," Garin countered, as if the location was the problem. "I would have preferred meeting in the Greek islands."

Annja knew that. Garin had even offered to send his private jet—one of his private jets—to pick her up from Brooklyn. But she'd refused. If she had to meet Garin for dinner, she wanted to do it under her own power.

Doing that meant she could also leave whenever she wanted. You could really run out of places to go on an island if you wanted to get away from someone.

"If you're trying to weasel out of our agreement," Garin said, "then that's fine. I've got other things to do."

The man's arrogance was monumental. In that instant Annja saw that she could break the date if she chose. She also realized that Garin sounded as if he had misgivings, as well.

That possibility irritated her. She knew she was good company, bright, articulate and attractive. She'd been told that by enough men to accept there must be some truth to it. So where was Garin getting off telling her he had other things to do?

"I'm at the police station," Annja said.

Garin growled a curse. "What did you do now?"

"I," Annja said, taking affront at once, "didn't do anything. Some men attacked the movie set today. They planted explosives that nearly killed several people and sent five stunt crewmen and women to the hospital. Maybe you heard about that."

"No."

"It was in the news." In fact, now that she thought about it, Annja wondered if she should have been upset that Garin hadn't called immediately to check on her.

"I wasn't watching the news."

Annja wondered what Garin had been doing.

"Were you injured?" Garin asked.

"No. Otherwise I'd be at the hospital."

"What are you doing at the police station?"

"Looking at photographs of potential bombers."

"Ah. You're giving a statement?"

"One of the local detectives *invited* me to come down and identify the men who planted the explosives." Annja stopped pacing and placed a hip on the edge of the table. "He hasn't been too amenable about letting me go. Of course, I haven't told him that I was meeting you for dinner. I'm quite positive," she said as sarcastically as possible, "that if I mentioned that he'd let me go immediately."

"Don't be crass." Garin didn't sound angry now, only grumpy.

"I tend to get that way when someone calls me and starts dumping blame on me."

"You have a phone," Garin argued. "You could have called me."

"Why? Dinner's still hours away. I can make it easily."

"I want you attired properly for the night," Garin said.

"I didn't know there was a dress code." Annja started to get angry all over again.

"This isn't an evening at McDonald's. I don't know how your other men treat you—"

"Kindly," Annja replied. "And with due consideration for the fact that I have a career and obligations. They even acknowledge that I know how to properly dress myself."

"Trust me. I've moved more on my schedule than you did to make tonight happen."

Annja was torn between being insulted and flattered. She also felt a little competitive. Being around Garin brought that out in her. She disliked the feeling, but she also knew it was impossible to circumvent given the company.

She also knew that what Garin said was probably true. He had several international business interests under several dummy corporations and holding companies. Managing an empire like his couldn't be easy. Especially if much of it was criminal, as she suspected it was. And Garin wasn't exactly the sort to have someone oversee it for him.

"You'd be better served if you just told the police that you didn't see the men who did this thing," Garin said.

"They knew I chased them."

"Well, that was certainly foolish."

"I didn't want them to get away with what they did."

"So now you're going to identify them for the police and be a witness at some time-consuming trial." Garin's distaste for such a prospect was clear.

"I don't want them to get away with this," Annja repeated.

"Then find them and kill them yourself. It's much simpler and not as dangerous as you might think if done properly."

Annja sighed. "Not exactly my choice of solutions."

"I find it very comforting," Garin said.

"Getting caught could be a problem."

"Did I need to mention that you'd have to be clever about it? You needn't claim your kills."

Annja rubbed the back of her neck. The headache wasn't going away. She wanted a hot bath and time to enjoy it. Stanley Younts, the writer she'd met while looking to solve a friend's murder, had couriered a draft of his new book to her because he wanted her to fact-check the history in the text. He was paying her quite handsomely. She'd had hopes of spending some time with it that day.

"I can have an attorney there in twenty minutes," Garin offered. "You'll be out five minutes after that."

"No," Annja said.

Garin cursed again.

"I'll handle this." Annja stared at the thick books of photographs. "And I'll be on time for dinner."

"I'll send a cab for you."

"You don't have to do that."

"I know. It'll be there." Garin hung up.

The quick dismissal stung Annja. She almost called him back. But she suspected she wouldn't get past Garin's personal assistant. Garin had an infuriating habit of becoming inaccessible.

Just get through tonight, she told herself. Then the debt's paid.

IN THE END, Skromach wasn't happy about releasing Annja before she could identify the guilty parties, but he didn't have a choice. He politely and patiently confirmed her hotel's information and told her he would be in touch.

A short cab ride later, Annja paid the driver and got out in front of her hotel. She'd chosen to stay in the Old Town where the surroundings were more Gothic than industrial. She loved the older sections of European cities. All she had to do was look at the buildings and she could imagine the wagons, carriages and horses clattering down the cobbled streets. History, hundreds of years of it, was ingrained in the architecture.

Her hotel boasted a collection of gargoyles that perched along the roof and looked ready to swoop down on her. She frowned a little when she realized they made her think of Garin. She didn't know if it was because they looked like predators or simply devious.

"Are you all right, miss?" the cab driver asked in hesitant English. He held the door open and stood with his cap in his hand.

Jarred back to the present, Annja looked at him. "I am. Thank you." She reached back into the cab for her backpack. She never went anywhere without it. Her notebook computer, GPS locater, extra batteries, cameras and other electronic equipment, as well as the change of clothes she habitually carried were inside.

She gathered the backpack by the straps and strode up the stone steps leading to the hotel.

"Ah, Miss Creed."

Barely in the foyer, Annja turned and found one of the hotel's assistant managers standing there. "Yes, Johan?"

The old man smiled. "You remember my name." He clapped in delight, then smoothed his long silver mustache with his fingertips.

Annja suspected he was old enough to be her grandfather, but he was thin and elegant and moved like an athlete. His dark suit was immaculate and fit the antique furnishings of the refurbished hotel. Soft yellow light gleamed against the surface of the stone floors.

"You've gone out of your way to make my stay here pleasant," Annja replied. "Of course I'd remember your name."

"You flatter an old man." Johan put a hand over his heart.

Annja smiled. During the past few days while she'd been a guest at the hotel, Johan and the other staff had taken good care of her. They'd seemed disappointed that she wasn't more demanding. As it turned out, several of them were fans of *Chasing History's Monsters.*

"There was a bit of a problem while you were gone," Johan said. He looked a little nervous. "It was most confusing. I was told it was supposed to be a surprise, but I could hardly allow such a thing."

That troubled Annja a little. "What thing?"

Johan crooked a finger at her and guided her off to the side of the foyer. "The man. I simply couldn't allow him into your room without you being there."

"A man tried to get into my room?" Annja thought at once of the men she'd chased. Maybe they had tracked her down.

Johan closed his eyes and shook his head. "Of course not. Had that been so, I would have called hotel security at once, and then the police. The hotel does not put up with such—" he fumbled for an American expression "—shenanigans."

"Of course."

"He claimed he was arranged for."

"Arranged for by whom?"

Johan shook his head. "Why, that is part of the problem. He wouldn't tell me."

"What did he want?"

"To dress you."

That threw Annja off stride. "To *dress* me?"

"That's what he said. He said he was arranged for and sent here at his employer's request. I have his card."

"The employer's?"

"No. The man who is here." Like a magician, Johan's hand exploded into motion and a card was produced as though he'd plucked it from thin air.

The card was heavily embossed and decorated in an understated manner with pale pink flowers that assured affluence. It had only one word—*Gesauldi*.

There wasn't even an address or phone number. Nothing on the card suggested what the man did.

Johan studied her face. "I was hoping that you would know him, Miss Creed."

"No." Annja slipped the card into her pocket. "Did he leave?"

Johan shook his head. "I wouldn't so casually turn away a man such as he."

"He's still here?"

"But of course. I put him into a room for the moment."

"Then let's go talk to him," Annja said with a sigh.

6

Gesauldi answered the hotel door but didn't look happy about it. He had the air of a man who didn't answer doors, not even his own.

"Mr. Gesauldi," Johan said. "I present to you Miss Annja Creed."

Annja had automatically dropped into an L-stance and prepared to defend herself. Lately there hadn't been many social calls in her life, and danger had dogged her heels. She didn't think she was being paranoid. She thought more of it as recognizing potential threats.

Gesauldi was slim and elegant, and roughly Annja's height. His neat black hair was clipped short, and his cheeks looked freshly shaved. His suit fit him like a glove. He looked to be in his late twenties, but her immediate impression of him was that he was older.

"Miss Creed," he cooed in a soft voice. "I'm enchanted to meet you." He took her left hand in his.

Annja stopped herself from recoiling as he lifted her hand

briefly to brush his lips against the back of her hand. Gently but firmly, she reclaimed her hand.

Gesauldi shifted his attention to Johan. "Could we perhaps have some tea? A nice Chinese green tea with mango or peach would be splendid. And some biscuits if that wouldn't be too much trouble." He glanced back at Annja. "After all, we want you in the proper mood for the fitting, or course."

"What fitting?"

Gesauldi's eyebrows rose toward his hairline. "Why, for your date tonight."

Annja took a deep breath. "Did Garin Braden send you?"

Gesauldi lifted his hands and spread his elegant fingers. "Please. I don't like to bandy names about. Especially when I've been asked to keep a confidence."

Unable to believe what Garin had done, Annja was just about to tell the man politely that she wasn't interested in being dressed by him. Then she saw the evening dresses on a free-standing clothes rack.

"Was there something you wished to say, Miss Creed?" Gesauldi asked.

Despite her irritation at Garin, Annja was mesmerized by the dresses. "Wow," she said.

Gesauldi gestured grandly toward the rack. "These are some of Gesauldi's very best. And, I might add, people do not usually get fitted by Gesauldi himself."

"May I?" Annja asked.

"But of course. Your attention and your pleasures warm Gesauldi's heart." The man took her by the elbow and walked her over to the dresses.

Annja ran her fingers along the material. It was smooth and silky, and she could only imagine what it might feel like against her skin.

"Wow," she said again.

"Of course you would feel that way. Gesauldi knew you would feel that way. Gesauldi's creations always leave people feeling this way."

"You're a dressmaker?"

He scowled. "Dear woman, Gesauldi is an artist!"

Annja examined the dresses. "Of course you are." She didn't know whether to be flattered or angry. "Garin really didn't think I could dress myself, did he?"

"Did you have a Gesauldi dress for tonight?"

"No."

"Then you couldn't have dressed yourself."

For a moment Annja considered telling the man to take his dresses and go. But she couldn't. She'd never worn anything that glamorous in her life.

She turned to Gesauldi. "Are you in the habit of delivering your dresses yourself, Mr. Gesauldi?"

He grinned at her, obviously pleased that she was so enraptured. "Only for *very* special clients or very beautiful women, Miss Creed." He inclined his head in a respectful bow. "Tonight I am honored to do both."

Johan leaned forward and whispered behind his hand to Annja. "Do you see, Miss Creed? I could hardly have thrown such a man from the hotel."

"No," Annja agreed. "You couldn't have."

LATER, soaking in a fragrant bath while Gesauldi arranged the dresses and his tools, Annja sipped green tea and thought about her *date*. She wondered what Garin was up to.

The attention was extremely flattering. Or quite unflattering, depending on how she chose to view Garin's efforts. Either he wants to treat me like royalty or he wants to make sure I measured up to his standards. That was an unhappy thought. Annja sipped her tea and chose not to think like that.

THE PHONE RANG while Annja, feeling much refreshed and looking forward to Gesauldi's fitting, was drying off from the bath. She'd soaked to just preprune stage. She wrapped a towel around herself and picked up her phone.

The phone number was European, but that was all she knew.

"Hello."

"Don't tell me it's true."

Annja recognized Roux's voice at once. The old man had a raspy voice that was unmistakable.

"It's not true," Annja said, sensing from Roux's tone that he wanted confirmation.

"Good." Roux sounded minutely appeased.

"Now," Annja said, "what's not true?"

Roux took a deep breath and it made the phone connection sound cavernous.

"That you're going out with Garin," Roux snapped. "Tell me that's not true."

Despite having grown up in an orphanage in New Orleans, Annja suddenly got the idea of what it might have been like to have to deal with a displeased father. Not surprisingly, it felt a lot like dealing with an irate nun.

"Where did you hear something like that?" Annja asked.

Roux cursed. "So it *is* true."

"Who I go out with is hardly any business of yours." Annja put her phone on hands-free mode, tightened the towel around her and reached for another to wrap her hair.

"It is when it's Garin," Roux said.

"I can take care of myself."

"Not against Garin. Are you going out with him?"

"We're having dinner."

Roux cursed again. "Do you find yourself so enamored of him that you can't control your hormones?"

"I resent that," Annja said.

"By all means, feel free."

"I'm in perfect control of my hormones."

Roux vented a derisive snort.

"I'm going to dinner with him to pay off a debt," Annja said. "Garin helped me out while I was in India."

"A *debt?*" Roux sounded as though he couldn't believe it. "You don't pay off a debt like that. At the very least not in the manner in which you're doing it."

"Dinner's not exactly the worst thing that I could imagine having to do."

Roux snorted again.

"And," Annja went on, "as I recall, you don't mind waving the debt card around when you want my help with something."

"That's different."

"How?"

"I helped you find the sword."

"So what? I'm going to owe you forever now?"

"No," Roux said. "Having the sword means you have a duty and an obligation to the powers behind that sword."

"Whatever powers might be behind this sword, it's definitely not you."

Roux sighed in displeasure. "I help you with what you're supposed to do. We're on the same side."

Although she didn't say anything, Annja doubted that. Roux, like Garin, had his own agenda. Neither of them chose to entrust her with it. Roux was always exactly on the side of Roux.

"Harboring any leniency with Garin is a mistake," Roux said.

"There's no leniency," Annja said. "There's dinner."

A knock sounded at the door. "Miss Creed," Gesauldi called out. "Gesauldi doesn't wish to hurry you, but time is of the essence."

"I'll be right there," Annja replied.

"Was that Gesauldi?" Roux demanded.

Annja furrowed her brow. "Do you know Gesauldi?"

"He sent the dressmaker?" Roux shouted.

"Gesauldi heard that," Gesauldi called from the other room. "Gesauldi is no dressmaker. Gesauldi is an *artist.*"

"He heard you," Annja said.

"I don't care," Roux snapped.

"How do you know Gesauldi?"

"If Gesauldi is involved," Roux said, "then Garin is seeing this as more than a one-time date."

Annja smiled, then caught sight of her reflection in the mirror and turned away. You're not going to think past tonight, she told herself. But she knew she was.

"I don't get that impression," Annja said.

"Annja," Roux growled, "Garin sent Gesauldi."

"Of course he did," Gesauldi said from the other room. "You only send for Gesauldi when you want the very best."

He must, Annja thought, have ears like a bat.

"Maybe you should ask Gesauldi how many times Garin has sent him to dress his women," Roux suggested.

That thought had crossed Annja's mind, but she hadn't given in to the impulse.

"Gesauldi will never tell," Gesauldi said. "A promise from Gesauldi is like a little piece of forever. Because Gesauldi will take such knowledge to the grave with him."

Terrific, Annja thought. "You know, Roux," she said, "it wouldn't have hurt you to let me have my little moment here."

"You're making a mistake," Roux said.

Annja hung up.

AT SEVEN-THIRTY, Johan called Annja. "Miss Creed, there is a gentleman here to see you."

Dressed in the spectacular black dress Gesauldi had tailored so that it showed her body to its best, Annja surveyed the results in the full-length mirror. She had to admit it—she looked exquisite.

Gesauldi had also brought along a hairdresser and makeup artist, who worked their magic, as well. She wore her hair pulled back, held by jeweled combs. The only thing missing was a necklace, but she hadn't brought anything with her. This was supposed to have been a working trip, not one of leisure.

"Tell him to come up," Annja said.

"I have suggested that," Johan replied. "The gentleman refuses. He insists that such behavior is rude and unseemly."

Annja thought about that.

"Given the circumstance," Johan said in a lower voice, "I would have to applaud the gentleman on his sense of decorum. If you wish, I can come up for you."

"That's all right," Annja said. "I'm on my way down."

7

The sight of Annja Creed stepping from the elevator momentarily stole Garin Braden's breath from his lungs. She was stunning. Even before Gesauldi's magic, Annja possessed a natural beauty that made men glad they were men.

Now—she was a goddess.

Garin was aware of the effect her appearance had on the men in the lavish hotel lobby. Heads turned in her direction and conversations came to a standstill. And it wasn't just the men who were affected. Women looked and quieted, too.

Thin straps crossed Annja's smooth shoulders and supported the dress. The black material clung to her figure in all the right places. Handmade Italian slingbacks glittered like polished anthracite.

For a moment, Garin forgot himself in the hush that fell across the lobby. Although he'd seen Gesauldi work his magic before, Garin had never seen any woman as striking as Annja. He'd seen more beautiful women—that was true—but none of them possessed the innate qualities that he'd found at once appealing and unnerving about the young woman in front of him.

"Excuse me, sir," the old assistant manager who had helped Garin whispered. "But if you don't mind me suggesting it, perhaps this would be an ideal time to give the young woman the flowers."

Garin's senses returned. He remembered the flowers in his hand. He chided himself for being so overwhelmed.

When everyone stared at her, Annja felt extremely self-conscious. She knew other women dreamed of making this kind of entrance, but it had never once been in her thoughts. She found that kind of attention uncomfortable.

She saw Garin as he approached her. He looked every inch the warrior, and as he stood six feet four inches tall, that was impressive. He wore his dark hair long and sported a goatee. His eyes were blacker than oil. He wore a tuxedo that suggested Gesauldi didn't just handle women's clothes.

Johan stood at Garin's side, dwarfed by the bigger man.

Garin carried an extravagant bouquet of flowers. He stopped in front of her and looked down. The fragrance of the flowers rode the air between them.

"You're beautiful," he said.

This is so not a date, Annja told herself. "Thank you. You look very handsome," she said quietly.

Garin handed her the flowers, then offered his arm.

Annja took it and let him lead her out of the lobby. She knew everyone in the hotel watched them go, and she didn't know if she'd ever have a moment as perfect as that one again.

As soon as they stepped out of the hotel, a silver limousine glided to a halt at the curb. The hotel doorman got the door, smiled and tipped his hat.

"There is one thing, if I may," Garin said. He took a small case from his jacket pocket and opened it.

What Annja saw inside took her breath away. A string of black pearls as shiny as drops of oil gleamed on the white fabric lining the case.

"I thought they would set the dress off," Garin said.

Annja thought so, too, but she wasn't ready to give in to temptation. "I usually don't wear a lot of jewelry."

"These will look beautiful on you." Garin plucked the string of pearls from the case and held them up in his fingers. They looked ready to spill loose at any second. "Unless, of course, you'd rather not wear them." He started to put them away.

"Wait," Annja said.

Garin looked at her and smiled. "I didn't think so. May I?"

Annja turned her back to him. Gently he strung the pearls around her neck. For just a moment Annja thought that maybe the pearls were actually a disguised garrote. *If you're thinking he might kill you, what are you doing here?*

The necklace fastened and she felt the cool weight of the pearls against her skin. She turned to face Garin.

"I was wrong," he said. "The pearls don't make the dress. You make the pearls."

"Thank you." *And you're just too smooth at knowing the right things to say,* Annja thought.

Garin helped Annja into the car and she slid across the seat. She felt uncomfortable and out of control. She didn't like either feeling.

"Would you care for anything to drink?" Garin opened the well-stocked built-in bar as the limousine slid into motion and pulled out into the busy street.

"Water, please."

He frowned in displeasure. "I've got a good selection of wines."

"No. Thank you."

Garin poured her a glass of sparkling water and poured wine for himself. "Well," he said.

"Thank you," Annja said. "For the dress. For Gesauldi." She held her glass in both hands so she wouldn't spill it.

Garin grinned a little. "Nervous?"

"No." Annja paused. "Yes."

After a brief hesitation, he said, "Me, too."

"You?" Annja raised an eyebrow.

Garin shrugged. "A little, perhaps. I have to admit, the feeling is quite unexpected."

"Just because I'm a little overwhelmed doesn't mean I can't take care of myself," Annja warned him.

"Of course not." Garin waved the thought away.

"In case you get any ideas."

"If getting ideas was going to get me in trouble, that dress would make me a dead man."

Annja didn't know how to respond. For a time, neither one of them spoke.

THE RESTAURANT WAS NESTLED between business offices downtown. After Garin helped her from the limousine, Annja gazed at the hand-lettered sign above the door. It read Keshet. A homemade sign tacked above an entrance that looked as if it let out onto an alley wasn't exactly awe-inspiring.

"Is something wrong?" Garin asked.

"After the buildup of the dress and the limo, this isn't quite what I'd expected," Annja admitted.

Garin grinned. "You were expecting me to take you to one of those flashy restaurants."

"Maybe."

"Are you disappointed?"

Annja gazed at him warily and wondered if this was some kind of trick. "Should I be?"

"If you are, I'll buy you dinner in any restaurant of your choice. In the world." Garin offered his arm again. When Annja took it, he led her toward the burly doorman.

"Good evening, Mr. Braden," the man said in English.

"Good evening," Garin responded.

The doorman opened the door. Annja turned and found Garin almost filling the tiny hallway that led from the door. Muted lights illuminated the way over a plain concrete floor. She joined him.

Another doorman opened the next door. When she saw inside, Annja was even more surprised.

The restaurant was even smaller than she'd imagined. A quick estimate of the tables in the room meant that fewer than fifty people could sit in the room at one time.

Instead of a wall separating the cooking area from the diners, the kitchen was exposed for all to see. A squat woman in her late sixties ran the kitchen staff with the ironhanded control of a Marine Corps drill instructor. Her gray hair was cut short. She wore black pants and a green blouse with the sleeves pushed up past her elbows. The kitchen staff responded to her orders like a well-oiled unit.

"Mr. Braden." A young hostess with olive-colored skin and a perfect smile joined them. "It's been too long since you've visited us."

"Merely growing my appetite for Mama's cooking," Garin said.

"She was excited to learn that you would be coming." The

hostess led the way to the only table in the room that wasn't occupied.

Located at center stage, the table had a perfect view of the activity in the kitchen as cooks worked the stovetop and kept bread rotating through the ovens. Garin took Annja's chair and seated her.

"Thank you," Annja said.

"You're welcome." Garin sat beside her at the table so he could watch the kitchen.

After taking their drink order, the hostess returned with water for Annja and wine for Garin. "Mama will be with you in a moment."

"Thank you, Petra," Garin said.

"Of course, Mr. Braden." The young woman's fingers trailed softly across Garin's when she handed him his glass.

Annja was surprised at the sudden jealousy that struck her. She took a deep breath and focused on the kitchen. It's not jealousy, she told herself. No one would like watching her date get hit on by another woman.

And even if Garin wasn't a real date, he was accompanying her tonight. There were lines that weren't supposed to be crossed.

Servers brought heaping plates out to the guests, who clapped and exclaimed appreciatively in a half-dozen languages. The diners still waiting looked on in envy.

Annja's stomach growled in anticipation. The smell of the food was divine. The aroma of fresh-baked bread permeated the air.

"Hungry?" Garin asked.

"Famished," Annja replied. "So what's on the menu?"

"I don't know." Garin sipped his wine. "Mama arrives in

the morning and decides then. She could walk into any kitchen in the world and get a job."

If she had to make a decision to believe that based on the smells in the dining room, Annja would have. She also noticed the pride in Garin's voice when he talked about the woman.

Mama left the kitchen area with two salads and walked to their table and put them down. Garin stood immediately and hugged the woman. He dwarfed her in size.

"Ah," Mama said, turning to Annja, "and you must be Annja Creed." Her eyes glittered as she surveyed Annja. In just that brief second, Annja knew that her measure had been taken, and she had no clue if she'd been found acceptable or wanting.

8

"It's very nice to meet you," Annja said, not at all certain if the statement was true. Still, she smiled and made the best of it she could.

"I have heard so much about you." Mama spoke with a thick accent. "This one—" she poked Garin in the chest with her forefinger "—I know him a long time. And before him, his father."

Father? Annja gazed at Garin in idle speculation. "Do you mean Roux?"

Mama waved that away. "No. I know Roux, as well." She shrugged. "I like him okay, but he can be an old goat."

"Roux tried to cook in Mama's kitchen one night," Garin explained.

Mama held a hand to her ample breast. "He has so much nerve, that one." She whispered behind her hand. "That was long ago. When I was much younger and more beautiful. He also pinched my bottom." She rolled her eyes in feigned shock. "I slap his face for him, I tell you."

Annja chuckled. She knew how Roux was around women.

And she knew how women were around Roux. They seemed drawn to each other.

"No, I am talking about Garin's father. The first Garin. Did you ever meet him?"

Annja looked at Garin and realized that the woman had known Garin in her much younger days. Since Garin didn't age, he had to disappear from his previous lives after a few decades.

"No," Annja said. "I never did."

"This one—" Mama pinched Garin's cheek "—he is so much like his father. Handsome and powerful. This one, he could be a twin brother to his father."

Annja nodded. She wondered how much longer Garin—and Roux—would be able to keep up the pretense of being normal humans. Not dying in an age filled with computers and record archiving—including digital images—was going to be harder to cover up than in centuries past.

Garin gazed down at the woman, and for a moment Annja thought she could see honest emotion in the man's eyes. She wondered again how anyone could live five hundred years—and in Roux's case probably more—and have any emotions left.

"This one, though," Mama said, "he is not so much like his father. He is more gentle. More respectful."

Garin almost looked embarrassed, and Annja couldn't help but smile at his discomfort. After everything she'd seen Garin do, the almost offhanded way he killed people when they threatened him, she couldn't imagine him being vulnerable. Venal, criminally so at times, but not vulnerable.

Mama looked at Annja. "His father, he was much the man." A dreamy expression showed in her eyes and Annja knew that—just for the moment—the woman was no longer in the restaurant. "He was so much the lover." She sighed.

"Please," Garin protested. "Not before we've eaten."

Playfully, Mama slapped him on the arm. "You. Sit. You should know to leave an old woman her idle passions. All I have these days are memories. The flower of youth is gone far too quickly."

"The flower of youth," Garin replied, "to the uninitiated, is oftentimes a weed."

Mama shook a finger at him. "Your father, he say such a thing to me one time."

"Father was fond of chiding me about my lackadaisical approach to my life. Perhaps he said that to a lot of people."

Annja knew that Garin had slipped up and had tried to cover his mistake.

"I liked your father very much," Mama said, "but he was not husband material, that one. He have an eye for the ladies. Like you. You won't be any good as a husband unless you find a woman strong enough to claim you as her own. That kind of woman doesn't come along so very much, you know." She looked a warning at Annja. "Better you should keep this in mind."

"Oh, believe me," Annja said, "I won't forget."

Garin scowled.

"The problem is," Mama said quietly to Annja, "that sometimes a woman, she likes the bad boys. At least for a little while, no?"

"Yes," Annja agreed.

"It is kind of like the sweet tooth. And it give us many problems." Mama laughed. "Now I go get you plates. You enjoy. I have a special dessert tonight." She stopped long enough for a final hug from Garin, then yelled at the kitchen crew.

"Quite a woman," Annja commented.

"An amazing woman," Garin agreed. Wistfulness stained his words. "You should have seen her when she was young.

She was incredible. And it wasn't just the way she looked, though she was stunning. It was her spirit. She almost seemed like she was on fire."

It was really weird, Annja thought, to be sitting there discussing an ex-flame with the man she was having dinner with. That had on occasion happened in Annja's life, but never when forty years had passed.

"So what happened between you two?" she asked.

Garin hesitated. "She got older. I didn't."

"You don't like older women?"

Garin grinned. "I love older women. A woman in her forties can be a tigress under the right conditions."

Annja felt no inclination to ask what those conditions might me.

"But it's selfish of me to get so involved with someone."

"You are a selfish person," Annja pointed out.

"I am. I'll admit that. I'll take a few weeks, a few months, perhaps even a year or two of a woman's life if I'm truly infatuated. But I won't ask any more than that."

"You could marry them."

Some of the humor went out of Garin's face. "I made that mistake. A few times."

"Marriage didn't agree with you?" Annja taunted.

Despite Garin's roguish grin, pain glinted in his eyes. "They died, Annja. No matter how fiercely I loved them, they died. They got old and perished and I remained. Alone." He paused. "Those weren't experiences I relished. Nor would I ever do something like that again."

Annja knew what it felt like to be alone. She picked up her fork and turned her attention to her salad.

"Tell me about the men who attacked the movie set today," Garin requested.

Annja didn't think Garin was truly interested in what happened earlier, but she couldn't think of anything else to discuss. Evidently they both realized they were on safer ground with other topics. She gave him the gist of the events. When she got to the matter of the tattoo on the man's neck, Garin stopped her.

He touched his own neck. "You said this tattoo was of a sword?" He took a handheld device from his jacket and quickly sketched an image on the screen with the stylus.

"I have to admit I'm surprised," Annja said as he sketched. "I figured you more for a pen-and-cocktail-napkin kind of guy."

Garin frowned at her. "I love technology. Roux doesn't care so much for it. But I love it. I own several companies that specialize in software and hardware research and development." He showed her the screen. The sketch revealed a sword that was heavy bladed and curved. "Was this the sword?"

"Yes. What do you know about this?" Anxiety and suspicion warred within Annja.

Garin studied the image. "A scimitar. You said it was green?"

Annja nodded.

A low curse escaped Garin's full lips.

"Do you know who these men are?" Annja asked.

"Pawns. If they belong to the man I think they do, they're very highly trained. You're lucky to have escaped with your life."

"Who are they and why would they be interested in me?"

"I think I know who they are, but I don't know why they would be interested in you. Unless they want to get to Roux. They might know about the connection you have to Roux. And to me."

"They're enemies of Roux?"

"Their master is." Garin took his cell phone from his pocket.

"Excuse me for just a moment." He punched in a number. The phone was answered almost instantly. "We may have a security problem. Make sure my dinner is uninterrupted."

"Who was that?" Annja asked.

"The security chief of the team watching us."

"Do you always travel with a security team?"

"I do. Except for those times I don't care to live my life in a fishbowl." Garin shrugged. "And during those times when it's better if no one knows what I'm doing."

Annja picked at her salad. She wasn't nervous, not really. But the thought of the man with the scimitar tattoo lurking around outside did give her pause.

"Who are you afraid of?" Annja asked.

"I'm not afraid of this man," Garin growled. "But I'd rather err on the side of caution where he's concerned."

"Should we go?"

Garin blew out a short breath. "No. I'm not going to be chased from my dinner like some timid little mouse. We're going to have a fine meal, and we're going to enjoy it." He looked at her. "Why? Do you wish to leave?"

Annja thought about it. She knew she should. But she was stubborn, too. Growing up in the orphanage had been hard. She'd never liked quietly going away, either.

"No," she answered.

"You don't care much for playing the mouse, either, do you?" Garin asked.

"I'm hungry."

Garin chuckled.

"Who do those men work for?" Annja asked.

"He calls himself Saladin."

"Like the Saladin who fought Richard I during the Crusades?"

"Yes." Garin looked pained. "But also like Honest Saladin, the camel dealer I met in Cairo when I was tomb hunting with Howard Carter."

Annja stared at Garin. Curiosity filled her like a tidal wave. "You were in Egypt with Carter?"

Garin shook his head. "Focus, Annja. What I'm telling you now may save your life if Saladin truly is after you."

"Why would he be after me?"

"Weren't you paying attention? Saladin would take you to get to Roux."

"What does he have against Roux?"

"He wants the Nephilim."

Annja had to think a moment. "The child of a fallen angel?"

"A painting of one."

"Why?"

"I don't know. Roux never told me. That old man has been keeping secrets for hundreds of years."

Annja's mind spun with questions.

"What was the importance of the painting?" Annja asked.

Garin shook his head. "I don't know."

"Roux never offered any hints?"

"Roux," Garin stated, "never offers hints, and he never slips up. If you think he has, he's merely setting you up. Trust me on that."

9

"What do you know about the Nephilim?" Annja asked.

"I never found out much. It was supposed to be a painting that at one time hung in a church in Constantinople. The painting, if it truly ever existed, disappeared when the city fell."

"That was 560 years ago," Annja said.

"I know."

"How do you know those men belong to Saladin?"

Garin touched his throat. "I know Saladin's mark. The green scimitar you saw on that man's neck."

Annja thought about that as she pushed her empty plate away. The food had been superb, but she had a lot on her mind.

"And they want the painting of the Nephilim?" she asked.

"Yes."

"But why?" Annja shook her head in frustration.

"I don't know. That, so far, has remained one of Roux's secrets."

Annja took out her phone and glanced at the number she'd stored in memory.

"What are you doing?" Garin asked.

"I'm calling Roux." Annja punched the button and held the phone up to her ear as she listened for the rings.

"He's not going to tell you anything."

Annja ignored the negative response. The phone rang six times before it was answered in French.

"Hello," she said, speaking French.

"How can I help you?"

"I'm looking for a man named—" Annja stopped because she had no idea what name Roux was using.

"Yes?" the man inquired.

"I'm looking for the owner of this phone," Annja said.

"That would be me, of course."

"And who are you?"

"Jean-Paul." The man's voice lowered. "You know, you sound very sexy. Perhaps you and I—"

"Do you know a man named Roux?"

"No, but if you like men named Roux, you may call me Roux."

"He called me from this phone."

Jean-Paul laughed. "Then this man Roux has very good taste. This is a very expensive phone. I can afford expensive things. Tell me, do you like the ride in a BMW?"

"Where are you?"

"Monte Carlo. I came here to gamble."

Okay, Annja thought, at least that made sense. The old man loved playing Texas Hold 'Em and other games of chance.

"Have you let anyone borrow your phone?" she asked.

"No."

Annja knew Roux was quite the magician, though. It would have been easy for him to pick someone's pocket, use the phone and replace it. But why go to all the trouble?

So you couldn't call him.

That realization made her angry. She told Jean-Paul good-bye and hung up despite his protests.

"I take it the old fox didn't call on his phone," Garin said.

"No."

Garin laughed. "He's worth millions and he stints on a long-distance bill."

Annja slipped her phone back into her purse.

Garin sipped wine. "Why did he call you?"

"Someone," Annja said, pinning Garin with her gaze, "told him I was having dinner with you."

Garin held up his hands. "It wasn't me. I know what he would say."

"He said it. I don't suppose you have a phone number where he can be reached?"

"No. Where is he?"

"Monte Carlo."

Garin stroked his chin. "I know where he might be. You and I could—"

"No," Annja said. Dinner had been far too comfortable for her liking. She didn't want to spend any more time in Garin's company because doing so was all too easy. "Whatever's going on, it's going to have to go on without me."

"Where's that driving curiosity that I've noticed is so much a part of you?" Garin taunted her.

"I'm going to turn it in other directions," Annja said, but she knew it wasn't going to be easy.

Roux and Garin were never forthcoming about information they had that she lacked. Thankfully, there were institutions all around the world that had more knowledge than both of those men combined.

In fact, when it came to pure history and the science of archaeology, she knew more than they did. Just not on a personal basis.

A few moments later, Mama served a cherry torte topped with homemade ice cream. For a time Annja forgot about the Nephilim.

"DID YOU HAVE a nice time?" Garin asked.

With the heavy meal sitting in her stomach, topped by the rich dessert, Annja felt sleepy. She stared through the limousine's tinted windows at the streets.

"I did," Annja said.

"I thought perhaps we might go dancing," Garin told her. "Unless you're too tired."

Annja considered that. She'd worked late on the movie set each night for the past few days and hadn't really seen much of the local scene. Several of the movie crew had mentioned the clubs throughout the downtown area.

Dancing sounded fun, but it sounded almost *too* attractive.

Noticing her reticence, Garin said, "I know you have an eclectic taste in music."

That was true. Annja liked what she liked, and the gamut ran from jazz to R&B to African tribal songs.

"I know a great club," Garin said. "It's not far from your hotel."

Annja wavered. It had been a long time since she'd last been dancing. She wanted to relax and let go. The offer was extremely tempting.

"I've got an early day tomorrow," she said.

"So you'll miss out on some sleep. You've done that before." Garin smiled. "Come on, Annja. A night of revelry and wild abandon. Doesn't that sound like fun?"

It did. It sounded like exactly what Annja needed.

"I'm going," Garin said, "whether you go with me or not."

Was that intended as a challenge or a threat? Annja wondered.

"I'm just saying," Garin continued, "that you're free to choose. My plans are already set. But I'd love the company and I think you'd have a good time."

So he isn't pressuring you, Annja thought. Before she could make up her mind, two cars roared into motion along the street.

Garin saw them, too. He yelled a warning to the driver as he pulled out a pistol and his cell phone.

The lead car slammed into the limousine hard enough to knock it from the street and across the sidewalk. The luxury car struck the corner of the building on the other side of a narrow alley, and the sound from the impact echoed inside the vehicle.

"Get someone up here!" Garin barked in German over the cell phone.

The seat belts had snapped tight and kept Annja from being thrown from her seat. Liquid fire traced her chest as the straps jerked the breath from her lungs.

Men boiled from the car that had rammed the front of the limousine. All of them carried assault weapons and pistols. They darted through the glaring headlights as they raced to surround the limousine. Annja saw at least two green-scimitar tattoos.

"Apparently your friends haven't given up," Garin growled.

"They're not my friends," Annja shot back. But she couldn't imagine why Saladin's men—if they were Saladin's men—were so driven to get to her. More than that, though, she didn't know how she and Garin were going to escape.

10

Quiet and composed, contemplative almost, Roux sat at the Texas Hold 'Em table in one of the casino's private rooms. He smoked a big cigar and watched the other players.

Six men and one woman still remained at the table. Only four of them, including Roux, were still in the hand currently being played out. The other three had thrown their hands onto the felt tabletop in disgust and studied their dwindling pile of chips. The game was all about skill and luck and husbanding the resources on the table.

Roux studied his own stacks of chips. They looked positively anemic.

The dealer politely called Roux's name. At least, the man called the name Roux was currently employing. The identity was a conceit that could conceivably backfire on him. He tried his best to live in the world without a paper trail. However, in order to qualify for the Texas Hold 'Em tournaments and other games he liked to play, he had to provide an identity that had some depth and texture. That was inherently dangerous.

"In or out, sir?" the dealer asked quietly. He was an older man with a jowly face and short-clipped hair. All night he'd acted as a seasoned veteran with cards.

Roux seethed inside. The cards had been so good to him at first, and now they ran cold. He didn't know if he could trust what he was seeing, and he hated to take long shots. It was absurd and intolerable.

He kept his frustrations locked in, though. Even so much as a deep breath could have given away crucial knowledge about him to the other players. Those behaviors were called "tells" in the trade, and they were dangerously destructive to a player.

Declan Connelly was an Irish launderer worth millions. He sat solid and imposing on the other side of the table. As if he didn't have a care in the world, he sipped his whiskey straight up. He could drink for hours—and had been—and still play as though he were stone-cold sober.

He'd also apparently brought the luck of the Irish with him. He'd hit on combinations during the night that had at first appeared all but impossible.

"C'mon, old man," Connelly taunted. "You're squeezing onto them chips like they're the last ones you're likely to see in your lifetime." He snickered. "'Course as old as you are, I guess maybe that could be the case."

Roux ignored the insult and concentrated on his cards. He wasn't going to let himself be baited.

Two queens—hearts and diamonds—had shown up in the flop, the spill of the initial three community cards across the felt. Roux felt certain Connelly was holding another queen in his two down cards because the river was widely split unless someone was holding a queen. There was nothing really to build on in the river and more than likely winning the hand would depend on pairing up cards. The third card was the jack of spades.

"We really need to get on with this," Ling Po said. "I'd like to get in another hand before I go for the massage I've scheduled." She was British and from old money. Besides her money, she also possessed her youth. She was in her twenties and was a beautiful porcelain doll of a woman.

"Now, honey," the big Texas wildcatter, Roy Hudder, drawled, "you ought not rush a man at two things in this life. One's romance and the other's poker. Give the old-timer a little breathin' room."

Roux hated being called old-timer by the Texan. Hudder was in his sixties and dressed like a television cowboy in a rhinestone-studded suit. Eyes flicking over the cards showing on the table, Roux knew that he still had a chance to put his hand together.

He held the ten and the king of spades as his hole cards. Together with the jack of spades showing, he had a chance at a royal flush. Provided that the next two cards dealt were the right ones.

Roux knew that his luck hadn't been running like that. It was just that he couldn't let go of Connelly's constant heckling.

"It takes nerve to play this game, boyo," Connelly said. He bared his teeth in a feral grin. "Maybe you've already spent yours, eh?"

Roux called, matching the bets that had been made on the table.

The dealer burned a card and slid the turn card onto the felt. The ace of spades stood neatly beside the two queens and the jack.

Now a potential straight lay in waiting. Some of the betting picked up pace.

Roux reluctantly parted with his chips. One card in his favor didn't mean much. And he hated bidding on luck, but he couldn't walk away from the table.

"Growing a spine, old man?" Connelly taunted.

Roux ignored him.

The dealer dealt the river, the final community card that finished the seven cards the players had to make a hand from.

It was the queen of spades. Roux couldn't believe his luck. He kept his face neutral and didn't move.

Connelly's left nostril twitched. It was a tell Roux had spotted hours ago. The man definitely had a queen among his hold cards. He now had four of a kind.

The bet went to Ling Po. She raised the stakes a little.

Roux pushed the rest of his chips into the pot. "I'm all in," he said.

Ling Po tossed her cards onto the table and Hudder did, as well.

Connelly stared at Roux from across the table. "So now it's just you and me, old man." His grin grew wider. "You're so desperate you're trying to buy this pot, aren't you?"

Roux said nothing.

"That's what this is all about, isn't it?" Connelly asked. "A big bluff at the end to show everybody you're not afraid to lose your money."

Roux returned the man's gaze without comment.

Connelly cursed. "Bit of theatrical nonsense is what it is." He tapped the table with a forefinger. "For you to beat me, you'd have to have the ten and king of spades. But you don't have them, do you?"

"The bet is to you, Mr. Connelly," the dealer informed the big Irishman politely.

With an impatient wave, Connelly quieted the dealer.

"You're just smoke and mirrors, old man. I still remember that bluff you tried to run when we opened this game."

Roux had done that purposefully because the pot had been small enough that getting busted running a bluff wouldn't cost much. And he'd gotten caught doing it, as he had intended.

"I hate bluffers," Connelly said. "Either you have the cards you need to win, or you need to go home. This game's about luck and skill, not about drama."

"Actually," Ling Po said, "I prefer a man who knows how to make a production of things. Otherwise this game becomes tedious. Except for the winning and losing, of course." She folded her arms on the table and leaned forward. "That's what we're all here for, right, Irish? The winning and losing? So are you going to talk and try to figure out if our friend is bluffing, or are you going to play cards?"

The red in Connelly's face deepened.

Roux knew the woman's words had seared Connelly, and they had sealed the deal. Although Roux had fewer chips, by going all in he'd shoved enough into the pot that losing a matching amount would seriously impact Connelly's game. Roux was counting on the hand playing out and doing that very thing.

"You don't have it," Connelly said.

Roux kept silent as the Sphinx. Anything he said would potentially tell Connelly something.

"Mr. Connelly," the dealer said quietly.

Like an impatient child, Connelly blew out his breath. It was the most out of control Roux had seen the man all evening. He also knew he'd never have a better chance to break Connelly's confidence.

"You don't have it," Connelly repeated. Angrily, he pushed in stacks of chips to match Roux's wager. As if delivering the death stroke, the Irishman flipped over his hole cards and exposed the queen of clubs. "I've got four ladies, boyo. Unless you can come up with three kings or three aces in those two hole cards, you're beaten."

"I can't do that, I'm afraid." Without fanfare, Roux flipped his cards over to reveal his royal flush.

Connelly screamed a curse and pushed back from the table.

"We have a scheduled break at this point," the dealer said smoothly.

Roux got up from the table and walked out into the main casino.

Standing on the second-floor landing overlooking the main pit, Roux took in a deep breath and let it out. There wasn't anything that felt as good as victory. If he ever lost that feeling, if he ever grew jaded with it, he honestly didn't know what he would do with himself. Living a long life could be incredibly boring and repetitious.

Especially in modern times.

In the past, when the world had been wide open and a man had been free to fight wars and love women indiscriminately, when there had been so many things to discover, Roux had felt better about his long years.

He had dined with kings, helped them slay their enemies and aided them in seizing their crowns. He'd raised armies and fought tremendous battles. Every day, those stakes had been for his life or the lives of those around him.

Now, though, he couldn't do those things. Warmongers tended to draw too much attention and the enmity of the world. World conquerors, he feared, were a thing of the past when all it took was one man with a satellite and a long-range missile to put that would-be world conqueror in the grave.

The times were so different these days, and he had started

to fear sometimes that if he lived too much longer he wouldn't be able to blend in.

Thankfully he had gambling, though the money was never an issue. He had more than he could ever spend in his long life, and there was more to be had if he needed it.

One of the reasons he loved Annja Creed as he did was that she had that fire in her that he could barely remember. Still, she had Joan's sword, and that thing had never proved helpful in living a long life.

He took out a hand-rolled cigar. It was a blend that he specially ordered. Cigars were one thing he'd never grown bored with.

Action was heating up at a craps table. Whoever was rolling the bones had evidently been inordinately lucky. The crowd was two and three deep, all of them cheering the shooter on as she threw the dice again. Another cheer rose.

Despite the movement going on around him and the steady current of conversations, Roux heard the light tread and sensed the movement behind him. He took another puff off the cigar and didn't react.

"They're happy."

"Yes," Roux agreed, "they are."

Ling Po stepped to his side and joined him at the railing above the pit. "You knew I was there."

Roux glanced at her. "Yes."

"Yet you ignored me."

"Trust me, dear girl, you're not easy to ignore."

"Well, then, why don't you pay more attention to me?"

11

Roux took in Ling Po's slender figure. It was obvious from the graceful way she moved that she paid attention to her physical health and was athletically inclined. The black pants, black jacket and white blouse almost looked like a business suit, but the tailor had made certain the material didn't hide the curves beneath. There was a generous expanse of cleavage.

"How did you know I was there?" Ling Po's brows knitted, and the effort almost made her look like a little girl.

"ESP?" Roux suggested.

Ling Po smiled. "No, I don't think so." She paused. "You're a very interesting man."

"I am," he agreed, and he silently thanked the gods that gambling wasn't the only interest left to him. His infatuation with young women, especially those who felt they had to compete with him on some level, was huge.

Ling Po laughed. "And you certainly don't lack for confidence."

"I find myself emboldened by your beauty," Roux said. "I find my spirit made larger for being in your presence. You'll have to forgive me."

Her cheeks turned slightly pink. That had been unexpected. With all of her wealth he would have expected her to be hardened to any form of flattery.

"You talk a lot of nonsense," the young woman responded.

"Do you think so? I thought it sounded much better than telling you that you had a great set of hooters." Roux smiled.

Ling Po laughed, but she didn't bother to hide her cleavage. She seemed genuinely amused rather than put off by his crude remark. "You know, I could think you're hitting on me."

Roux lifted his eyebrows. "I'd be devastated to know that you approached me with anything less in mind."

"You're entirely too confident."

"I've always been very successful with women."

"Have you?"

"You came over to meet me, didn't you?"

"Not because of any sexual allure."

"Are you certain?"

"You're old enough to be my grandfather."

"And that makes me even more intriguing, doesn't it?"

Ling Po didn't deny it. "I like the way you handled Connelly."

Roux shrugged. "The man was positively begging for a comeuppance of the rudest sort. Although, if the cards hadn't favored me, that could have been embarrassing."

They shared a brief laugh.

"He didn't know that you allowed yourself to be caught bluffing earlier," Ling Po said.

Roux managed an innocent look but couldn't help grinning just a little. Ling Po was sharper than he thought. It would be good to keep that in mind.

"Did I do that?" he asked.

The young woman nodded. "Yes. It was very carefully done, by the way."

"Thank you."

"I don't think anyone else caught on."

"Yet you did."

"Truthfully, I think I'm better than anyone else in that room."

"Ah, I see."

"I don't mean to take anything away from you. You're a very good card player," she said.

"Again, you're too kind."

"No. I've seen some of the best. That's why I'm surprised I've not crossed paths with you before."

"I play a small game."

"By choice. You could be on television, playing in one of the tournaments that get broadcast."

Roux waved that away and took another puff off his cigar. He rounded his ash into a nearby ashtray. "I've no interest in that. Entirely too much attention." And there was too much of an opportunity for too many people to see him and perhaps recognize him.

"I can't believe you'd be shy."

"Perhaps I just prefer a gentleman's game among friends."

Ling Po shook her head. "After the way you ambushed and baited Connelly, I don't think so. That wasn't very gentlemanly."

"He isn't—by any stretch of a generous imagination—anywhere close to being a gentleman."

"No, but I have to wonder what you're all about."

"Then I'll just say that I like being mysterious. I've found that women think that's attractive."

"It is."

Roux turned to face the young woman. "So is your intent

in meeting me merely to get a better sense of my game? Or do you have something else in mind?"

Her stare returned his challenge full measure. "You honestly don't care if I take you up on that or not, do you?"

"I do," Roux said, "but if you feel disinclined, I won't be devastated." That was true, but he seriously doubted she was going to walk away. She was much too competitive. She was going to have to find out if she was his equal at the poker table and elsewhere.

Ling Po traced the back of Roux's hand with her forefinger. "We do have time for dinner before the game resumes," she said.

"We do."

"I've got a big room. We could order in."

"That," Roux said, "sounds absolutely delightful." After crushing Connelly as he had, Roux found his appetite for other things had been whetted, as well.

"Then you'll come as my guest."

"I wouldn't have it any other way."

"Still robbing the cradle, I see," a woman stated laconically. Her accent was South African, a mix of English and German with sharp edges.

The voice came to Roux from the past. Pleasant memories and warnings accompanied the words. He turned to face the woman.

"Jennifer," he whispered. Dread, anticipation and wariness all spun a web within him.

JENNIFER BAILEY WAS a goddess of the night. When Roux first met her that thought had leapt into his head and never left. Her skin was flawless warm toffee, and her eyes were a brown that seemed to glow with an inner fire.

Five feet eight inches tall with generous curves, she turned heads and silenced conversations every time she entered a room. Her hair was cut short and framed her beautiful face. She wore a scarlet dress that dipped low and was cut high, stopping just short of being tacky.

As he gazed at her, Roux tried to remember how long it had been since he'd last seen her. At least ten years had passed. That meant she had to be in her early forties, but she did not look her age. Anyone who saw her would have guessed she was in her early thirties.

Scarlet lipstick turned her frown florid.

Ling Po bridled at once, obviously irritated that their conversation had been interrupted. Roux smiled at that, but when it came to class, Jennifer Bailey beat the younger woman hands down.

"It's good to see you again," Roux said.

"Is it?" Jennifer cocked her head to one side to regard him. "The last word I received from you was a note on a pillow telling me you had things to do. That was thirteen years ago."

"Thirteen. Really? A wretched number filled with ill-fated consequences," Roux noted.

"It's been a long time." Jennifer gazed at the young woman at Roux's side. "I can see you haven't changed a bit."

"My predilections remain as constant as the North Star."

"And remain as predictable. That's how I found you."

"It took a long time," Roux pointed out.

Jennifer shrugged, an elegant shift of her shoulders.

"I've thought of you often," he told her, and part of him hoped she believed him enough to forgive him his trespasses.

"And I've often thought of kicking your skinny arse for leaving without a proper goodbye." Jennifer put her hand on her hip and stared at Ling Po. "I'd also dare say you haven't thought of me for at least ten or fifteen minutes."

"Do you know this woman?" Ling Po stepped close enough to Roux to partially claim him as her territory.

"I do." Roux made the introductions. "Ling Po, I'd like you to meet Jennifer Bailey. She's an artist. Maybe you've seen some of her work."

"I'm not much into greeting cards, I'm afraid."

Roux coughed delicately. "Actually, Jennifer's work has hung in some of the finest European and African galleries. Jennifer, this is Ling Po. Her family owns the Topaz Hotel in London, among others."

Ling Po didn't appear to be impressed. Nor did Jennifer.

"Perhaps you didn't notice," Ling Po said icily, "but we were engaged in a *private* conversation."

"That's all right," Jennifer said dismissively. "We're old friends. Evidently you're going to be another new friend. He doesn't make many friends who turn into old friends."

"You've certainly got the old part covered."

For a moment Roux thought Jennifer would physically attack Ling Po. Jennifer wasn't one to mince words. She also preferred a direct line of action.

"After thirteen years and a note on a pillow," Ling Po went on, "I'm surprised that you'd consider yourself a friend."

"Youth can be diverting," Jennifer replied, "but it's also flighty and annoying. Especially on a self-indulgent, high-maintenance narcissist."

"A man prefers new challenges to old conquests," Ling Po said.

"Maybe we should let him be the judge of that," Jennifer suggested sweetly.

Roux, a master strategist on the battlefield and leader of warriors, suddenly found himself in the worst possible position any man could face.

Both women looked at him expectantly.

Roux decided to double down on the risk. He'd gone in search of neither of the women. He could just as easily dine alone. And the night was still young. There would be other opportunities.

"Perhaps we could have dinner and reach some kind of accord that would be less adversarial. Though not without mutual reward and benefit," he said. He smiled. In the past such a suggestion had often netted surprising results.

"Really?" Ling Po gazed at Jennifer in open speculation.

Jennifer frowned. "You really haven't changed, have you?"

"There was a time when you weren't so quick to turn down new experiences," Roux said. "I seem to recall you introducing me to one of your girlfriends shortly after we met."

Jennifer looked at him. "I have a lead on the Nephilim."

Excitement filled every molecule of Roux's body. Jennifer was one of the few people he'd told about the Nephilim painting.

"Do you know where it is?" he asked. His voice was hoarse and tight.

"I've found someone who might know," Jennifer replied.

Roux couldn't believe it. None of the sources he had looking for the painting had offered even a whisper of the Nephilim's location in years.

"Where is he?" he asked.

"*She,*" Jennifer replied. "And I'm not going to tell you. I'm going to take you there."

Sour bile burst at the back of Roux's throat. "You know how dangerous that is. You've seen how Salome can be."

Jennifer smiled at him, and fear laced with sadness showed in her bright eyes. "I still wear the scars."

"You're lucky to be alive. Tell me—"

"No." Jennifer shook her head to emphasize her answer. "I've worked on this since you've been gone. I'm not just going to hand it to you and watch you walk away."

"It would be better if you did."

"We're not going to live forever. Isn't that what you used to say?" Jennifer smiled. "But look at you. You haven't aged a day."

"Jennifer—"

"No. I'm in or I'm gone. That's the deal."

Roux held her gaze for just a moment and saw no compromise there. "All right."

"What?" Ling Po stepped in front of him. "You're just going to leave with this woman?" She made Jennifer's gender sound like a terminal condition.

As gallantly as he could, because he never liked to sour an unexplored potential conquest, Roux took Ling Po's hand in his. He kissed the back of her hand gently.

"Until we meet again, dear girl." Roux released her hand and stepped back.

Ling Po looked as if she was in shock.

"Beat Connelly for me. I'll see you when I can." Roux turned and took Jennifer by the arm and headed down the sweeping staircase.

His thoughts centered on the painting of the Nephilim and the secrets it hid. He knew he was the most excited he'd been in decades. Except for finding the final piece of Joan's sword and watching it mend itself in an eye blink in Annja's hand.

But he was also afraid.

12

Annja stared at the armed men on the other side of the limousine's tinted window. They threatened her with the handguns and machine pistols they held. At least three of the five wore green-scimitar tattoos at their throats. If the others did, the shadows hid them.

"Come out!" one of them shouted. His voice barely penetrated the muffled confines of the luxury car.

The driver attempted to reverse and break away, but the second car crashed into the rear of the limousine. The tires spun but couldn't get any traction.

"I suppose getting out of this while in the car is out of the question," Annja said.

"Yes." Garin looked irritated.

"We could stay in the car and call the police."

"Until they decided to blow us up or drill holes in the car roof and flood the interior with gasoline."

"Aren't you the pessimist," Annja said. She couldn't believe she was as calm as she was, but she'd been in bad situations before. Since claiming Joan's sword, those situations seemed to come along more often than not.

"No. It's what I would do under similar circumstances," Garin said.

"It's a good thing you're not out there, then."

"Yes. But I, much as it grieves me to say so, am not wholly unique."

"On the other hand, we might be able to stay in the car long enough for the police to arrive."

"That," Garin said, "would present a whole new set of troubles. I'd rather keep the authorities out of my business. Besides, the Prague police aren't overly fond of charging into small armies of men armed with assault weapons."

"That leaves us with trying to escape," Annja said.

One of the men slammed his clenched fist against the tinted window. Hollow booms echoed within the limousine.

"Get out! Now!" the man ordered.

"It's a pity about the dress," Garin said. "I'd rather hoped you might get to have it as a keepsake. No matter how the evening turned out."

"What?" Annja couldn't believe what she'd just heard. There was no way the evening was going to end up with her doing anything other than going back to her hotel. *Alone*. And if Garin was so egotistical that he wouldn't acknowledge that, then she was—

"Excuse me." Garin put his hands on her thigh. He gripped the hem of her dress and tore it up to her hip.

Immediately, Annja slapped him. The open-handed blow landed hard enough to split his lower lip.

Garin released the dress and slid back out of reach. Anger darkened his face. "You couldn't move in that dress as it was. I was trying to help you."

"Oh." Annja felt a little unsettled. "You should have said something."

Gingerly, Garin wiped blood from the corner of his mouth. "I did. I said, 'Excuse me.' It was, I thought, polite enough."

"Your intentions weren't exactly clear."

"Trust me," he said, "if I ever moved on you in an amorous fashion, it wouldn't be as clumsy or heavy-handed as that."

"You're just lucky I didn't break something."

Garin growled a curse.

The man at the window used his gun butt to rap against the glass this time. Then he reversed it and shoved the barrel against the glass.

"Is the glass bulletproof?" Annja asked.

"Against those weapons it should be," Garin said in displeasure. "Of course, that also means that I can't shoot back at them. By the way, would you like a pistol?"

At Garin's touch, a section of the wall slid back to reveal a dozen handguns, two shotguns, three assault rifles and two machine pistols. Oil gleamed on the metal.

"You don't have a rocket launcher in there?" Annja asked drily.

Garin pressed a recessed release button on the seat in front of them. The cushion flipped over to expose three rocket launcher tubes. "I keep it fully stocked," he said.

"You normally need this much firepower?" Annja asked.

"Every day I hope that I don't. But I'd rather be prepared than struggle to get that way." Garin grimaced at the repeated hammering on the window. "So, would you like a weapon?"

Annja hesitated. Although she had killed from time to time to save her own life or those of others, it wasn't something she was comfortable with. Nor was it something she wanted to ever get comfortable with. But she knew that violence was often best met with violence.

"It's us or them," Garin told her, "and I'd much rather not be the only one shooting back. I thought maybe if you were armed we could mix it up a little. Divide their attention."

Annja took two of the 9 mm pistols.

"Good," Garin said.

Expertly, Annja tucked one of the pistols between her knees and used the release button behind the trigger guard to drop the ammunition magazine. The bullets gleamed in the clip.

"They're both loaded," Garin said. "It's foolish to keep a weapon around and not keep it ready, as well."

Annja checked the magazine in the second pistol. It, too, was loaded.

The man at the window stepped back and warned his companions. For a moment, they all fell back.

Then another man came forward with a trenching tool and a can.

"That," Garin said, "would be the gasoline."

The man stepped up onto the limo's trunk.

"We do have one thing in our favor," Garin said.

"I'd love to hear it," Annja replied.

"At this point I don't think they want to kill you. I think they want to use you as a bargaining chip against Roux."

"Not getting that warm, fuzzy feeling," Annja said. She listened as the man hammered the trenching tool against the car's roof. A dent took shape at once. She knew the roof was reinforced when the tool didn't immediately rip through.

"We don't have a lot of time." Garin reached for a remote control in a pocket on his door. "And I do have one surprise left. Be prepared to move."

"I am." Annja just wished her stomach would stop flip-flopping.

"We go straight into them and hope they hesitate about firing into the middle of each other." Garin took up a cut-down pump-action shotgun. "Then we cross the street and try to take the high ground."

"Okay."

The man atop the car roof hammered the trenching tool down again.

"Ready?" Garin asked.

Annja kicked her shoes off, sucked in a deep breath, then blew it out. "Ready."

Garin pressed a button on the remote. Immediately the man on top of the limo started jerking and jumping. Annja watched the man's shadow on the ground. If he hadn't been trying to kill them, his antics might have been amusing.

Then he fell from the car and lay prone on the ground. The trenching tool and the gas can landed beside him.

"The car's exterior can be lethally charged with electricity for a short time," Garin said. He reached across Annja and opened the door. "Go!"

Annja stepped out into the alley and swiveled past the open door. She started to slow, but Garin put a hand into her back and shoved her forward. Thrown off stride, she stumbled, but quickly recovered.

The men faced her, but their attention was still partially on the quivering man on the ground. She ran toward them and hoped that Garin was right about them wanting her alive.

They brought their weapons up, then hesitated as they realized their companions were in their line of fire. Instead, they transformed into a solid wall of flesh and blood to block her.

Garin ran at Annja's heels. He scooped the can of gasoline

and flung it at the men. Annja sensed what Garin was about to do because she knew how destructive he could be.

"Drop!" Garin ordered.

As she spun and dropped into a crouch, Annja watched the gas can fly above the heads of the men. When the metal container reached chest level, Garin fired the shotgun. Pellets tore through the container and through the hapless man standing directly on the other side.

At least one or two of the pellets scraped sparks from the metal can. The descending gasoline suddenly turned into a maelstrom of liquid fire that fell across the center of the line of men.

Instantly engulfed in flames, the line broke. Men concerned themselves with beating out the fire rather than continuing to pursue their quarry.

Annja winced at the heat and the thought of what the gasoline fire would do to the men it covered. Then Garin shoved her into motion again.

"Run!" he shouted.

Annja sprinted for the opening. Men shrieked helplessly around her. Others cursed and someone ordered them to grab Annja. A man clawed at her arm. She pointed one of her pistols in his direction and quickly squeezed off two rounds. The offending hand dropped away.

A fire-enshrouded man blocked her way and lunged at her out of mindless terror rather than by design. Garin's shotgun boomed again. The fiery man whirled like a top and fell away. Most of his head was gone. Annja ran across the street.

A racing engine warned her of a car's approach. She glanced to her left and was almost blinded by the vehicle's lights. The car came straight at her. The engine raced even harder as the driver stepped on the accelerator.

Unable to turn back, slow or outrun the car, Annja did the

only thing she could do—she leaped up and forward. The incredible speed she sometimes acquired during periods of increased adrenaline saved her.

Her foot touched the car's hood and she leaped again, throwing herself forward. As she flipped, she brought both of her pistols to bear and fired as quickly as she was able. She lost track of how many shots she fired.

The bullets smashed through the side window, then the rear glass. Fist-size holes appeared in the windows, mirrored by smaller ones in the car body.

Annja landed on her feet, arms thrown out for balance. Garin had been right. If he hadn't torn the dress, she'd never have pulled off that move. Still, the draft was incredible.

"No time for a victory dance," Garin growled as he ran by her and caught her by the arm. He yanked her into motion. Somehow she managed to stay on her feet as she went from zero to sixty in one of his strides.

13

Bullets chopped into the street and the buildings as Annja fled toward the alley. People at an outdoor café a block away screamed and took cover.

Annja felt the rough street surface slap at her bare feet. Yowling and spitting cats scattered from the crooked line of garbage bins lining the walls. The cloying stench of rotting food was overwhelming.

A glance behind her revealed that men were in pursuit.

"Don't look." Garin caught hold of a fire escape zigzagging up the side of the building. He rounded the corner and headed up. Bullets from their pursuers' weapons licked sparks from the iron structure.

Annja paused at the bottom of the stairs and took aim. No one was out in the street except the men chasing them. She triggered her shots quickly, aiming at the center of the mass of men, and felt the pistols buck in her hands.

Two of the men sprawled onto the street. Others broke ranks and dived for cover. A few stood their ground and fired assault rifles on full-auto. Bullets rattled the fire escape as Annja took cover.

In the next instant, the limousine blew up. A concussive wave rolled over the men and knocked them flat. White noise filled Annja's hearing. She heard Garin yelling at her from above.

"Hurry!" Hard, dark shadows lined his face. "Are you going to wait around for them to recover?"

Annja grabbed the railing and started up. Only a few sporadic bullets skidded off the stairs.

Garin waited for her at the top of the four-story building. Below in the street, the men had regrouped and charged for the fire escape.

"Why did the car blow up?" Annja asked. She tried to ignore the pain in her bare feet from the rocks across the rooftop.

"I blew it up." Garin pulled a remote control from his pocket. "I don't like to leave incriminating evidence behind. The explosion should at least confuse the police and help build a case for deniability. There are some drawbacks to the modern technology."

"We were riding around in a car filled with explosives?" Annja was horrified.

"No," Garin said. "There were just enough explosives in the car to dispose of it."

"What about the driver?"

"He's long gone by now." Garin gazed down at the street.

As Annja watched, four sleek black cars screeched to a halt in the street. Men got out of the vehicles with grim efficiency and unlimbered weapons. For a moment Annja thought that reinforcements had arrived. Then the men started firing on the would-be kidnappers.

"Your security team," Annja said.

"A little late, but that was my fault. I had them securing the club I was going to take you to."

"I hadn't agreed to go."

He grinned at her wolfishly. "You would have."

Harsh cracks sounded out in the street. Annja took partial cover behind a gargoyle at the corner of the rooftop and looked down. Methodically, the new arrivals killed the men left in the street. Only a few escaped. The security team checked the men on the ground and shot those still alive.

Sickened, Annja turned back to Garin. "Call them off. That isn't necessary."

"I think it is," Garin said coldly. "They tried to hurt you."

"That's my problem," Annja said angrily.

"While you were in *my* care," Garin stated. "That's intolerable. I didn't get to where I am by being weak or showing compassion to those who declared themselves my enemies. You know history. That's true of every ruler that claimed territory as his own."

Annja listened to the flat cracks that grew further apart. She tried not to think about what was happening down there.

Sirens reverberated in the street and grew rapidly closer.

"Let me get you somewhere safe," Garin suggested. "Staying to answer questions for the police isn't going to help you any."

Not knowing what else to do, not relishing the possibility of returning to the police station, Annja nodded.

"THIS ISN'T the safest place for you."

Annja met Garin's glower with one of her own. "I might point out that being with you didn't prove safe." She walked along the hallway to her hotel room in her bare feet.

An older couple passing by stared at her and Garin in consternation. It didn't help that four of Garin's men in black suits followed them.

"We were mugged," Annja explained, feeling the need to say something.

The woman made sympathetic noises, but neither she nor her husband stopped.

"I was the one inadvertently in danger," Garin protested. "If I hadn't been with you, they wouldn't have tried to kill me."

"So this is *my* fault?"

"It's hardly my fault," Garin objected.

Annja slid her hotel door card through the slot. The light turned green and the electronic lock disengaged. She stopped inside the door and blocked Garin's way.

He stared at her. "Surely you're jesting."

"Nope."

"You're not going to let me in?"

"Not by the hair of my chinny-chin-chin," Annja confirmed.

"That's stupid."

"I don't think so."

Garin cursed.

Annja tried to close the door. Garin blocked her efforts with a hand.

"Take your hand out of the door," Annja directed. "Unless you don't need those fingers anymore."

"You need me."

"Never."

Garin heaved a sigh. "We were having such a good time."

Annja pressed on the door. She knew it had to hurt.

Garin wiggled his fingers. "Annja, in all seriousness, you're probably not safe here. You should let me take you somewhere else."

Although part of her knew that Garin's argument was valid, she didn't want to place her fate in his hands. She didn't trust him, and she also didn't want to depend on him.

"I can manage," she said. She renewed her efforts to shut the door.

"You're hurting my hand."

"Take it out."

"I can't." Garin sounded totally put out. "You've got it trapped with the door."

Annja eased back on the door. When she did, Garin leaned into it and shoved it open.

"Get out," Annja ordered.

Garin ignored her and went to the couch. The room was small and he seemed to fill the space even while seated.

"I'm not leaving until I know that you're safe," Garin insisted.

"You don't like me, remember? I'm the reason Joan's sword is whole again. The reason you might not live forever."

"Don't tempt me. I'm feeling favorable toward you at the moment, but if I ever find one gray hair, that might change. And as difficult as you're being, that could happen tonight."

Annja glared at him. "I could call hotel security."

"You could. But they don't have enough people here to throw me out. They'll have to call the police. Then the police will have questions they want answered. They won't make me leave. They'll take both of us into custody."

"I'm willing to go. Are you? Or are you afraid of being inconvenienced?" Annja said.

"I have friends everywhere," Garin said. "The local police will hold me only as long as I allow them to." He grinned at her. "You, however, they would hold longer. If only to spite me because they might think we're *involved*." He raised his eyebrows suggestively. "That might be quite amusing. And I have no reason not to believe you'd be safe with the police. Let's do that, then. Make the call."

"No."

"Coward."

"You're a jerk."

"Stick and stones…"

Annja folded her arms. She took a deep breath and let it out. "Tell me about Saladin and the Nephilim again."

Garin let his head drop in obvious frustration. "I've told you everything I know."

"I don't believe you."

"Of course you don't. Believing me would be entirely too easy."

A phone shrilled for attention. Irritably, Garin took his phone from his pocket and glanced at the caller-ID panel. Then he pulled it to the side of his head.

"What do you want, Roux?" Garin asked.

Some of the anger and frustration Annja had been feeling drained away as she listened intently. But she couldn't hear Roux's side of the conversation.

Garin remained quiet for some time. Then he stood and said, "I'm on my way. As soon as I make arrangements I'll let you know when to expect me." He closed the phone. "Well, that certainly changes things."

"What?"

"I've got to go." Garin walked to the door and let himself out. The four security men stood post in the hallway.

"Where are you going?" Annja followed him.

"Roux called."

"I know that. The two of you hate each other."

"Not always."

Annja knew that was true. At times the two men seemed

to care for each other deeply. Then they would try to kill one another. Keeping up with their relationship was confusing.

"Now?" she asked. "Now you like each other?"

Garin shrugged. "We'll see how it works out."

"This is about the Nephilim painting, isn't it?" Annja asked.

Garin grinned at her. "So now you want to be my friend."

That brought Annja up short. "For the moment," she agreed.

Garin laughed.

"I'm going with you," she declared.

"No," he replied. "You're not."

Without warning, Garin leaned forward and kissed Annja.

14

Annja felt Garin's lips pressed to hers, and her synapses fired in warning and excitement. After a moment, she recovered enough to draw back to punch him. Instead, he pushed her back into her room and closed the door.

Annja opened the door and tried to step out, but she was instantly confronted by Garin's four security men. They didn't move out of her way, and Annja got the distinct impression that any physical effort she put forth would be countered.

"Take care, Annja," Garin called from down the hallway.

"Come back," Annja told him.

Garin paused at the elevator. "Thank you, but no. Tonight has been an exercise in frustration. On any number of levels. And I don't know that Roux is going to offer anything better."

"Where are you going?"

The elevator doors opened behind Garin.

"If you're really interested, maybe I'll tell you someday." Garin stepped into the elevator cage and pressed a button. "Over dinner. The next time, you can cook."

"I wouldn't bet on it."

"You're too curious." Garin smiled. "I like steak. Potatoes. Maybe a wedge of apple pie and ice cream. I'm really a simple man with simple tastes." He waved to her, still smiling, and the elevator doors closed.

Angrily, Annja drew back and slammed the door shut on the security men.

LESS THAN TWENTY MINUTES later, someone knocked on the hotel room door. Annja was in the bathtub soaking and trying to push past the evening's frustration.

She wanted to ignore the knock. If it was Garin, she was certain he wouldn't tell her anything. If Saladin's men were knocking—and there was no reason they would, she told herself—she didn't want to be caught in the bathtub.

Grudgingly, she climbed from the scented water and toweled off.

The knock sounded again, more insistent this time.

"Coming," Annja called. She dressed quickly, pulling on her bra and panties, then covering that with jeans and a long-sleeved white shirt. She padded barefoot to the door. Before she arrived, the knock was repeated.

"Open up, Miss Creed," an authoritative voice demanded. "We know you're in there. This is the police."

Anxiety pulsed through Annja. She peered through the peephole.

Two men stood in the hallway. One was Skromach, the police detective who'd investigated the bombing on the movie set. The other was younger and slimmer, but he looked as much like a cop as Skromach.

"Miss Creed," the younger man called. He knocked on the door.

"I didn't call for the police," Annja protested. She felt like an idiot saying that as if she were protesting a pizza delivery. .

"We need to speak with you, Miss Creed."

Desperation set in then. Annja knew that a police visit at this time of the evening couldn't bode well. She retreated from the door and crossed to the bed where her backpack and boots were.

After grabbing both, she headed for the balcony. She was only four floors up. The climb wouldn't kill her. The fall might, but the climb wouldn't. And she could claim, especially if they were investigating the violence that had broken out earlier, that she was afraid for her life. She slung her backpack over her shoulder and opened the balcony door.

Three men, all of them dressed in tactical riot gear, stood on her balcony. They looked at her.

"Good evening, Miss Creed," one of them said politely in accented English. "Perhaps it might be better if you went the other way and accompanied the detectives."

"Sure. That would be just great." By the time Annja turned around, the detectives had let themselves through the door with a hotel passkey.

"Ah, Miss Creed," Skromach said, and he looked almost happy. "So we did catch you at the hotel."

Annja knew the verb was an intentional choice.

"We'd just like you to come with us down to the police station," Skromach said.

"Why?"

Skromach shrugged. "We have just a few questions we'd like to ask you." He pinned her with his gaze. "About a dozen or so men that were killed earlier this evening."

"Don't I get to call the United States Embassy?" Annja asked.

"Perhaps," Skromach said. "We're hoping that such a thing won't become necessary. We're certain that all of this is just a misunderstanding and can be cleared up in a short time." He gestured toward the door. "Please?"

Knowing she wasn't going to get out of the investigation, Annja sighed. "Can I put my boots on first?"

"Of course."

ANNJA WOKE when the door to the interview room opened. She lifted her head from her forearms. Her vision was blurry at first, and a headache throbbed at her temples.

Her return visit to the police station was less friendly than the first time. Earlier that day—*yesterday,* she reminded herself—she'd almost been a guest.

She'd been questioned off and on for the past fourteen hours. Skromach hadn't gone home, though she suspected that he was catnapping somewhere because he seemed to come in bright eyed and ready every time he questioned her. The Prague policemen weren't pushy with their questions, but they were persistent.

"Good morning, Ms. Creed." A man approached the table. He wore an expensive suit and looked elegant. His dark complexion spoke of a history of outdoor activities.

Annja knew at once that the man wasn't a policeman.

"May I sit?" the man asked.

"I'm not here in the position of hostess," Annja said.

The man grinned, then pulled out the unadorned straight-back chair on the other side of the conference table. Unlike Skromach and his companion, this man didn't carry a file folder with her name on it.

"Thank you," he said.

"Who are you?"

The man spread his hands in front of his face and smiled again. "I could be your friend."

Wariness filled Annja. She crossed her arms and studied the man.

He was in his late thirties and physically fit. A thick shock of black hair and a small, neat goatee framed his lean, hard-planed face.

"I've got enough friends," Annja said.

That brought another smile to the man. "I've found in my business that a man cannot have too many friends."

"I don't usually meet my friends in police stations. I think I'll pass on the offer," Annja said.

The man gestured at the room. "It seems to me you could at least use one more friend at the moment."

Annja paused for a moment as if considering. "What would this *friendship* cost me?"

"I'm sure we could arrive at something."

"No, thank you."

Something hardened in the man's dark eyes. "Perhaps you shouldn't act so rashly."

"Do you call yourself Saladin?" Annja asked.

"As a matter of fact, I do. My father named me that. As his father named him. That name has been handed down in my family for generations."

"I suppose it saves on monogramming," Annja said, "but it must be confusing at family gatherings."

A trace of a scowl tightened Saladin's mouth. "Do you amuse yourself with your own wit, Ms. Creed?"

"I do. But you're the one who chose to barge in and play. How did you get past the police?"

"I'm not without resources. As I said, I could be a good friend to have."

"Trust is a big issue with me."

Saladin favored her with a smile. "You can trust me."

"You sent those men after me," Annja argued.

Saladin shrugged and grinned again. "All work and no play tends to dull the minds of the men working for me." He gazed at her intently. "You're a cipher to me, Ms. Creed. I don't like ciphers. How is it you know both Roux and Garin Braden?"

"That's none of your business, but I will tell you this—the Nephilim painting you're after? I don't know anything about it."

Saladin studied her and she noticed that one of his eyes was of a slightly different color than the other. The left one held a splash of green in the upper-right quadrant.

"Even if that were true," he said slowly, "those two men value you."

"Those two men," Annja countered, "left me to my own devices while knowing full well that you were hunting me. Does that sound like they value me?"

Annoyance deepened Saladin's scowl. "I guess the only way to truly know that is at your funeral." He got up from the chair and left the room. Annja heard the lock click behind him.

HOURS LATER—Annja didn't know how much time had passed because she didn't have access to her watch or any of her electronics—another man entered the room. He looked around cautiously, almost a little fearfully.

"Miss Creed?" he asked. He held his briefcase in front of him like a shield. He looked as if he was barely into his twenties. Youth left his face soft and round. Glasses gave him a vulnerable look. His hair was already getting thin on top.

"Yes." Annja made no effort to get up from her chair.

"I'm Walter," the man said in a nervous voice. "Walter Gronlund. I'm with the State Department."

"Don't tell me. The United States government wants to place me under arrest also."

Walter pushed his glasses up his nose with a forefinger. "Actually, no. I'm going to get you out of here."

Annja breathed a sigh of relief and hoped that what the little man was saying was true. "Forgive me, but do you happen to have any identification?"

"Of course." Walter reached into his jacket and took out a leather identification case. The photo ID looked just like him and announced that he worked for the United States Embassy in the Czech Republic.

Nervously, Walter settled his briefcase on the table. "I think they've got someone coming with your things from the hotel."

That puzzled Annja. "Why are they bringing my things from the hotel?"

"That way you don't have to stop on your way to the airport." Walter checked his BlackBerry. "We're getting a police escort to the airport, so getting there in time for the flight shouldn't be a problem."

"What flight?"

"Your flight, Miss Creed. Your visa has been canceled. Effective immediately."

Annja couldn't believe it. "They're kicking me out of the country?"

"That's an awfully blunt way to look at it, Miss Creed."

"Is there any other way to put it?"

"Actually, I believe I did put it another way. They're rescinding your visa."

Stunned, Annja slumped back in her chair.

15

Despite the impatience that screamed through her, Salome forced herself to sit quietly in the plush chair amid all the other potential buyers. She knew many of them. Over the years, they'd all crossed paths. Many of them watched her covertly and quickly glanced away when she looked in their direction.

She had a reputation, and she was quite aware of it. In fact, she took a certain amount of pride in that reputation. She'd worked hard over the years to attain it.

The auctioneer called for the buyers to bid on another item. He was a fastidious man in a good suit. His voice, though quiet and controlled, was far larger than he was.

Two young women, both dressed in low-cut gowns that threatened to expose them, presented an antique silver tea service. After they had the item properly positioned to show it off to its best advantage, the young women stepped aside.

After referencing the three-by-five card that accompanied the piece, the auctioneer said, "This six-piece tea service was once owned by President Andrew Jackson while he resided in the White House. The set has been authenticated as having been made by Jabez Gorham himself very early in his career."

Salome checked the details of the tea set in her catalog out of habit. The tea service was worth quite a bit.

Salome quietly wondered how and where the auction house had gotten its hands on such a prize.

Once the bidding began, it went fast and furious. Bids were increased with the movement of a finger, the tap of an identifying number or simply the wiggle of an eyebrow.

Salome kept track of the bidding, not at all surprised at the brisk pace. Major buyers had known the service was going to be present. Auction houses in the Hague didn't often get such things.

Salome immediately wondered if the tea service had been stolen at some point, or was even a very good replica. Either was possible. If a theft had occurred long enough ago, and if it had happened in another country, it was possible to get away with such a thing. Especially if documentation was provided that checked out against art-theft lists generated by Interpol and other international police agencies.

The tea service finally sold, but it was for at least, she judged, twenty percent over fair market value. That told her whoever had purchased it had bought it out of love, not as an investment. It was worth making note of, and she did. But it was a mental note. Nothing she ever thought or observed or noticed was recorded anywhere. Her insight was much too valuable.

Once the tea service was taken away, the two buxom beauties brought out the next piece. When Salome saw it, she stopped breathing for just a moment.

She trusted that she gave no outward sign. To the room she was prim and proper. The elegant Versace business suit—with pants, not a skirt—was the foundation of her professional image. Her brunette hair, parted on the left, hung to her shoulders and stayed carefully in place.

"The next item up for bid," the auctioneer announced, "is a painting by a little-known Venetian artist Virgil Carolini."

Salome knew that was not true. Virgil Carolini's brush had never touched the canvas in the antique frame sitting at the front of the room.

"Carolini's works are starting to find favor with collectors around the world," the auctioneer said. "Some said he was a madman, that the visions he wrought so carefully on the canvas were merely fever dreams he'd trapped in paint."

A naked man lounged on a bearskin rug in front of a fire. He was beautiful. The fire warmed the man's dusky skin and backlit him so that the shadows gave him partial modesty. His black hair gleamed and framed his face in ringlets. He was huge and proportioned evenly, godlike in every way.

"Oh, my," one of the female buyers gasped.

Salome regained control of herself. During her thirty-six years, twenty-nine of them spent chasing objets d'art beginning with her father when she was very young, she'd only felt this near the loss of control a handful of times. She took a slow breath and let it out.

Another woman laughed.

"He's rather…large, isn't he?" the woman asked, but Salome could tell from the woman's reaction that she hoped this was no fantasy.

"Who was the model?" another woman asked.

"It doesn't matter," a man grumbled. "Whoever he was, he's long dead. And the artist probably embellished that anyway."

The auctioneer smiled a little, and it was the first emotion Salome had seen out of the man the whole long morning.

"Actually, if the rumors about this piece are true—" the auctioneer couched his terms salaciously "—the model could still be alive."

Salome's pulse quickened. She hadn't expected the auction house to have any of the real history of the painting. The secret was about to be exposed, and she wondered who was responsible. She knew that Roux would never have told anyone. In fact, when she'd let him know how much she knew, he'd nearly killed her.

That was nine years ago. The incident had happened in Luxembourg after an art show. Despite the fact that she'd been checking for Roux's presence since she'd stepped into the auction house, she looked around again.

There was no sign of the old man. Or of Saladin. She would be doubly blessed.

How did I find the prize before you did? she wondered. Then she admonished herself for feeling so fortunate. She hadn't made off with the painting yet.

"According to the legend surrounding this piece," the auctioneer went on, "the figure in this painting is a fallen angel." He used a laser pointing device to indicate the fireplace. "If you gaze into the fire, you can see tormented souls twisting in Hell."

At her distance, Salome couldn't see the figures, but she knew they would be there. The notebooks she'd studied, the ones found in Cosimo de' Medici's private collections, had shown sketches of the Nephilim.

"And this shadow?" The auctioneer traced the curved shadow barely visible on the right side of the painting. "This is supposed to belong to the artist who painted this piece."

"Unless I'm mistaken," one of the men said, "that shadow belongs to a woman."

The auctioneer smiled. "You're not mistaken. Virgil Carolini was actually the pseudonym of a woman painter."

"There weren't many of those in the seventeenth century," someone observed.

Salome was relieved to realize they didn't know the painting was actually painted earlier than that. No one, except perhaps for Roux, knew the painting's true origins.

And the old man wasn't telling.

"No," the auctioneer agreed. "There weren't many female painters for a long time." He let that sink in.

Salome knew he'd expertly moved the piece from art to a definite acquisition for possible investment. Collectors and investors alike treasured the unique in that regard.

The auctioneer moved the laser pointer again. "If you look in the shadows here, you can see what appear to be wings folded beneath the man."

An appreciative murmur came from the crowd.

"I see them," a woman said.

Salome did, as well. She slipped her phone from her purse and opened it to the keyboard. She typed quickly without looking at the keys.

"It's here."

The response came almost immediately. "It won't escape us."

"Make certain that it doesn't." Salome put the phone away.

The bidding started gingerly at first. Since there was no real knowledge of the piece or the artist, buyers were hesitant. Salome stayed out of it.

Eventually the painting sold to one of the women in the room.

Salome sat through eight more items. She bid on a few, always stopping short of where she knew the final price would hit. She even purchased a clock handmade by Jens Olsen, the internationally known clockmaker who'd designed and built the world clock in the Radhus, the Copenhagen City Hall. The price was low because most of those assembled didn't know that it was an original. Salome knew she could sell it to a collector she knew for at least forty thousand dollars more than she paid for it.

Then the woman who had bought the painting got up to make arrangements for the acquisition. Salome did the same. While she was in line, she also rifled the woman's purse and found her identification without getting caught.

As SALOME LEFT the auction house, she was met at the curb by a car. The man in the backseat got out and helped her inside.

Riley Drake was a big man. He headed his own private security company and rented his shock troops out to countries around the globe. He'd grown up in England, but he'd learned his trade in the killing fields in Africa. He kept his head shaved and looked deadly earnest at all times. It was a quality that influenced CEOs and heads of state to do business with him.

"Her name is Ilse Danseker," Salome said. "I got her address."

Drake nodded. He was also not much of a talker, which many of his employers appreciated. He only spoke when he had something to say.

"She's having the painting transported to her house," Salome said. "But I don't know when."

"We could take it during transport," Drake suggested.

Salome shook her head. "Then it looks like we were targeting the painting. No, this will play better if it looks like a home invasion."

Drake looked at her. "You're afraid of that old man you told me about, aren't you?"

Salome considered that. "I'm not afraid. I'm just knowledgeable enough to be wary."

Reaching over, Drake took her hand. His felt warm, confident and strong. "I could have him removed."

Salome touched his face and smiled gently. "I would rather that be a course of action we have to follow rather than one we choose. For all I know, Roux doesn't even know the painting has surfaced."

"You're sure this is the one?"

"The painting is right. I haven't seen it up close yet, but it matches the sketches in Cosimo de' Medici's journals."

Drake nodded. "And this thing is going to give you enough power to do anything you want?"

As she listened to him, Salome's excitement grew. She couldn't help herself.

"With what that painting hides," she said seriously, willing him to believe her even though he seldom believed in anything that he couldn't see with his own two eyes, "a person will have the power to remake the world."

"And if it's just a story?"

Salome refused to believe that. "It's not just a story. Too many people are chasing after it."

"You mean the old man."

"More than just the old man," Salome said.

Drake frowned slightly. "I thought you said not many people knew about this."

"They don't." Salome knew that Drake was upset because she hadn't trusted him with everything she knew. Men were like that. They got their egos bruised easily. Even big men.

"It's just that these things can be difficult to control, love," Drake said as he took her hand to his mouth and kissed her palm.

The kiss sent tingles through Salome. "There's only one other," she said. "His name is Saladin. He's a very dangerous man."

Drake regarded her with his pale blue eyes. "I'm more dangerous, love."

Salome silently hoped so. But it wouldn't matter after they had the painting.

16

Fall chill had settled into New York by the time Annja returned. As the jet came down, she glanced at the cold, slate-gray ribbon that was the East River and tried to convince herself it was good to be home.

She didn't buy it.

She didn't get to stay and work on the movie, hadn't been able to follow up on the King Wenceslas piece she'd planned for *Chasing History's Monsters,* hadn't explored more of Prague's Old Town and didn't find out anything about what Garin and Roux were doing.

Or even if they were still alive. Saladin hadn't struck her as someone who would be easy to deal with. Probably none of the Saladins had been.

She felt incredibly grumpy after the plane landed. Rather than stand in line with the rest of the passengers as they waited to be released, she reached into her pocket, took out her phone and turned it back on.

Her menu showed six missed calls. Four of them were

from Doug Morrell, and she didn't want to talk to him at the moment. Two others had come from Bart McGilley's cell phone and were only minutes old. Knowing that Bart had called lifted her spirits somewhat.

Detective Bart McGilley of the New York Police Department had been Annja's friend almost from the time she moved to Brooklyn. One of Bart's superiors had seen Annja on Letterman and decided to call her in to consult on a case involving artifacts stolen from one of the smaller private museums in the city.

Bart and Annja had hit it off from the beginning. Both of them had been working to get their careers started, and the case had ultimately helped them do that in their respective fields.

Despite the fact that Annja's relationship with Roux and Garin sometimes caused problems because she couldn't tell Bart everything that was going on, they'd remained friends.

She punched his number in and listened to the ring.

"Hey," Bart answered after the first ring. "It's you."

"It is me," Annja agreed. She felt a little happier just connecting with him. "As it happens—"

"You're back in NYC," Bart said. "I know."

"How did you know that?"

"Well, you get kicked out of a country, that country kind of lets your home country know about it. So they can check and make sure you make it home. A guy from the State Department—"

"Walter Gronlund," Annja said. The little man had been very kind but very firm about her departure. He'd stayed with her until she'd boarded her flight.

"That's him," Bart agreed. "Anyway, he called and wanted a background run on you. Locally. I guess the Feds have got a whole other book on what you've been doing elsewhere."

"Terrific." Annja suddenly felt worse despite Bart's warm,

friendly voice. She stood, retrieved her backpack from over-head storage and shrugged into it.

"Naturally, the captain sees your name, he calls me. I think he figures I'm the Annja Creed specialist."

"You're stuck babysitting me." Annja wasn't sure, but she felt entitled to be more than a little angry at the turn of events.

"Nope. Not even." Bart sounded incredibly chipper. "I got to fill out the background check for Walter. Talked to him over the phone. He explained about the dead guys in Prague. I thought about telling him about the dead guys you've some-times left over here."

"Thanks. Heaps."

"I said I *thought* about telling him. I didn't actually do that. Figured it would have complicated things for you."

Annja fell into line and followed the passengers out. She even managed a smile for the flight attendants.

"I called to let you know you're in luck," Bart said.

"How's that?"

"I'm here. Waiting on you. You've got me to tote and carry the baggage, give you a ride home, and I'm going to take you to dinner. Sort of a 'welcome home, glad to have you' thing instead of 'sorry you got kicked out of a country' thing."

"Thanks, Bart." In spite of the turn of events, Annja was actually smiling by the time she deplaned.

"Hey, I see you." At the end of the boarding tunnel, Bart stood outside the ropes. He was six feet two inches tall and solidly built, not a guy to trifle with. His dark hair was razor cut, and a permanent five-o'clock shadow tattooed his jaws and chin. He wore a lightweight dark gray trench coat.

He waved in a good-natured way that didn't befit the pre-conceived notions of a homicide detective, and she couldn't help but grin like a loon. Suddenly it did feel good to be home.

"SO," BART SAID while they stood in line at the baggage carousel, "what's it like?"

"What?" Annja kept careful watch for her baggage.

"Getting kicked out of a country. I mean, man, that's gotta suck."

"I've really missed that sympathetic shoulder you always offer."

Bart chuckled. "At least they didn't throw you so far under the jail that they had to pipe in sunlight."

"I didn't do anything wrong." Annja excused herself and leaned through the crowd to collect a bag. She placed it beside Bart.

"Is this it?" Bart asked.

"No."

"No?" Bart looked worried.

"Be brave."

Bart sighed. "Anyway, it looked like you did plenty wrong. There were fourteen dead guys. Some of them were shot, but there were a half-dozen killed when the car you were riding in blew up."

"I didn't do that."

"Didn't kill anybody?"

"Blow the car up." Annja snared another bag.

"Is this it?" Bart asked.

"No."

An unhappy look crossed his face.

"You volunteered," Annja argued. "I was going to grab a cab."

"I didn't know you were caravanning through Prague," Bart said. "When I saw it on the Travel Channel, it looked like a party spot."

"I wasn't caravanning." Annja pulled another suitcase from the belt. "And I didn't get to party." Then she reflected on a couple of the movie soirees she'd been to and amended her answer. "I didn't get to party much."

"This much luggage, there shoulda been camels involved." Bart looked around. "You know, maybe I need to start looking for a camel."

"You're a big boy. You can handle this. I got it to the airport."

"All the time I've known you, I've never seen you pack this much stuff. What could you possibly have needed? And is there anything left at home?"

"I was working on a movie," Annja said. "Not exactly a regular gig for me. I didn't know what I needed. They make a lot of extras for the DVDs these days. I knew I was going to be in some of them. I wanted to make sure I was dressed right."

"Were you in the movie?"

"A couple of times when they needed background people. But I worked on three of the features regarding the artifacts they're using in the movie, as well as the history of Prague."

"Did you meet the main actor, what's-his-name?"

"I did," Annja replied. "Terrific kisser, by the way."

Bart frowned. "You're making that up."

"Yes."

Bart looked a little relieved about that. Annja knew they were attracted to each other. They always had been. But Bart was the marrying kind, the kind who'd want to put down roots and raise a family. That meant his wife couldn't be out in the field digging through broken Mayan pottery and possibly getting sniped at by grave robbers.

And there was no way he was going to understand the sword and the problems it seemed to bring.

Bart had recently called off an engagement he'd had, or the

woman had. Annja wasn't exactly sure how that had gone down because Bart was busy pretending it had never happened.

"Back to this shoot-out in Prague," Bart said.

"They were trying to kill us."

"Us? You mean you and this guy, Garin Braden."

"No. Me and the Earps and Doc Holliday."

Bart grimaced.

"Yes. I mean Garin Braden." Annja hadn't known what name Garin was doing business under in Prague. Besides, if the Prague police could track him down and make his life miserable for a while, he deserved it for running out on her.

"Well, nobody seems to know who that guy is. I looked him up and didn't find anyone by that name who fits the information you gave the Prague police."

Annja pulled her last bag from the carousel. "He's got a lot of names."

Bart blew out a disgusted breath. "You know, you really ought to watch who you hang out with. You might not get in so much trouble that way."

"I'll try to do better." Annja looked at the pile of luggage, then looked around the baggage area. "Did you spot a camel?"

"AH, THERE YOU ARE! My movie star! Back from so far away!" Maria Ruiz, the owner of Tito's Cuban restaurant, threw out her chubby arms and wrapped Annja in a bear hug.

Thankfully it was after eight o'clock and most of the dinner crowd was gone.

Annja hugged the big woman back. A feeling of seriously being home washed over Annja. She hadn't realized how much she'd been gone lately until that moment. Of course, maybe getting tossed out of a country made her a little more grateful for the old neighborhood.

"I hope it's not too late to get something to eat," Annja said.

Maria dismissed the thought. She was short and stout, a pleasant, hardworking woman who drove her son Tito crazy while she managed the restaurant and he ran the kitchen. Together they'd created a restaurant clientele that kept them busy all day long.

"Never too late for you," Maria said. "Come. I get the two of you a table. Then I fix you something special. You need something to put meat back on your bones. You're getting too skinny. It's not healthy."

Annja knew better than to protest. She followed Maria back to the rear of the restaurant. In the next moment, Annja and Bart were seated. Tortillas, chips and an array of salsa and cheeses were placed before them.

Bart, never shy when it came to eating, dug in at once.

"So," he said as he rolled a tortilla, "you didn't blow up the car, but you maybe shot a few guys."

"I don't know. Probably. It all got pretty crazy." Annja poured salsa onto a tortilla, added cheese and started rolling.

Bart looked at her for a moment, as if deciding whether to say what was on his mind. Then he said it. "You know, you've been involved in more gunfights than anyone I know."

Annja was just glad she hadn't told him everything she'd experienced since she'd found the sword.

"That wasn't exactly my choice," she replied. "I'm an archaeologist."

Bart ticked his fingers off. "And television host, author, consultant—to museums, private collectors and the NYPD on more than one occasion—and gunfighter."

"I never set out to do those things. I just wanted a better, deeper look at the world."

"I guess you do that during the reloads."

"I suppose you had time to figure out all this comic dialogue after you heard I was coming back."

"I may have fine-tuned it a bit," Bart admitted.

"My advice? Find an appreciative audience. I just got kicked out of a country, remember?"

"How much trouble are you in?"

"I don't know." Annja sipped the Diet Coke one of Maria's servers had brought. "I don't think it's going to follow me back here."

Bart rolled his eyes. "I hope not. The captain and commissioner haven't forgotten the last debacle. Good times were *not* had by all, I assure you." He sipped his soft drink. "Are you planning on returning to Prague?"

"Not anytime in the near future." Annja popped a cheese-dipped chip into her mouth. "How good is my credit in the favor department?"

"You'll never get out of debt."

"Then it won't matter if I go a little more in debt."

"It's that kind of cavalier attitude that really gets you into trouble."

"I need to know about a guy."

"You seem to know more about Garin Braden than the rest of the world."

"Not him. Someone else."

Bart reached inside his jacket and took out a small notebook. "Is this going to be like the time you asked me to check out a set of fingerprints and they turned out to belong to a person of interest in a 1940s Hollywood murder?"

That had been Roux. Annja still didn't know what to make of that.

"I hope not," she replied.

"Okay." Bart waited, pencil poised.

"He calls himself Saladin."

"First name or last?"

"I don't know."

"Helpful. *Not.*"

"He came to see me while the Prague police had me. Actually, he came to threaten me."

Most of the levity left Bart then. He took threats to his friends seriously. "Saladin, eh?"

"That's what he said."

"The Prague police should know who he is."

"If they're willing to tell you. They let him in to see me, and I got the distinct impression they were willing to let him do whatever he wanted to." Annja started to take another sip of her drink, but she suddenly felt eyes on her.

The sensation of being watched was uncomfortable but not frightening. She'd experienced such things before. Women generally did. Usually it was better to just ignore things like that, but Annja was aware that she no longer lived in a *usually* world.

She glanced at the window overlooking the street. Night had settled in over the city, and darkness hugged the doorways and alcoves.

A figure stood at the window and he was staring at her. Gaunt and dressed in rags, the old man looked more like a scarecrow than a human being. A ragged beard clung to his pointed chin. His hat had flaps that covered his ears and gave his face a pinched look. His eyes were beady and sharp, mired in pits of wrinkles and prominent bone.

He lifted a hand covered in a glove with the fingers cut off. His dirty forefinger pointed directly at Annja, and even from across the room she read his lips.

"Annja Creed."

A chill ghosted through her. How did the man know her name?

"Annja Creed," the old man said. "The world is going to end. Soon."

17

"Annja Creed," the old man repeated. His mouth moved, making her name clear even though his efforts carried no sound. His forefinger tapped against the glass.

"What are you staring at?" Bart asked. He turned in his seat. "That homeless guy?"

Without answering, Annja got up and walked toward the front door of the restaurant.

"Where are you going?" Bart asked.

"He knows my name," Annja explained.

"A lot of people know your name. You've been on television."

Still, Annja felt drawn to the man for reasons she couldn't explain. Maybe it was his apparent helplessness.

"Do you know this guy?" Bart was suddenly at her side.

Annja saw Bart's reflection in the glass next to hers. Both of them overlaid the old man for a moment.

Terror filled the old man's eyes and he opened them wide. He placed both palms against the window and shook his head.

Annja kept moving and Bart matched her step for step.

"What is the matter?" Maria called out. She hurried over as she wiped her hands on a bar towel. "You don't have to go, do you? Your food, it is not ready."

The old man turned and fled before Annja reached the restaurant door. By the time she was out on the street, he was gone. She jogged to the corner, but there was no sign of him.

"Do you know him?" Bart asked again as he surveyed the street scene.

Annja shook her head. "No. But he knew me. He called me by name."

"Television," Bart replied.

"Does he look like the type to watch television on a regular basis?"

"He looks more like the type to have aluminum foil packed into his hat," Bart admitted.

Annja turned back to Maria, who stood in the doorway and peered out. "Did you see that man?"

"I did."

"Do you know him?"

"That one?" Maria shook her head. "Not so much. I'd never seen him before, then—poof—he is here. Like a wizard."

"He's here?" Bart asked.

Maria nodded. "Yes. The last two or three days, maybe. Always looking in the windows."

"Maybe he was just looking for a handout," Bart suggested.

Annja couldn't forget the way the old man had called her name. She didn't think it was just because he'd recognized her from television. Those rheumy old eyes had madness in them.

"Come back inside," Maria coaxed. "Your food will be up soon."

AFTER DINNER, Bart drove her to her loft. He parked in front of the building and placed his police identification sign on the dashboard as Annja got out. She checked the time and found it was a little after nine.

Bart reached into the car's trunk and started removing suitcases. He put them on the sidewalk. "We'll just take out a few, no more than we can carry, and we'll leave the rest safe in the car."

"Wait here," Annja said. "Wally has a cart we can use."

Inside the building, Annja knocked on Wally's first-floor apartment. The building superintendent had one of the smaller units in the structure, but he kept it clean and neat. Wally took care of Annja's mail and her plants while she was gone.

Wally answered the door himself, still clad in his work clothes. Behind him, a baseball game was on television.

"Annja!" he boomed. "It's good to have you back."

Annja smiled. "It's good to be back."

"I figured you'd call first."

"I would have. I apologize. I came back early."

"Nothing to worry about." Wally waved the apology away. "You need help with anything?"

"I'd like to borrow the cart if I can."

"Sure, sure." Wally stepped back into the apartment and returned with a small four-wheeled cart. "You're not gonna try to carry that stuff in yourself, are you?"

"Bart's with me."

Wally grinned. "Good. I like to watch a young man work." He guided the cart through the door and walked out with Annja.

"CAN I BORROW a sleeping bag?"

Startled, Annja looked up from her computer at Bart. He'd

taken off his coat, and his pistol was visible holstered on his hip. "Planning a vacation?"

"No, I'm staying here for the night and you only have the one bed."

"Did I miss the part where I invited you for a sleepover?" Annja asked.

"There was an implicit invitation when you left dead guys in Prague."

"I had to leave them. They'd never have cleared customs."

"You're making bad jokes," Bart said. "I know you're tired."

Annja actually felt a little guilty about that one. She didn't take death lightly, but she'd been serious for far too long these past few days. Verbally sparring with Bart was always fun, and his humor ran dark occasionally.

"I'm going to be fine," she told him.

"With me here, you'll be finer."

"You can't stay here forever."

"You're right. I've got to throw on the Batman suit and get up early to fight crime in the morning. But for tonight I can be here and not worry about you."

"You're not exactly bulletproof yourself," Annja pointed out.

"Let's just hope I don't have to be." Bart smiled. "Humor me. I'm tired after carrying all that luggage."

Annja got up and located a plush sleeping bag and gave it to Bart.

"Can you tuck yourself in?" she asked.

"Yeah. Gee, thanks, Mom." Bart laid out the sleeping bag in the corner. "Will the TV bother you?"

"No."

"Good. I can catch the rest of the Yankees game and compare notes with Wally in the morning."

"You're going to see Wally?"

"To let him know to keep an eye out for you, and to make sure he still has my cell number." Bart picked up a small bag from the floor.

Annja didn't recognize the bag. "That's not mine."

"It's mine. Shaving kit. Change of clothes. Clean underwear."

"Always prepared."

"My mom trained me well." Bart took out his toiletry bag, a pair of gray sweat shorts and a T-shirt, then headed to the bathroom. "I take it you're going to be up for a while."

"I slept on the plane. And I've got some research I want to do." Annja turned and put her face back into the computer.

While waiting for her flight out of Prague, Annja had logged on to the archaeology sites she often used for research. She'd sent out queries regarding Nephilim and paintings of them.

She weeded through the discussions, finding most of it centered around horror movies—some good and some bad—and the mythology that Nephilim were the children of fallen angels and human women.

It wasn't helpful, but it was interesting. There was also conjecture that the Nephilim were a race of giants mentioned in the Bible, and that the Flood had been caused to wipe them and their wicked ways from the earth.

Annja leaned back in her chair and tried to get comfortable. Her mind kept pulling at the mystery. She kept thinking about Garin and Roux and wondering if they were all right.

More angels, in paintings and statuary, were mentioned. She started scanning those entries, and one instantly grabbed her attention.

Don't know if this helps, but there's a legend about a painting of a Nephilim that the Medici family was interested in. Cosimo de' Medici supposedly sent an emissary to retrieve the painting from Constantinople during the siege by Ottoman forces under Mehmed II.

Annja responded.

Would love to talk to you more about this. Can we meet for IM?

The time frame sounded right, and Garin had mentioned the fall of Constantinople.

Annja sent the e-mail and continued to prowl restlessly through the Internet. Bart had gone to sleep on the sleeping bag. He snored gently. The blue glow from the television fell over him.

Annja got a blanket from the closet and spread it over Bart. He was a good friend, and she felt badly that he was sleeping on her floor rather than at home in his own bed. With all the artifacts and books she had crammed into the loft, Annja barely had room to live there herself, much less the luxury of a guest room.

Bart wasn't like Roux and Garin at all, Annja thought. He wouldn't ever leave her in the lurch the way those two had so often.

Bereft of energy and still full after the meal at Tito's, she took a shower and went to bed. She kept hearing the old man's voice in her dreams.

"Annja Creed. The world is going to end. Soon."

18

Garin got out of the cab in the Hague and knew he was being watched. He reached up to the earpiece that connected him to the security team he'd placed inside the city.

"I'm being spied on," he said quietly.

"Yes, sir. We expected that. We're looking." The man's voice was calm and self-assured. Garin wouldn't have paid for anything less. The problem was that such a man also wouldn't acknowledge if things got out of control.

Garin didn't think Saladin would have been able to find him so quickly. Since leaving Prague, Garin had changed identities four times as he traveled ever closer to his destination.

But Saladin wasn't the only one who might be interested in whatever prize Roux was after.

His phone rang. "Yes."

"Call off your men," Roux said. "It's only us here."

Garin stopped and looked around. "You see me?"

"And your men, yes."

"How many men?"

"So far?" Roux sounded bored and impatient. "Five."

Garin had eight men flanking him. After being surprised in Prague, he'd decided not to take any chances for a time.

Still, Roux spotting five of them was impressive. Of course, he'd known for several lifetimes that the old man was a canny individual.

"Where are you?" Garin asked.

"Where I said I'd be."

Garin looked up at the second-story window of a building a half block down. A small French restaurant occupied the first floor.

Roux appeared in the window for the briefest instant. He held a phone to his face and quickly stepped back. Even though he'd said no one else was there, the old man obviously wasn't taking any chances.

"Don't dawdle," Roux said.

Garin unleashed a scathing retort, then realized he was speaking to dead air. He looked at the caller-ID screen, thought about calling back and knew it would be a wasted effort.

For a moment, Garin thought about just turning around and leaving. But he couldn't do that, either. He was certain Roux knew that. The mystery of the Nephilim painting had hung in the back of Garin's mind for hundreds of years.

Angry, Garin pocketed the phone and headed for the building.

AN IMMACULATE MAÎTRE D' approached Garin. "Would you like a table, sir?"

"He's with me," Roux announced. Dressed in slacks, a windbreaker and a golf shirt that made him look like a casual diner, the old man stood near the door. From the way the jacket hung, Garin knew that Roux carried a pistol in a shoulder holster. He led Garin toward the wall farthest from the windows.

"You should have had that jacket tailored," Garin said in German. That had been the first language they had shared.

Roux spoke in the same language. "That would have been a waste of money."

"Ever the skinflint, and you're sitting on more money than you'll ever spend."

"No," Roux said. "It's just that I don't see a reason to advertise my affluence to call forth pickpockets and muggers. We've got enough problems." He pointed his chin at a nearby table.

Garin stared at the woman seated there. She wore a light peach blouse that accentuated her dark skin. She was stunningly beautiful.

"You didn't mention you had company," Garin said as they approached the table.

"She's an old friend," Roux explained. He made the introductions.

"It's nice to meet you, Mr. Braden," Jennifer said.

Garin captured one of her hands and kissed it. He bowed slightly in a gentlemanly manner.

"Aren't you suave," Jennifer said, chuckling. Clearly she wasn't impressed with his behavior.

"He's obviously in one of his elegant moods," Roux groused. He sat himself on the other side of the table. "There's no need to be flattered. It merely signifies that he's measuring you up as a potential romantic fling."

Jennifer's dark eyes sparked. "Really? Well, I find that quite interesting, actually. As you know, I happen to like a man who knows what he wants."

In just those few words, Garin knew that Roux and the

woman had been lovers at one time. She casually flirted with him not to catch his eye, but to catch Roux's. Garin pocketed that little bit of trivia and sat at the table.

"Did you have a safe trip?" Jennifer asked.

"Yes. Thank you." Garin spread his napkin in his lap.

"We have wine. May I pour you a glass?"

"Please." Garin sipped the wine when she gave it to him. It was a robust red, but it wasn't expensive. That told him Roux had ordered the wine. "I'd like to know what's going on."

"Jennifer believes she's found the painting," Roux said.

"After you've been looking for it for all these years?" Garin arched a mocking brow at Roux.

Roux ignored the slight and swirled his wine.

"Luck has as much to do with a find as diligence," Jennifer said. "Surely Roux taught you that while you were with him."

Knowing that Roux had told her at least *something* about him put Garin on notice. Roux wasn't one to let anyone into his business. "So you were luckier than the old man?"

Roux curled a lip in displeasure. "I wondered if you were going to be more hindrance than help. I guess you've answered that question."

"No." Garin turned fully toward Roux and shifted back to speaking German. "When the chips are down and your back is to the wall, there's only one person you'll ever send for. And you know it." Even as he said that, though, he knew Roux was incapable of admitting it. The old man had never been one to give praise willingly.

Then a realization hit Garin. "This is about Annja, isn't it? That's why you didn't call her instead of me. You're upset that she went out with me."

"She didn't go out with you," Roux said icily. "You took advantage of her."

"I," Garin stated forcefully, "was the perfect gentleman."

"You forced the situation."

"The situation, yes, but not her." Garin leaned back in his chair. No one would ever force Annja Creed to do anything. He'd known that before he'd arranged the evening.

Roux cursed.

"Stop it," Jennifer said sharply. "I don't know exactly what's going on between the two of you, but I do know that there's been bad blood in the past."

Idly, Garin wondered what she'd think if she'd known that bad blood had been brewing for hundreds of years.

"The bottom line is that you called—" Jennifer nodded at Roux "—and you came." She nodded at Garin. "And that the painting of the Nephilim, for whatever reason you want it—" she looked at Roux again "—might be here."

"Might be?" Garin snorted derisively. "You don't know?"

"Not yet," Jennifer said.

"Then I've wasted my time."

"Not yet," Jennifer repeated.

Roux turned to Garin. "There's every likelihood that the painting is here. Jennifer has worked with me regarding this matter before."

"Until he ditched me thirteen years ago," Jennifer said, staring daggers at Roux.

Despite his own troubled mood, anxiety and confusion about his own motives, Garin had to laugh at the woman's thinly veiled rancor. "She's not exactly part of your fan club, is she, old man?"

Roux pointedly ignored Garin and turned his attention instead to the arrival of the food. "I took the liberty of ordering for you."

Watching carefully, Garin studied the plates as the servers burdened the tables with them. The dishes were all French, which wasn't Garin's favorite, but his favorites among that fare were clearly represented. Roux had forgotten nothing.

"That's fine," Garin said. "Thank you." He turned his attention to the food.

One of Roux's first lessons to him had been to eat when he had food before him. They'd lived like wolves much of the time in those long-ago days. Often they'd never known where their next meal was coming from.

"Where is the painting?" Garin asked.

"With a collector," Roux said. "Here in the city. There was an auction earlier today. We couldn't make it in time."

"Pity," Garin said. "I might have been able to finish my *date.*"

Roux visibly bristled.

"As it was, I believe she was quite upset," Garin went on.

"She returned to Brooklyn," Roux countered. "Don't make her out to be heartbroken."

Garin smiled. Roux would never had handed out the thought if it hadn't been in his mind.

"How did you find the painting?" Garin asked. His eyes locked with Jennifer's.

19

"For the last thirteen years," Jennifer stated, emphasizing the number of years and flicking a glance at Roux, "I've been searching for the painting."

"Because Roux told you about it?" Garin asked.

"Partly. And partly because it was the only chance I thought I'd ever have of meeting Roux again."

Garin peered at her over his glass of wine. "The old man must have left you with quite an impression."

Some of Jennifer's edgy emotions showed. "This isn't about then. It's not even about the future. It doesn't concern Roux at all. This is about the painting."

"Nothing like a vindictive woman," Garin said in German. Roux ignored him.

"How did you find it?" Garin asked Jennifer.

Jennifer looked at him. "This isn't a trap."

Garin shrugged. Just because she said so didn't mean it wasn't. And even knowing something *was* a trap didn't mean the intended victim would be clever enough to stay clear of it.

"I followed up on the painter's family," Jennifer said.

"They didn't have the painting." Garin flicked his glance at Roux. "We talked with them."

Jennifer looked startled. "Recently? Because they certainly didn't mention it."

"Quite some time ago, actually," Roux said. "It doesn't matter."

All the people they'd asked, Garin knew, had died generations ago.

"They didn't know what they had." Jennifer cut off a bite-size piece from a stuffed crepe. "Artists back in those days lived by the grace of a patron. Not from selling their work."

Garin held his thumb and forefinger a fraction of an inch apart. "Condensed version."

Jennifer flashed him a disdainful look. "Roux told me the two of you had talked to the family once. But you pursued the paternal family. As it turns out, the painter, Josef Tsoklis, was an illegitimate child."

Even after all the years that had passed, Garin still felt the physical impact of that description. He felt Roux's eyes on him and didn't dare look at the old man. Garin would never completely forget his upbringing.

"Josef took the name of his mother's husband," Jennifer said, "but he was always closer to his mother and her people."

"All right, he was really a mama's boy," Garin said. "What of it?"

"Josef's family has been trying to track down the painting. They've heard the legend."

"What legend?" Garin asked.

"That Josef hid most of the gold he earned from patrons and the painting reveals the hiding place."

"Do you know how little those artists were paid?" Garin

shook his head. "I'm telling you now that whatever amount they've imagined, it's either not real or far less than what they believe."

But that only made Garin wonder all the more why Roux was looking for the painting. He turned his attention to his food.

"There's also conjecture that Tsoklis stole an immense fortune from one of his benefactors."

Garin snorted, and knew from the angry look on Jennifer's face that he'd offended her.

"I don't believe in those old stories for a minute," she declared.

But Garin could see that she wasn't completely telling the truth.

"Finding the painting became a family project for Josef's cousins on his mother's side of the family because of their beliefs, not mine. Over the intervening five hundred years, they've been looking for the painting, as well. You're familiar with Cosimo de' Medici?"

"Yes."

"Some—those few that knew of the painting's existence— also knew of Cosimo's interest in it."

"Looking for a lost fortune isn't something Cosimo de' Medici would have done," Garin challenged. From the corner of his eye, he watched Roux for a reaction.

The old man blithely ate and seemed content to listen.

"No, he *was* interested in the painting's ability to bring about the end of the world."

Garin paused. Now *that* would be something to catch Roux's interest. During their years together, Roux had hunted such objects and talismans of power. At first, Garin hadn't believed in any of those things. But he had soon realized that those things—like the sword Annja carried and whatever power had kept him ageless for five hundred years—existed.

"Of course," Jennifer said quickly, "I don't believe in any of that."

"Of course," Garin replied. He glanced at Roux, but the old man wouldn't meet his eyes. "Then what do you believe in?"

"That painting has a lot of history. Whatever secret it's been hiding has been there for hundreds of years. People are willing to kill to get it."

"What people?" Garin asked.

"Salome," Roux said. "She's chasing the painting, as well."

The name resonated inside Garin's skull. "Now, there's as pretty a viper as you'd ever want to meet."

"Yes," Roux said.

"I see now why you called me."

The old man shrugged.

"Salome?" Jennifer looked confused. "I don't know the name."

"You weren't the only one Roux has used to bird-dog his little artifacts," Garin said. "Salome was a few years ago." He smiled mirthlessly. "She's a particularly nasty piece of work. I'm surprised she's still alive." He glanced at Roux and spoke in German. "You must be getting soft if you let her live."

"You're still alive," Roux replied.

"I've had a long time to learn how to survive. And I never betrayed you the way that woman did."

"No." Roux sighed. "You didn't."

"Then we kill her this time?"

Roux thought about that for a moment. "If circumstances permit."

"We're not committing murder," Jennifer said in flawless German.

Surprised, Garin turned to her. "You speak German?"

"I'd heard Roux speak in German during the years we were together."

It wasn't any great leap of logic on Garin's part to realize that Roux had probably been talking to him. They'd always kept in touch—even when they'd been trying to kill each other.

"After he left," Jennifer went on, "I thought I'd learn the language."

Garin switched to Latin. It was the first language Roux had taught him that wasn't his own. "This woman is going to be trouble. We should get rid of her."

"No," Roux replied. "She's resourceful. And more in tune with this world than you or I. Annja would be better to have, but this one will serve."

Although neither of them spoke of it, Garin knew that Roux didn't want Annja there because Roux wasn't certain how to deal with her yet. Their date behind his back had thrown their relationship into a murky state of affairs.

Not only that, but Roux wouldn't have wanted to bring Annja anywhere near Salome, who was pure poison. And she was as deadly as any woman Garin had ever met.

"This is stupid," Jennifer said in English. "I'm not going to learn every language in the world just to talk to the two of you."

"All right," Roux said.

"No more…whatever it was you were speaking."

Roux inclined his head.

"And you." Jennifer pointed her fork at Garin.

With a smile, Garin spread his hands and said, "Of course." But if he got the chance to kill Salome, he intended to.

And he'd drive a stake through her heart to make certain she stayed dead.

DRAKE TOOK Salome into the estate shortly after darkness consumed the tree-lined grounds along Koningskade Quay. She was dressed all in black, had her hair pulled back, and wore a Beretta 93-R at her hip. She carried a cut-down shotgun tucked in a scabbard that ran down her back.

"All right," Drake said as he studied the BlackBerry in his hand. "Byron and his lads have taken out the security system. We're good to go." Cosmetic blackface disguised his features.

Salome wore the paint, as well. She hated it because it was so hard to clean off, and it was hard on her skin. Her beauty meant a lot to her. Her features were the most potent weapon in her arsenal.

Drake carried a silenced H&K MP-5 in both gloved hands as he broke into a trot. Salome knew weapons because she often dealt in them. No product translated into cash as readily in so many countries as weapons. The same couldn't be said of drugs. She knew because she'd dealt in those, too.

As they neared the security gatehouse, a black-clad warrior stepped from within. He gave Drake a thumbs-up. Salome glanced briefly through the darkened window and saw the men slumped over inside. Blood dripped down the inside of the bulletproof glass and offered mute testimony that the men inside hadn't gone down easily.

Their deaths didn't bother Salome. She was prepared to kill everyone inside the large house within the security walls.

"Do you really think this painting has magical properties, love?" Drake asked.

Salome walked behind the man, two steps back and one step to the right to give herself a proper field of fire. "It's supposed to," she replied.

"According to this old duffer you've talked about? Roux?" Drake sounded as if he spit every time he said Roux's name.

Salome answered without hesitation. "Yes."

Although Drake didn't make a reply, she knew he was somewhat disappointed in her. When they'd first met, while he'd been providing security for a man who'd owned one of the artifacts she'd been after, they'd been enemies. But only professionally. As Drake had insisted, he hadn't known her well enough to dislike her.

That night she'd killed two of his best men. One of them had been a good friend. He'd almost been unable to forgive her for that. But he had. When it came to the bottom line, they were both professionals.

He just didn't like the fact that she believed in magic.

It would be better, Salome thought, as she often did, if I could show him the things I've seen. The problem was, of course, that she couldn't. She'd only seen those things while she'd been with Roux. Talking about those times always left Drake in a foul mood.

The one drawback she'd found in him was that he was insanely jealous. Other than that, he was perfect. He was a talented and generous lover. And he was a flawless killing machine when he was in action.

She followed him through the darkness that filled the estate's inner courtyard. Her hands firmly gripped the pistol.

ILSE DANSEKER SNORED softly. She was in her late forties. Strands of her henna-colored hair lay across her slack face. She'd had plastic surgery done to preserve her looks. Without makeup, the scars under her chin were just barely visible.

She lay cuddled in the arms of a man who was not her husband. Salome had seen a picture of Edward Danseker. The shipping magnate was in his early seventies, a quiet and distinguished man from his appearance. He was also rich enough and selfish enough to overlook a wayward wife nearly half his age while he was out of town.

The bedroom looked as though it had been transported from a child's book of fantasy stories. The huge four-poster bed was the centerpiece. One wall contained electronic entertainment equipment. The blue glow of the television washed over the woman and her lover.

Drake looked at Salome. They weren't really on a timetable, but he'd trained her to recognize that any moment spent in hostile territory was a risk.

Salome held the Beretta in one hand while she reached out to tap Ilse on the cheek with the other. The woman stirred but didn't wake. Salome patted her more firmly.

This time the woman's eyes fluttered open. Then they locked open and she started to scream. Salome clapped a gloved hand over the woman's mouth.

"No," Salome said firmly but quietly. "No screaming. We're going to handle this like civilized adults."

The man shifted. Salome knew he was awake from his posture beneath the silk sheets. He sprang up and tried to grab Salome's wrist. She thought it was possible that his eyes hadn't adjusted and he didn't see Drake and the others standing in the room's shadows.

"Let her go! Get out of here!" the man shouted. "Who are you?" Obviously he didn't see the pistol in her fist, either.

Without hesitation, Salome shifted the Beretta slightly and squeezed the trigger. A trio of bullets sang free of the sound suppressor and thudded into the man's face. His hands on her arm relaxed, and he slumped back onto the bed. Blood stained the sheets.

The woman opened her mouth to scream.

Salome shoved the Beretta's suppressor between the woman's lips and shushed her as if she were a child.

"Well," Salome whispered as she stared into the woman's wide, frightened eyes, "perhaps this will be a little less than civilized."

20

"Is that man your father, Ms. Creed?"

Annja knew, without turning around, that the homeless man was back. He'd been watching her for almost two hours. Frankly, she was surprised it had taken this long for the museum's assistant curator to notice the old man standing there.

"No." Annja didn't look up from the exhibit she was working on. The museum had recently received acquisitions from a benefactor who had died, and she'd been hired to catalog and certify the artifacts.

Since most museums existed more or less by the sufferance of their patrons—especially so in the case of a small museum like this one—she knew they would have rather continued the man's yearly donations than accept his collection after his death. After all, the collection acquisition only came in once.

The pieces were good, but by no means spectacular. They were worth putting on display. Most visitors to the museum wouldn't recognize their significance, though.

"Oh, he's not your father."

"No."

Evan Peably, the assistant curator, frowned in confusion. He was in his early twenties and looked as though he'd just graduated university. His appearance was deceiving, though. Black hair hung long and lank, as if he'd only just returned from an excursion in the Gobi Desert or someplace, and he maintained a five-o'clock shadow through the use of a beard trimmer set to leave only stubble behind. His khakis held straight lines, and his shirtsleeve cuffs, rolled to midforearm, looked crisp and carefully measured.

Peably tapped his upper lip with a forefinger and gazed at the man. "I was just wondering—"

"Because he's been there for the last hour and a half."

"I didn't know he'd been there that long."

"He has."

Peably sighed. "Well, do you think he means the museum any harm?"

Not *me,* Annja thought. He's worried about the museum. She straightened, put both hands on her hips and stretched. Vertebrae in her spine popped and she felt better almost immediately. She looked at the assistant curator.

"I think if he'd meant any harm," Annja said, "it would have happened by now."

Peably folded his arms over his chest. "Perhaps I should alert the security guard."

Annja smiled at that. The security guard was Oswald Carson, a retired seventy-year-old NYPD policeman who had never drawn his weapon while on the job. The guard looked like a rake dressed in a security uniform.

"He knows," Annja said. "He's watching."

Carson stood near the bronze exhibit beside a Spartan warrior holding a spear and shield.

"Maybe he could do something more than watch," Peably suggested.

"Like what?" Annja took pictures of vases.

"He could chase that man off."

"Why?"

"Because he's creepy-looking, that's why."

"Being creepy-looking isn't against the law," Annja said.

Peably tapped his foot in agitation. "It's obvious that he's stalking you."

"Is it?" Annja glanced over her shoulder at the old man. He stood beside a model of Athens that had taken someone months to construct.

"Was he here when you got here?"

"No." Annja was pretty sure she would have remembered that.

"Then I submit to you that he followed you here."

"I doubt that."

"Why?" Peably seemed irritated that Annja refused to take his advice.

"Because I came straight here from my loft. If he followed me here, he would have had to know where I live." That particularly unsettling thought had popped into Annja's mind the moment she'd seen the old man. Wally had mentioned that he'd seen an old man around. But that didn't mean anything.

Maybe more than one of them was following her. In an instant she imagined an army of old men handing off surveillance on her.

Now that's definitely a paranoid thought, Annja chided herself. Still, she glanced over her shoulder to make sure that the old man was the same one from Tito's last night.

The truth was that she didn't know. Old men tended to look the same. And this one wore nondescript clothing. Furthermore, the wild look in his eyes could be seen in a lot of people these days.

She supposed, given the right circumstances, that she might even see it in hers.

"I think you should take his presence here a little more seriously," Peably admonished her.

"I am. I took his picture and sent it in to a detective friend of mine. He's trying to find out who he is and where he belongs."

When she'd turned around with the camera she was using to capture images of the artifacts, Annja had fully expected the old man to cut and run. Instead he'd stood his ground as if he was posing for a photo op.

"Maybe he'll do something," Peably said.

Annja hoped Bart could at least identify who he was and where he belonged.

Then, as she knew it would, Peably's mind got around to recognizing the fact that if Annja was in danger, so was he because he was standing so close.

"It looks like you're doing well here," he said nervously.

"Don't you want to go over everything?" Annja barely kept from grinning.

"Not today." Usually Peably was only too happy to question her every spare moment she had regarding whatever she was working on.

Annja was pretty certain that he resented the notoriety she had. It didn't help when some of the museum's guests recognized her and asked for autographs while they were trying to work through an authentication.

"Just finish up quickly," Peably said. "We're going to lock up the museum promptly at seven. What you don't finish tonight, you'll have to come back tomorrow and do."

Annja didn't intend to let that happen. The authentication job didn't pay well enough to spend two days on it. Besides that, she still had the King Wenceslas piece she wanted to put together for *Chasing History's Monsters*.

She glanced back toward the old man. He was still there. And he was still watching her.

"CAN I HELP YOU?"

Annja knew at once that the old man had shuffled over to her. She looked over her shoulder at him. Up close, she realized that he was taller than she'd believed.

For a fleeting moment she wondered if she should run. Then she decided that if she thought she had to run from a skinny old man, she was really losing it and needed to just stay home.

"I don't mean to impose," the old man said. He smiled and revealed crooked teeth. "It's just that I thought you might use a hand. I heard that young fellow say you had to be out of here by closing time, and it's a quarter to now."

Annja glanced at the time on her phone lying nearby and was surprised to find that it was six forty-five. There was no question that she needed help. She'd counted on Peably's presence to help get everything finished on time.

"I've got steady hands, if that's what you're worried about. I'm not an alcoholic. I just get a little mixed up from time to time." The man held out his hands. They were steady as rocks. They were also scarred. His fingers were twisted and his knuckles were misshapen. They looked arthritic at first glance, but he still possessed supple movement. "I won't drop anything."

"Okay." Annja handed an urn to the man. "Just hold that there so I can take pictures of it."

"Of course." He smiled as if pleased to be of use.

Annja settled behind her camera lens and took pictures. She took several of the old man, as well. But she didn't think she succeeded in taking them without his knowledge.

"What's your name?" she asked.

The man smiled as he turned the urn under her direction. "I've had several names. Do you have a favorite?"

"For me?" Annja asked, confused.

"For me," the old man said. "Your name is Annja."

Even though he'd called her by name the night before, it was still weird to hear him do it again and she wondered how he knew her.

"I don't have a favorite name," Annja said.

"Of course you do," the old man said. "You love stories of the past. You've heard many names. Surely you have a favorite among them."

"Not really," Annja replied. But she found herself thinking of Charlemagne instead of Wenceslas. The king of the Franks had been a true warrior and recognized as one of the Nine Worthies, one of the nine historical figures that were thought most chivalrous.

"You can just call me Charlie." The old man turned the urn. "I haven't been called Charlie in a long time."

It was just luck, Annja told herself. She didn't give in to the temptation to believe that the man had read her mind. That was impossible.

So is the sword you carry, a voice whispered in the back of her mind.

BART CALLED at five minutes to seven.

Annja transferred the call to the clip-on earpiece she wore so she could keep her hands free. Together, she and Charlie had almost completed the pictures she needed to take. With them in hand, she'd be able to finish the authentication at home and send the museum a bill.

"Hello," Annja answered.

"Hello," Charlie said.

Annja pointed to her ear, hoping the old man would realize she was talking to someone over the phone.

Charlie smiled and nodded agreeably. He leaned to that ear, then he spoke more loudly. "Hello!"

"Hello," Bart said. "Who's the guy you're with?"

Annja handed Charlie the last piece. "I'm talking on the phone," she told him, and pointed to the earpiece.

"Oh. Sorry. All this new technology is hard to comprehend." The old man grinned as he held on to the urn.

"Is that him?" Bart asked. "Is that the old man?"

"I'm here with Charlie," Annja said.

Charlie nodded. "Hi."

"Charlie says hi," Annja said.

"Great."

"He's friendly." During the past few minutes Annja had been surprised to find herself warming up to him.

"He says Charlie is his name?" Bart asked.

"Yes. Unless you have something different." Annja felt hopeful.

Bart heaved a sigh. "No. I ran him through the photo database of missing people and came up with nothing."

"Maybe it hasn't been reported yet."

"I thought of that all by myself. I went through missing-persons' reports. It's scary thinking about how many of them disappear every year," Bart said.

"Did you find anything?" Annja asked.

"No. So how are things going there?"

"Fine. I've got help working through the authentication."

"He's working with you?" Bart sounded incredulous.

"Yes."

"No end-of-the-world speeches?"

"Not yet."

"Need me to come by?"

Annja thought about that and was grateful for the offer. "No. Not if you're busy. I think I can handle this."

"Okay." Bart sounded tired.

Even though he claimed to have rested well in the sleeping bag at her loft, Annja knew he hadn't.

She heard someone call Bart's name.

"Look," he said. "I've got to go. A triple homicide just got called in. But I've got my phone. If you need anything, call."

"I will," she said.

"And don't trust this guy."

"I won't." Annja broke the connection and pocketed the earpiece in her jeans.

Charlie stood nearby and smiled pleasantly to himself. "It seems the curator is in a hurry to go." He nodded toward the front of the museum.

Peably stood by the main doors. The PA system had already blared out the news of the museum's closing. Within minutes the museum patrons had filed through the door. It hadn't taken long because there weren't many of them.

Determined to beat the clock, Annja grabbed the files and papers she'd been working with and shoved them into her backpack. She was ready in seconds.

Without a word, Charlie fell in step behind her.

"What are you going to do?" Annja asked the old man.

Charlie shrugged. "I thought maybe I could take you to dinner."

Annja pulled at her backpack straps. There was no reason to go with him. In fact, there was every reason *not* to go with him.

Thunder rumbled outside. The concussions shook the museum's plate-glass windows. For the first time Annja realized the darkness outside wasn't just from the lateness of the hour. The smell of rain blew in through the door Peably was pointedly holding open.

"Ms. Creed," the curator invited in a strained voice. "If you please."

"Dinner?" Annja repeated.

Charlie nodded. "There's a nice soup kitchen not far from here. They might still be serving."

Annja felt terrible. If Charlie had stayed at the museum past serving time, he might be going to bed hungry.

Bart's advice not to trust him echoed in her head. Thoughts of serial killers bounced around in there, too. But there was something about the old man—except for the fact that he seemed a little spotty when it came to reality—that drew her in.

While she'd worked with him, she'd seen his gentleness and innocence, as well as his quiet strength.

Peably cleared his throat in a rude fashion.

You're going to be in a public place, Annja told herself. You'll be able to protect yourself even if something happens. He doesn't exactly look like a kung-fu master.

"All right," Annja said. She headed out into the rain, which by that time had increased to almost a deluge. Peably didn't even offer to let them stay within the doorway until the rain slackened.

Annja stood at the curbside and searched for a taxi. There was never one around when it was raining.

Without warning a voluminous pop sounded behind her.

Annja took one step to the side and bladed automatically, turning so that her body was presented in profile to the old man. Her left hand came up to defend and her right reached behind her and felt for her sword in the otherwhere.

"I didn't mean to startle you." Charlie stood unconcernedly and worked with a battered umbrella he had pulled from under the ratty trench coat he wore. Annja didn't know how she'd missed it before. "I thought maybe you would like to be out of the rain."

He shook the umbrella and it made creaking noises that didn't sound encouraging. Incredibly, the umbrella opened to gigantic proportions. The black fabric had turned gray from age and hard use. Small slits allowed the rain to drip through in places, but it blunted the downpour.

"There," he said. "That's better." He grinned, and for a moment Annja could see the young man he had once been.

Annja gazed down the darkened street. She was grateful for the shelter of the umbrella, but the possibility of being picked up by a taxi didn't look good.

"I think we're going to have to walk," she said.

"Nonsense," Charlie said. "We're on a quest to save the world. Just as the forces of darkness align themselves against us, those of light will favor us."

"Maybe we'd better get started," Annja said.

Charlie smiled at her benignly. "Maybe you should have a little faith, Annja Creed. You've been given a great responsibility in this world. You've also been given a bit of luck." He nodded down the street.

Annja looked. Incredibly, the headlights of a taxi bored through the darkness. Even more incredibly, despite the number of pedestrians trying frantically to wave the taxi down, it pulled to the curb in front of Annja.

"See?" Charlie took a step forward and opened the door. "Just have a little faith."

Annja slid inside and made room for Charlie. She stared at the old man as he closed the umbrella, raked his hair from his face and slid inside.

"But you still have to make your own luck," Charlie said. "Without that, the world will end for certain."

21

Seated in the darkened cargo area of the panel van he'd rented for the night's excursion, Garin studied Roux. He and Jennifer sat on the other side of the van. Both of them wore black clothing.

Members of the security team Garin had hired bookended them. That hadn't happened by chance. Garin didn't trust Roux ever.

Roux had remained strangely quiet through the meal, and on the ride back to the hotel where he'd rented rooms for all three of them. There were only two rooms. As it turned out, Jennifer was rooming with Roux.

Why are you so quiet, old man? The question kept banging through Garin's head.

The only time Roux got so quiet was when he was fretful. Of course, there was plenty to fret about. Both Saladin and Salome were after the painting. Saladin was a dangerous man. And Salome was definitely deadly. Garin still wore the scars she'd given him.

"Sir."

Garin turned his attention to the earpiece he wore. "Yes."

"We're coming up on the estate now."

"Good." Garin reached up and flipped down a video monitor from the vehicle's roof. The cargo area only had windows in the back door. Both of those had been blacked out.

Instantly, an image filled the screen. The monitor showed the road leading up to the estate. A soft glow of light from a guardhouse could be seen.

Roux snorted.

Jennifer looked at him.

"The old man doesn't much care for technology," Garin said. He touched the screen and shifted through the different perspectives available to him.

The security team had outfitted the van with a satellite relay that allowed Garin to stream video coming in from the camera mounted on the front of the van. Select members of the group also wore more cameras.

"A child and his toys," Roux muttered.

"Don't knock it," Garin said. "I've found it most helpful." He turned to Roux. "Plus, the last time I was at your estate, you seemed to have the latest security measures."

"It only serves to keep the idiots out."

Jennifer frowned as she stared at Roux. "You have an estate?"

Roux took a moment to answer. "A small one."

"Since when?"

Roux shrugged.

Exasperated, Jennifer glanced at Garin.

"I love technology," Garin said. "He likes secrets. You'll never get anything more out of him than he's willing to give."

"It seems like he could have mentioned he had an estate," Jennifer said.

"The same way he could have mentioned why this painting is so important. But he chose not to."

"Perhaps we could concentrate on getting inside *this* estate," Roux suggested.

The team leader interrupted. "Sir, are you ready for us to approach the outpost?"

Garin surveyed the front of the estate. Nothing moved there.

"Go," he said. He touched the screen again and shifted through the views until he'd selected the camera mounted on the man in the approach team.

In the camera's view, two men took advantage of the brush on the side of the guardhouse as they closed on their objective. The camera bounced slightly as it followed.

"Do you want to tell me how you were going to break into this place if I hadn't decided to lend a hand?" Garin asked.

"I have resources," Roux said as he watched the screen.

Garin almost delivered a derisive response. The only thing that kept him from doing so was the fact that Roux did know people who could do exactly what he was doing. The old man preferred subtlety and subterfuge. Those had always been his weapons of choice.

A moment later, the two men entered the guardhouse.

So far, so good, Garin thought.

Then the whole operation went to hell.

"Sir," one of the men said, "we have a problem. Somebody killed these guys."

The cameraman stepped forward. The image carried back showed corpses lying where the bullets had left them sprawled.

Roux cursed. "Salome beat us here."

HEART RATE ELEVATED, senses flaring as adrenaline flooded his system, Garin held a sound-suppressed pistol in his gloved right hand. He focused his attention on the monitor as the van hurtled toward the house.

"Invading the premises at this point isn't the smartest thing we could do," Jennifer said. "If Salome got here before us—"

"She did," Roux grated. "We waited too long."

Garin didn't say anything. It had taken time to get his team in place. Besides that, no matter how things went tonight, he'd known going in that he'd be blamed for any mistakes. That was how his relationship with Roux generally worked.

"Then we'd be better off leaving," Jennifer finished.

"She might still be here," Roux said.

"And the police might be on their way," Jennifer added. "I didn't come here to get arrested for murder."

"That," Roux declared, "will be the least of our worries if Salome gets her hands on that painting."

"Maybe if we knew what was at stake," Jennifer suggested, "we'd all feel better about the risk we're taking."

Roux ignored her as Garin knew he would.

The view of the main house grew bigger as the van sped across the landscaped grounds. A few lights glowed softly inside the structure. Two of Garin's teams closed on the back door and left the front entrance to the van crew. Snipers positioned on the security walls kept watch over the site.

"I think Salome is already gone," Jennifer said.

"If she was, then the police would be here," Roux said.

"What makes you so certain?"

"She'd do that to make the situation even more insufferable," Roux grated. "As a final insult."

Or, Garin thought, she might set up a trap. He scanned the front of the house less than fifty yards away. Shadows cloaked the facade.

Without warning, the sound of a heavy-caliber rifle

cracked through the radio frequency. An instant later, it rolled over the ground.

"Look out!" one of the snipers warned. "They've got a rocket launcher set up on the second floor!"

"Get us out of here!" Garin ordered. He slammed a fist against the metal plate that separated the front seats from the cargo area. He slammed against the side of the van as the driver took evasive action.

THE SAFE WAS LOCATED behind the entertainment center. Ilse Danseker had given up the location quickly after she'd seen her lover killed.

Salome tripped the electronic locks with the same remote control that operated the television, surround sound, DVD player and other entertainment devices. Evidently the woman's husband liked having everything linked to the same controller.

After Salome keyed in the special code, the entertainment center slid away to reveal a safe built into the wall. The safe was the size of a regular door. Another key code spun the tumblers inside the lock. They fell into place with loud clicks.

When she glanced at Drake, Salome saw the man was grinning in anticipation.

"Excited?" she asked.

"Positively brimming," Drake assured her. "A man builds a safe like that, he's not casual about what he puts in there. I expect to find a few other things to pick up besides the painting you're after."

Ilse Danseker sobbed at the foot of her bed. Disposable cuffs bound her wrists and ankles. She rocked on her knees, unable to keep still. A whispered prayer poured from her lips in a litany. "Please don't kill me, please don't kill me."

The temptation to put a bullet through the woman's head was almost more than Salome could bear. But until she had her hands on the painting of the Nephilim, she wasn't going to lose her only avenue of information.

Drake nodded at one of the men in the room. He stepped forward and started to pull on the door.

"Wait," Drake said. He looked at the sobbing woman. When he aimed his pistol at her, he depressed the trigger just enough to bring the targeting laser to life.

The ruby beam was steady between the woman's eyes. The reflection turned her tears pale scarlet.

"Are there any booby traps on the safe?" Drake demanded.

"No," the woman whispered.

"Because if there are, if something happens to my man or if the police suddenly decide to arrive," Drake said, "I'm going to kill you."

"There aren't. I swear." The woman closed her eyes and ducked her head so she couldn't look at him.

Drake turned back to the door and nodded to the man at the door. The man went inside and found a light switch. Illumination filled the safe.

Salome entered. It almost looked like a bank vault. Stacks of currency from a handful of countries sat on a shelf in neat bundles.

Drake stripped a pillowcase from the bed and swept the cash into it. "Nothing wrong with walking away with a little extra."

Salome barely noticed. Her eyes locked on to the painting that sat inside a protective case. She took a small penlight from one of the many pockets in her Kevlar vest. She shone the beam directly on the painting.

The brooding figure of the angel glowed.

Carefully, Salome took a reagent from her pocket, applied it to a handkerchief and knelt to swab it on a corner of the painting. She waited patiently. For a moment nothing happened and her hope remained intact.

Then, slowly, paint lifted from the canvas.

She cursed as she took the reagent from her pocket and upended it across the painting. Applied in greater volume, the paint bubbled from the canvas in strips.

"What's wrong?" Drake stood nearby in the midst of helping himself to the jewelry in the boxes on a shelf.

"It's fake," Salome snarled. "This isn't the original painting."

Drake finished adding the jewelry to his bag and glanced at the painting. "You're sure?"

"Of course I'm sure." Salome gazed at the painting in disgust. "It's a very good copy, but it's forged."

"You said it was a copy," Drake stated.

"It is."

"Not merely guesswork on part of the forger?"

In an instant, Salome saw where Drake was heading with the question. "You think the forger painted this from the original painting?"

Drake shrugged. "You said yourself that no one had seen this painting in years."

"Yes."

"Then how did you know what it was supposed to look like?"

"From reports of people who have seen it." Salome looked at the dripping mess of the painting oozing onto the floor.

"Whoever forged this knew what he or she was doing, love," Drake declared. "Stands to reason that maybe the artist was working from good source material. Like, for instance, the original painting."

"Find the painter, find the original," Salome said.

"Perhaps we can trace the painting's ownership back. Maybe we'll get lucky and find him."

"Someone could have hired the painter," Salome argued.

"Once we find him, love, we can ask him. This isn't the end of the world. Or a dead end."

Salome turned away from the false painting. She sealed away her frustration and anger. All of this could still be sorted out.

The radio receiver in her ear buzzed. She thumbed it on and watched Drake reach up for his receiver at the same time. "Yes."

"We have visitors," a man said quietly.

"Who are they?"

"We haven't identified them."

"Where are they?"

"Front of the house."

Salome crossed to the bedroom's window. One of Drake's men shut off the light inside the safe at his barked command.

She peered around the edge of the window at the estate grounds. A van sped up the road to the main house. They would arrive in seconds. She felt certain she knew who was inside. Roux had always been driven to succeed.

"There are also ground forces," the man said. "We've identified two separate units in addition to the van. They've placed snipers on the walls."

"We have the rocket team," Drake told Salome.

For a split second, Salome thought about Roux and the years they'd spent together. The old man had taught her a lot, but he hadn't taught her everything she'd wanted to know. In the end, she'd stolen part of his knowledge, taken a journal that talked about many wondrous things that she wanted to find.

So far, she'd found none of them. Twice before she had found items mentioned in that book, and twice before Roux had managed to strip them from her hands before she could realize her prize.

She knew what she had to do.

"Kill them," she commanded.

Drake gave the order. Immediately, a rocket shot from the second-story window on the other end of the building and streaked toward the van. The vehicle's driver was already trying to take evasive action, but it was too late. The rocket struck the van's left front bumper and knocked it aside like a child's toy. Flames engulfed the van at once.

So long, Roux, she thought. There was a twinge of sadness inside her as she watched the van roll over and over.

Drake gave the rocket team the order to reload.

22

"You have the most beautiful eyes."

The comment startled Annja as she sat across the small table from the old man. She and Charlie occupied one of the back tables at Luigi's, a small Italian restaurant that offered an evening buffet. Even Luigi, who prized Annja's patronage because she was—in his view at least—"a television star," barely admitted Charlie to his establishment.

Italian-themed bric-a-brac occupied the walls. Friezes of grapes outlined every door. Small fishermen's nets hung from the ceiling. Gallon wine jugs—empty, to prevent grievous bodily harm—hung in the net, as well as Italian stuffed toys that were often given to the children of patrons.

"I've never seen eyes quite like yours," Charlie went on. "They're like a cat's, but they have so much more promise. And maybe threat."

"Thank you," Annja said. "I think." She felt a little embarrassed. "But they'll be closing the kitchen before long. You should eat."

"I am eating. I was merely letting my stomach settle a little. The food here is very filling."

Annja knew that. It was why she'd brought him there. From the look of him, he hadn't had a decent meal in a long time.

"You don't find this kind of thing in the soup kitchens." Charlie picked up his fork and resumed his attack on the huge slab of lasagna in front of him.

"I suppose not," Annja said.

"It's true. The food there is very wholesome. It's just that all too often there isn't enough of it or it isn't prepared as well."

"Look," Annja said, "I can give you a little money. If you think that will help."

Charlie smiled beatifically. "Dear lady, I haven't asked you for tribute, have I?"

"No." Annja felt guilt for even offering. The reaction was foolish, but there was an air of pride about the homeless man that won her over. Even as she realized that, though, she could hear Bart's voice in the back of her head telling her not to trust the man.

You're not trusting him, she told herself. You're just feeding him a little. She looked at the lasagna piled high on his plate. Well, okay, maybe a *lot.*

"But it's also foolish to turn down generosity just because of pride when you're in dire straits," Charlie said. "Do you have money you could spare?"

Annja reached into her pocket and brought out two twenties. She'd use her debit card to settle the tab at Luigi's.

Charlie crumpled the bills into his palm, curled his fingers into a tight fist, turned his hand over, then opened it so the palm faced up. There was no sign of the money.

A moment of stunned fascination passed. Annja stared at Charlie's empty hand. It was a child's trick, a practiced maneuver of simple deception. Except she hadn't seen a single hint of misdirection.

"Surprised?" Charlie asked.

"How did you do that?" Annja asked.

"Magic," Charlie whispered.

"You're a magician?"

The bony shoulders lifted and dropped. "Some have called me that. I've never considered myself a magician."

Despite her need to get home and get to work on other projects she had going, as well as check on the research on the Nephilim painting, Annja found herself mesmerized by the old man. There was something about his voice, weak as it was, that drew her in and seemed to hold her spellbound.

"Have you been an entertainer?" Annja asked. With the feat of legerdemain, she found she was even more intrigued by him. Somehow the magic seemed to fit.

"For many years." Charlie forked more lasagna. "I've been throughout Europe. Trod stages and conducted performances 'neath leafy boughs."

"What was your act?"

"Why, magic, of course. That's the one thing that attracts everyone's attention."

Annja silently agreed. "But I thought you didn't consider yourself a magician," she said as she handed her debit card to the server who'd presented the bill.

"I didn't. I don't now. I'm a storyteller." Charlie smiled. "I tell most wondrous stories, but I find that if you don't keep an audience's attention they'll never stay with you to the end of the story." He shrugged. "It's the same thing Hollywood does with all the special effects they cram into movies these days."

"You watch movies?" That surprised her more than the magic did.

"Of course. Puerile entertainment at best, but Shakespeare entertained the common masses with the same aplomb," Charlie said.

"Shakespeare and special effects." Annja shook her head in amazement.

"They weren't unknown to each other. Shakespeare took advantage of stage presentation to get his tales told. He did have a limited landscape in which to perform, after all."

"What kind of magic did you do?"

"All kinds." Charlie waved his fork around to take in the room. "I once made a camel appear in downtown Cairo to amuse a handful of children. That little maneuver brought about far more attention than I'd hoped for."

"Besides magic, what other jobs have you held?" In spite of her fascination, Annja wanted to get enough information to help Bart find out where the old man belonged when he wasn't out wandering the streets.

"Oh," Charlie said, "I've been a soothsayer now and again for different kings and queens."

The statement saddened Annja because it reminded her how far from a balanced mentality he was. She hoped it was only a matter of his body's chemistry and that the remedy would be a simple one. Maybe he'd simply been off his meds for too long.

Charlie looked at Annja and smiled wistfully. "I find that people really don't change. No matter where you go, once they discover that you can foretell events, they all want to know what's going to happen to them. They never want to know what's going to happen to the world or how they might help the global community."

"People tend to be self-involved," Annja agreed. She got

that every time she dealt with Roux and Garin, and when she tried to explain true history to Doug.

Charlie sighed. "It's become embarrassing, if you ask me. Everybody always wants to know what's going to happen next in their lives."

"Not me," Annja said.

"Not you," Charlie agreed. "That's because you already know you've got a great destiny before you."

Annja smiled and played along. "How would I know that?"

"Because," Charlie said good-naturedly, "you have Joan's sword."

Surprised, Annja glanced around to see if anyone had overheard. She immediately wondered if she was being set up by an enemy of Roux's whom she hadn't yet met. Or if Garin had sent someone to try to get the sword from her.

Satisfied that no one had, she turned her attention back to Charlie. She also felt a lot more paranoid than she had previously.

"I don't have a sword," Annja said.

"You do. It belonged to Joan of Arc." Charlie stabbed another piece of lasagna and popped it into his mouth.

The low buzz of the few scattered conversations around the restaurant suddenly seemed threatening. She had the sudden sensation of being watched. She tried to dismiss the impressions and told herself she was imagining things. Neither of the feelings went away.

"What makes you think I've got a sword like that?" she asked.

"You positively glow with its possession."

"No." Annja couldn't keep the impatience out of her voice. "Who *told* you that I had a sword like that?"

Charlie smiled. "I'm afraid I can't tell you that. That isn't part of this tale."

Still paranoid and edgy, watchful of everyone around her, Annja asked, "What is this tale?"

"Why, the one where you save the world, of course. Why else would I be here?"

"I don't know."

"I do." Charlie looked pleased. "I came here to tell you that you have to save the world."

"How?"

"By stopping the king, of course."

"What king?"

"One of the sleeping kings."

Annja thought instantly of Wenceslas and how she'd been investigating the history of the man and the legend he'd inspired. Had she mentioned something to the old man about it? She was sure she hadn't, but she couldn't positively remember. There'd been a lot of talk about history in the museum. It was possible.

"One of the sleeping kings is going to end the world?" Annja asked.

"Yes." Charlie smiled as though she were a particularly bright pupil who'd made an overdue breakthrough.

"The mythology of the sleeping kings is that they're supposed to save the world," Annja said.

"Well, these things sometimes go astray," Charlie said. "That's why heroes—and heroines—like you were mixed into the weave. To keep everything on track. That's what you're going to have to do this time."

Annja sat and tried to figure out which way to direct the conversation next or even if she should bother. Charlie, as much as she liked him, wasn't in full possession of his faculties. It was a disheartening thing, but there it was.

How did he know about the sword? a voice in her head shouted.

"I don't mean to be indelicate," Charlie said in a low voice, "but do you happen to know where the men's room is?"

Annja pointed the way to the sign and watched him walk away.

As soon as Charlie disappeared, Annja made notes about their conversation. The small bells over the door rang. One of Luigi's servers went to the new arrivals and told them that the restaurant was unfortunately closed for the evening.

"Get out of my way," an accented voice ordered.

The sharp tone drew Annja's attention immediately. When she looked up, she saw three men in dark street clothes gazing directly at her.

The server, one of Luigi's young cousins or nephews, put a hand in the center of the man's chest to halt his forward movement.

"I told you, we're—"

The man caught the young server full in the face with a back-fist, then spun and delivered a roundhouse kick. The server sailed backward and landed in a crumpled heap on the floor.

The man's eyes focused on Annja. "Ms. Creed, if you come with me, you won't be hurt. My master has asked that you be taken without harm."

In that moment Annja caught a flash of a scimitar on the chain at the man's throat.

"If possible," the man added. "It doesn't matter to me." He reached under his jacket and pulled a pistol free from a shoulder holster.

23

The van jerked violently to the side, then flipped and rolled. Unfettered by a seat belt, Garin slammed against the vehicle's sides with bruising force. The front of the van was on fire. He felt it through the metal plate that cut the front section off from the cargo area. He didn't doubt that the men up front had died instantly.

Without warning, the van struck something and went sideways. Despite the reinforcement struts, the vehicle started to come apart. Smoke from the burning front section coiled inside the van. His nose and lungs burned with the noxious fumes.

Then, as suddenly as it had started, the vehicle stopped flipping, skidded a few more feet and smashed against something solid. Garin remembered the trees that lined the estate grounds.

They'd smashed into the trees. Garin saw them through the rents in the roof. A branch stabbed into the cargo area.

He also realized they were targets for a second attack.

"Take out the rocket launcher," Garin commanded. He wasn't sure if his radio was still operational. He hoped that it was. He also hoped that his snipers had already eliminated the rocket team. If they hadn't, he was overpaying them.

He reached into one of his pockets and pulled out a penlight. Before he could turn it on, another light came on with dazzling brightness.

Incredibly, Roux stood there looking for all the world as if he were out for a Sunday walk. Even standing amid the tangled sprawl of the mercenaries, he looked grim and capable.

"Get them out of here," Roux ordered. "If you don't, you're going to get them all killed."

Garin didn't bother with a response. He turned his attention to the doors. The van had come to a stop on its side. One of the mercenaries stood. Blood spattered the man's face from a broken nose. He looked unfocused and unsteady on his feet.

The doors were jammed. Garin pushed against them, but they wouldn't open. He stepped back, hampered by the sheer number of people inside the van. Then he braced himself and kicked at the doors. Nothing happened. He kicked twice more before the lock shattered and the twisted hinges screeched.

Conscious of the time passing and grimly aware of how quickly a rocket launcher could be reloaded, he grabbed the semiconscious man and heaved him through the open door. Then he reached for another. In the next second, Roux was there with him, helping him get the men out.

Two were dead. One's neck lolled at a sickening angle, and the other had a chestful of metal shards from the side of the van that had caught the rocket round blast.

Roux helped Jennifer through the door. The woman seemed dazed, as well. She had a large cut over her right eye.

Roux looked back at Garin.

"Go," Garin said gruffly. He shone his light around the cargo van's interior and found the pistol he'd dropped, as well as an H&K MP-5. By the time he'd grabbed his prizes and turned around, Roux was through the door.

Garin looked out the door. The mercenaries began to recover and took up positions among the trees. Flames licked at the front of the van.

Then a spark leapt from one of the second-story windows again. Evidently the snipers hadn't picked off the rocket team, who'd managed to launch another rocket.

"Garin!" Roux shouted hoarsely.

Garin started to respond, but the missile struck the middle of the van. The explosion knocked him from his feet. Everything turned black.

CONSCIOUSNESS RETURNED to Garin in a rush, as if he'd been deep underwater and suddenly surfaced. A face, blurred and indistinct, hung above him. He clenched a big fist and threw a punch. Almost at the same time, he realized the face belonged to Roux. The old man was kneeling beside him. His face was stretched tight in worry.

Roux slapped the blow away as if it were a bothersome insect. Garin thought he must really be out of it if Roux could block him so easily, but he also knew the old man excelled at self-defense.

"Can you get up?" Roux demanded.

Garin read his lips more than he heard him.

"Yes." Garin tried to get to his feet, but his coordination was shot. He kept expecting another rocket to strike them. With the twisted wreckage of the van burning nearby, he knew the darkness held no safety for them.

Roux stepped forward and Garin felt himself being

wrenched to his feet. He groaned in pain. Fiery agony wrapped his midsection, and he wondered if he'd broken his ribs.

In the next instant, a disturbance raked the ground where he'd been. Clods of black earth flew up and left small craters.

"Evidently Salome hires better killers than you do," Roux groused.

"Look, if all you're going to do is criticize, I'll save myself," Garin replied. He looked at the carnage spread over the estate grounds. "Some of these men worked for me for years. And I bought into your troubles. This is no trouble of mine."

"You're right," Roux said. "I apologize."

The announcement stunned Garin enough that he forgot about his pain and the fact that bullets tore through the trees around them. Roux rarely apologized for anything.

Roux put Garin up against a tree and looked at him. The old man's eyes held deadly intensity. "If possible, you need to regroup your men. We can't let Salome escape with that painting."

Garin put a hand to the side of his face and adjusted his earpiece. He quickly sorted the living from the dead. Most of the team in the van were alive. Two were dead and three were out of the action. The other groups held their positions around the main house.

"The snipers are still in position," Garin said. "Salome and her people know they're out there, though. The snipers took out the men with the rocket launcher."

"That's good. Let's just hope no one else picks up the damnable thing." Roux glared through the leafy branches at the big house. "True warriors fight with naked steel and close enough to see their opponents' faces. This is a sacrilege to honor."

"Honor gets you killed on the battlefield," Garin said. "It's better to have superiority. That way, if the other side can see your show of force, maybe no one has to die."

"Generals have thought that for centuries. It's not any more true now than it ever was. If a man has to fight you—if you're going to take something precious from him or threaten his life even if he surrenders—he will. And it won't matter who he has to go up against to do it. That's the measure of a man."

Garin forced the pain from his mind. Survival was all that mattered.

"Can you stand?" Roux asked.

"Yes."

Roux released him and stepped back.

Garin stood unsteadily, but he stood.

A shadow stepped out of the darkness and closed on Roux. Garin brought up the pistol in his fist and took aim automatically. His finger curled around the trigger.

Roux knocked the pistol aside as Garin fired. The bullet went wide of the target. Garin saw only then that it was Jennifer. She stared at him in shock.

"Sorry," Garin said. "Didn't know it was you." For a moment, he was back in that old mind-set, when it had been Roux and him against the world. Plenty of people had been willing to kill them in those days. Looking back on where he was now, Garin realized things hadn't changed much.

"Next time, *look*," Jennifer snarled.

Chastened, but only a little, Garin reached out for her at the same time Roux did. They both pulled her to the ground just before a fusillade of bullets slammed through the trees.

"The muzzle-flash of your pistol—" Roux said.

"Alerted the shooters still inside the house," Garin finished.

"Rocket launchers and machine guns," Jennifer whispered. "We never went up against people like this when we were together."

"That's one of the reasons I didn't stay," Roux said. "Things in this world insist on getting decidedly more dangerous." He hesitated. "I do apologize for the way I left."

"Don't you think it's a little late for an apology?" Jennifer replied.

It was a night for wonders, Garin decided. They still lived in spite of everything, and he was witnessing a side of Roux that he didn't think he'd ever seen.

"That's up to you," Roux said.

"Late or not," Garin told them, "this is an entirely inappropriate place. Maybe you could shelve the reunion until after we get out of here alive and are one step ahead of the police."

In minutes, Garin organized his men and they armed themselves again. He set himself with his back to a tree and called out to the snipers. "Ready?"

"Ready," they responded.

"Sir," the leader of the security team said, "you don't have to do this. One of the other men—"

"None of the other men on this side of the main house are in any shape to draw fire," Garin interrupted.

Four of the men from the van remained mobile. None of them were capable of a hundred-yard dash at the moment. Garin just hoped they could help provide covering fire.

"Let's do this," Garin said.

"Yes, sir."

Garin took a deep breath and ignored the flaming claws that raked his left side. He held the MP-5 in both hands.

Roux's hand fell on his shoulder. "They're going to be looking for you."

"That's what we're counting on," Garin stated.

"Be careful." Roux squeezed his shoulder and took his hand away.

Garin turned his attention to the seventy-plus yards that separated him from the next copse of trees.

Three snipers had the front of the main house in their field of fire.

"Now," Garin said, and he broke cover. He drove his feet hard against the ground and sprinted for the trees. Bullets cut the air around him.

24

Before the man's pistol had time to clear the holster, Annja slung her backpack over her left shoulder and reached for the sword with her right. She had her fingers curled around the hilt when she realized that Luigi and the restaurant staff would see it.

Annja pushed out her breath in frustration. She could explain muggers attempting to rob her in the restaurant, even though it seemed she was the only one they'd come for, but she couldn't explain the sword.

"Ms. Creed." The man pointed his weapon at her.

Unable to go on the offensive, Annja turned and ran. She took two long strides, vaulted into the air and threw her feet forward to slide across a table. She dropped her feet to the floor just as the table started to tip, then dropped to her knees. She caught hold of the table's edge and yanked so that it tipped over completely and formed a momentary barrier. Luigi didn't stint when it came to furniture. He bought it once and bought it to last.

Bullets hammered the overturned table but didn't penetrate. Annja hadn't thought they would. She'd seen a suppressor on the pistol's snout. That meant the pistol fired subsonic rounds, which generally meant less power.

I'm going to have to reimburse Luigi for that table, Annja thought.

"Get her!" the man roared.

Annja stayed in a crouch as she pushed herself into motion. She kept her attention riveted on the hallway off the main dining area. The hallway led to the back door that led into the alley.

She thought briefly of Charlie, feeling badly that she'd left him behind. They're not after him, she told herself as she grabbed the partition wall and made the sharp turn. They're after you.

Her fingers slipped from the corner of the low wall that separated the hallway from the dining area. Out of control, struggling to keep her feet under her, she slammed against the opposite wall hard enough to drive the air from her lungs. She threw her hand out and pushed off into a full run.

Bullets hammered the length of the partition wall. Wooden splinters and jagged pieces that had been colorful ceramic figurines became a dust storm in front of her. She aimed for the panic bar that sealed the door.

Feet slapped the floor behind her.

At the exit, she twisted and slammed a hip against the panic bar. The security system screamed to life as the portal swung open. She passed through and turned right immediately, away from the door as it opened.

Stale, hot air washed over her face as she stepped into the alley. Piles of trash lined the narrow thoroughfare. Homeless people were already working the bags.

"Get down!" Annja yelled. "There's been a robbery!"

Galvanized into action, the homeless people sought shelter at once.

Annja was tempted to hide, but she knew if she didn't allow her pursuers to see her they might search the alley and kill everyone in sight. She couldn't allow that.

So she ran. She stretched out her stride and concentrated on eating up the distance. Her backpack thudded against her back. Despite the adrenaline filling her system and the way she pushed herself, her breathing remained under control. She wanted to reach for the sword but she held off that impulse.

You can do this, she told herself. This is your city. Your turf. They can't catch you here.

Her phone rang. The noise sounded so loud in the alley that it jangled her nerves. She caught sight of the brightness behind her as the restaurant's back door opened. The discordant scream of the panic bar siren filled the alley again.

There was no warning this time. The man pursuing her merely opened fire. Bullets slashed the air around her and cracked against the alley wall.

Annja ran across the street as more shots were fired. A cab missed her by inches and slammed into a delivery van, which braked to an immediate halt.

The confusion disrupted the traffic flow and caused a sudden eruption of car horns.

Annja ran behind the taxi and cut in front of the stalled oncoming traffic.

Footsteps drummed up behind her, and Annja caught sight of a man in her peripheral vision at the same time she spotted a MINI Cooper bolting around the two cars ahead of it. She checked the distance and speed and guessed that she had just enough time before the small car sped through.

The man behind her threw himself in a dive. He managed to wrap a hand around her ankle, but he was on the ground when he did it. The MINI-Cooper driver was concentrating on Annja. He didn't even see the man on the street.

The man had time to give one startled yelp, then the MINI Cooper smashed over him. His fingers peeled away from Annja's ankle.

She tripped and went down, then forced herself up on one elbow. The heat from the MINI Cooper's engine blew over her.

"Oh, my God!" the male driver exclaimed as he got out of his vehicle. "I didn't even see him! He ran out of nowhere!"

Annja pushed herself to her feet and ran for the nearest alley. Her pursuers hadn't given up.

LONG MINUTES LATER, once she was certain she'd outdistanced the men chasing her, Annja finally slowed her pace to a walk. When she looked around, she got her bearings and aimed for a second-story cybercafé above a Vietnamese bodega. It operated twenty-four hours and was filled by hardcore gamers, crackers and scammers.

After checking and still not seeing any sign of her pursuers, Annja entered the small stairwell and went up to the cybercafé.

"Hey, Annja," the guy behind the counter greeted. He was in his early thirties, short and dark haired, with round-lensed glasses and an innocent face. Tattoos featuring koi and dragons covered every square inch of his arms.

"Hey, Graham," Annja replied. "Can I get a booth?"

"Always." Graham turned his attention to the massive control panel and performed a few keystrokes.

Graham's wife, Helen, worked the small kitchen area

behind the main counter. The café didn't offer much in the way of a menu, but the clientele wasn't picky. Anything with cheese accompanied by anything with caffeine or sugar generally met their needs for marathon gaming binges.

"Do you have a window booth open?" Annja asked.

Graham checked. "Yep. You want that one?"

"Please."

"Done." Graham looked up at her and smiled. "Anything else?"

"Hot chocolate?"

"Sure." Graham turned and called the order out to Helen. "It'll be a minute. I'll bring it out to you when it's ready."

Annja nodded and said thanks. She turned and started to head for the booth.

"You okay?" Concern showed on Graham's face.

"Yeah. I'm fine."

"You look a little discombobulated."

Annja smiled at him. It had always amazed her how many friends she'd made around the neighborhood. She was gone a lot, and she'd been raised in an orphanage. Either of those things was generally enough to kill any friendship potential in New York. But she'd still managed to get to know people.

"Mugger," she said.

Graham frowned. "You okay?"

"I'm fine," Annja said.

"She probably kicked the mugger's butt," Helen said from the kitchen.

"Actually," Annja said, "I might have set a new record for the hundred-yard dash."

"I've seen you make grown men want to beat their heads against a wall," Helen said. "I'm disappointed." But she was smiling.

"First rule of every fight," Annja said. "If you can, run."

"I know, but fighting just sounds so much cooler."

"My wife," Graham said, "the UFC wannabe."

Helen grinned and suggested a physically debilitating procedure Graham could do to himself.

"I'll bring that hot chocolate," Graham promised.

SALADIN'S MEN didn't give up easily. They cycled through the neighborhood in two-man groups.

As she took her seat in the booth, Annja glanced out the window and saw two men obviously walking a search pattern. She recognized one of them from Luigi's, and that made her wonder what had happened at the restaurant.

She opened her backpack and took out her digital camera. A nearby streetlight illuminated the two men as they strolled down the sidewalk. There was enough light to shoot by, and Annja managed a half-dozen frames before they disappeared back into the night.

She took out her phone and called Luigi's. The line was busy and she couldn't get through. Anxiety chafed her. She was just about to call Bart when her phone rang and his number showed up on caller ID.

"Hey," Annja answered.

"What's going on, Annja?" Bart demanded. "I just got a call from central that you'd been involved in a gunfight at an Italian restaurant." He sounded nearly apoplectic.

"It wasn't a gunfight," Annja said a little defensively. "A gunfight is when both parties have guns and they shoot at each other. I didn't have a gun. They just shot at me."

"Are you hurt?"

"No."

Bart cursed. Then he took a deep breath. "Where are you?"

"Do I need an attorney?"

"Why would you need an attorney?"

"I don't feel like being arrested. I didn't do anything wrong. They came into Luigi's—"

"Luigi's! Man, that was one of my favorite restaurants."

Irritation filled Annja. "It was still standing when I left. You don't have to refer to it in the past tense."

"Who were the guys that came after you?"

Annja hesitated. Then she felt she owed him that at least. "I think they were part of the same group that attacked me in Prague."

"You think?"

"I didn't exactly want to stand around asking for bad-guy references."

"What do they want?"

"Nothing I can give them."

"Obviously they don't know that or they wouldn't be chasing you."

Annja silently agreed. "Look, why don't you call someone and find out if Luigi and his employees are okay. I don't want to think any of them got hurt because of me."

"I need to talk to you," Bart said.

"You can. Just not at this moment. Find out about Luigi first." Annja paused and knew that Bart was going to erupt at any moment. "Please."

"All right," Bart replied.

"And find out if Charlie is okay, too."

"Charlie?"

Annja didn't know how to finesse that one. "The homeless guy."

"The homeless guy?" Bart's voice went up a few notches again.

"Yes."

"He was with you?"

"Yes."

"What were you doing with him? I told you to stay away from him."

"It's a long story, okay? Just find out about Luigi. I'll tell you all about it when I see you."

For a moment Bart was silent. Annja felt certain he was going to argue with her again. But he surprised her when he spoke in a quiet, controlled voice.

"You realize that old man could have led these guys to you."

"I don't think so." But Annja kept thinking about how Charlie had disappeared right before the arrival of Saladin's men.

"One phone call from him, they're all over you."

"I don't think he did that."

"You just told me you don't know what's going on."

"I don't," Annja agreed.

"Are you at home?"

"No."

"Good. Don't go there."

"I hadn't planned on it." Annja didn't know where she was going to go at the moment. She wasn't sure how much information Saladin had about her. As a television personality and archaeologist, her secrets weren't as impenetrable as Roux's and Garin's.

"I'll get back to you as soon as I can," Bart promised.

"Thanks. And if Luigi is okay, tell him I didn't mean to bring any of that there." Annja broke the connection because she knew Bart wouldn't want to let go.

Graham brought the hot chocolate and left without a word.

Annja gazed at her reflection in the window and thought about Roux and Garin. She hadn't had any contact with them in two days. A lot, she told herself, could go wrong in two days.

25

One of the bullets struck Garin's Kevlar vest high on the back of his right shoulder and nearly knocked him down. He stumbled but didn't fall.

Muzzle-flashes marked the positions of the shooters within the main house. Garin reminded himself again that the men he'd brought with him were good, and that they'd get the job done.

He threw himself the last few feet across the ground, then popped up behind the trees.

"Sir," the team leader said. "We confirm five men down inside. They won't be getting back up again."

Garin grinned at that. Despite the risk, there was nothing that made him relish life so much as potential death. For a while he'd thought maybe he'd gotten that trait from his father, through the blood that they shared. Then, over time, he'd realized that Roux was the same way. And Garin had thought he'd learned the recklessness that fired him.

He set himself. "Ready?"

"Ready."

Garin picked another spot, closer to the main house now, and broke cover again.

SALOME STOOD near one of the windows and watched as a man ran out of the darkness across a moonlit patch of ground. His destination was a stand of trees only thirty yards from the main house.

"Kill him," Drake ordered. He stood over a man with a machine gun in the window. Drake held a bolt-action sniper rifle and used the window frame for protection.

The mercenary opened fire and unleashed a stream of bullets at the running man. Without warning, the mercenary jerked back into the room and sprawled on the floor.

Another bullet tore through the window frame and dusted Drake in splinters. He cursed and drew back. Grimly, he worked the bolt to chamber a new round.

Anger surged inside Salome. This wasn't how things were supposed to go. The painting wasn't supposed to be a fake, and they weren't supposed to get trapped in the house.

But Drake had prepared for that eventuality.

"It's time to call in the air support, love," Drake said. "And time for us to get gone from this place."

Salome nodded. She didn't trust her voice. She hated retreating. In frustration, she listened to Drake make the call and silently cursed Roux for all she was worth.

WITHIN MINUTES the snipers cleared the windows. Garin reached the front doors of the main house and stood guard while the rest of his team arrived. The two other teams breached the back side of the house.

Roux and Jennifer joined him, as well. The old man had picked up an assault rifle.

"Sir," the team leader said.

"Yes." Garin took point as they battered the doors open and went inside. Nothing moved in the great room.

"Comm has been listening in on the local police band frequencies. Cars—a lot of cars—are presently en route."

"Understood. Pull in the exfiltration teams. We're going to clear this area." Garin had two helicopters waiting nearby. They were only minutes away from the coastline. If they ran hard and fast and stayed below radar, they could be gone before anyone could track them.

When the helicopter rotors sounded a moment later, Garin knew they didn't belong to the aircraft he'd arranged. These had arrived far too quickly.

He ran up the stairs and avoided the bodies of the servants left strewed there. At the landing, he gazed out the window and saw a helicopter slide into view. The moonlight barely brought the wide black body out into relief as it coasted toward the rooftop. Then it was out of sight.

Garin cursed.

"That isn't yours?" Roux asked.

"No." Garin ran up the next flight of stairs and gave orders to shoot down the helicopter.

"You can't do that," Roux said. "The painting may be aboard."

Garin immediately rescinded the order and told his snipers to take out any people they saw. His breath came hard and ragged in his lungs. Pain sliced at his side.

He followed the house design by instinct. Hundreds of years of dwelling in houses, many of them bigger than this house, gave him experience to draw on. He found the master bedroom easily. The information Jennifer had on the woman who had bought the Nephilim painting included the fact that they kept a safe on the premises.

When he shone his flashlight on the room's interior, Garin saw the dead man on the bed and the bound woman on the floor. She'd been shot once in the head. Her mouth gaped open in a silent scream.

"Salome doesn't leave any witnesses when she works," Roux said. If the violence touched him, he didn't show it.

The sight didn't bother Garin much, either. For the past five hundred years he'd watched thousands die at the hands of others. Sometimes it had been during a war, but most of the time death had been close and personal. He no longer remembered how many people he'd killed.

"She's headed for the roof," Garin said. "We still have a chance to catch her."

Roux entered the room and hunkered down beside a painting lying facedown on the floor. Cautiously, he turned it over. His light revealed the paint that had bubbled free of the canvas, but enough of the image remained that Garin easily identified it.

"Salome destroyed the painting?" Garin asked.

Roux touched the paint with a finger. "No. This was a fake."

Garin didn't question how the old man knew. It was enough that Roux did.

Sudden thunder erupted overhead. Garin knew the sound was heavy-duty machine guns.

"Sir," the security team leader called over Garin's headset, "their helicopter is at the back of the house. The snipers up front are blocked. I've got two men at the rear wall. They're reporting heavy machine-gun fire. They've taken cover."

"Understood." When he gazed around the room, Garin ran

the house design through his head. Where would a helicopter most likely be able to pick up people?

Then he remembered the widow's walk at the back of the house. He looked at the back of the bedroom and saw a doorway that let onto the widow's walk.

"Here," Garin called, and led the way to the back of the bedroom. He held the machine pistol in both hands as he whirled around the doorway.

Only a sixth sense he'd developed from long years of combat saved his life from the gunman lying prone along the roof.

Garin spun back inside and looked up at the ceiling. After measuring where he thought the man was, Garin emptied a clip into the ceiling. Roux stared at him, but Jennifer stepped back and covered her head with an arm.

Deftly, Garin changed magazines in the weapon as he turned back to the widow's walk. He stepped outside again just as the dead man rolled from the roof and dropped over the side.

The helicopter hung at the back of the house. Shadowy figures boarded through the cargo doors.

Garin lifted his weapon, but a door gunner mounted on the side opened up. Fifty-caliber bullets raked the widow's walk and drove Garin back inside. Several more rounds chewed through the walls at the corner of the room. Fortunately the angle was too acute to allow the gunner to fire into the bedroom.

"They're getting away," Roux shouted above the chatter of the machine gun.

"I'm not the only one lying here with my face on the carpet," Garin replied. The vibrations caused by the bullets penetrating the walls echoed in the floor. "Feel free to run out there and stop them."

Roux cursed.

"They're not getting away with anything," Jennifer stated. "They thought they had the painting. They didn't."

"I know," Garin replied. "But killing that woman would have given me immense pleasure. Sooner or later, it's going to have to be done."

The machine gun kept firing and the angle of the bullets altered, but the sound drew farther away. Garin pushed himself up and checked outside.

As he watched, the helicopter sped away and there wasn't anything he could do to stop it.

26

"Hey. Are you there?"

Annja stared at the instant-message window that floated to the top of her computer screen. It took a moment for her to recognize the name of the sender and associate it with the information she was looking for regarding the painting of the Nephilim.

Hey, Annja typed back. Good to hear from you.

Is this a good time?

It's fine, Annja wrote. She took a sip of her hot chocolate. Graham had replenished it from time to time. She glanced at the time.

Forty-three minutes had elapsed since she'd talked to Bart. There had been no news about Luigi or Charlie. The Internet news services had only stated that gunfire had broken out at the restaurant but there weren't any reported casualties. She chose to take that as a good sign.

You in the states? Her contact asked.

Annja hesitated over the question. She still wasn't certain how Saladin's men had found her at Luigi's.

Hey, it's cool. You don't have to tell me.

I'm in the States. Sorry. Was working. Clearing my head, Annja quickly typed.

Cool. You wanted to know about the Medici story and the Nephilim painting.

Excitement warred with wariness in Annja. Things didn't come easily in her field. She was prepared for disappointment.

Yes, she typed.

I heard the painting was sold in the Hague yesterday.

Annja's heart raced. Is that where Roux and Garin are? In the Hague? While I'm here dodging bullets and getting my friend's restaurant shot up?

I didn't hear that, she replied.

This whole thing seems kind of hush-hush.

Why all the secrecy? Annja asked.

Not really secrecy. Just nobody believes it.

What? Annja asked.

That the painting's got the power to destroy the world. I mean, the kind of crap you see in B movies. LOL.

I thought it was kind of intriguing someone had painted a portrait of a Nephilim and a Medici family member wanted it, Annja typed.

Cosimo, Yeah. He was an odd guy. But he was head of the family when Constantinople fell. He had a difficult job managing the family fortunes. Lots of stress.

Annja waited, willing the person to tell the story.

Cosimo was interested in the painting because of the power it was supposed to contain, her contact wrote. Back then, you gotta remember they felt like the fate of the whole world was being decided in Constantinople. Real Old Testament stuff. Everybody back then swore that God and demons took part in the battles.

Annja knew that was true.

Constantinople was the crossroads between the East-ern and Western cultures, Annja typed. It was an important place. A lot of people and ideas passed through there.

Are you a teacher?

Annja thought about that. Sometimes, she wrote.

Cool. So am I.

Where?

Naples.

Italy?

LOL. Florida.

How did you know about this painting? Annja wrote.

Got a double major. History and Art. A lot of people don't realize how much those two fields overlap these days.

I do.

What field are you in? the contact asked.

Archaeology.

Awesome. I thought about getting into archaeology. I still might. I want to take a doctorate before I'm through. Maybe then.

Annja didn't want to sound impatient, but she also didn't want to spend the night comparing degrees. How did you find out about the painting? she asked again.

I studied with a brilliant man named Dr. Anton Krieger. Ever hear of him?

Annja had. There had even been a Discovery Channel special on the man after his recent death. I have. Smart man. It was a shame to lose him.

Yeah. He was one of those rarities—a really good guy. But he was eighty-nine when he died. He'd lived a full life. The funny thing is, he'd never gotten to figure out the truth about the Nephilim Medici was trying to find. Dr. Krieger told me he had papers Cosimo de' Medici left behind. He felt certain the secret location of the Holy Grail was hidden in that painting.

Annja didn't believe that. If a code had been embedded in the painting it would have been figured out long before now. There were a lot of legends about paintings hiding secrets.

That's pretty hard to believe, she typed.

I know. I don't think I bought into it, either. But it was weird when you started asking questions about the painting.

Did Cosimo de' Medici find the painting?

Maybe. There's a rumor that he did. One of his men supposedly located it in Constantinople as the city fell to the Ottomans. He was supposed to have gotten out of the city with the painting, but something happened to him on the way back to Venice.

What? Annja asked.

According to the story Dr. Krieger ultimately got, this guy was killed by a jealous husband in an inn. Nobody said what happened to the painting.

What did Dr. Krieger think happened to it?

He thought there was every possibility that the killer or killers saved the painting and sold it. Or they might have destroyed it on the spot.

Or the innkeeper threw it out the next morning because the dead man bled all over it, Annja typed. Or because he thought it might have been cursed. The painting was incredibly suggestive from what I've read.

Right. There was even some conjecture that Cosimo had the man killed to prevent anyone from connecting him to the painting.

Do you know who the artist was? Annja asked.

The original artist was a man named Josef Tsoklis.

Annja took a moment and opened up another window. She Googled the name quickly but didn't get any hits.

Doesn't appear to be much on Tsoklis, she typed.

Except for this one painting, he was pretty much a nonevent. He died soon after he did the painting.

Then why did Krieger get interested? Annja asked.

Because of the Grail story. Dr. Krieger was interested in the aspects of the story that equated it to the horn the archangel Gabriel was supposed to blow that would bring about the end of days.

That was something Annja hadn't heard before. How did Krieger arrive at that conclusion?

There have been other papers written about that possibility. Dr. Krieger was just covering his bases when he did the work on this project sixty years ago. But it was interesting enough that it stuck with him. Shortly before he died a few months ago, we had a breakthrough.

What happened?

Dr. Krieger had discovered some sketches in Cosimo de' Medici's personal effects. They showed what Cosimo had been told the Nephilim painting looked liked.

That bothered Annja at once. If sketches existed, there was every possibility that the work had been copied more than once. If so, finding the original painting would be infinitely harder.

While I was working with him, her contact wrote, I noticed that some of the sketches were a lot like another painter with moderate success at the time. I was preparing a paper on Venetian artists.

The cursor sat blinking for a moment.

Anyway, I found some notes in Dr. Krieger's collection that he got from the Medicis' records. There's a possibility that this second artist was in Constantinople and did some touch-up work on the Nephilim painting before the city was sacked.

Define 'touch-up,' Annja wrote.

Bringing the color back into line. Smoothing out some of the texture. Back in those days, artists had a tendency to glop the paint onto the canvas.

Who was the other artist? Annja asked. She waited, wondering if she'd scared him off.

27

If Dr. Krieger was alive, her contact wrote, I wouldn't give you this. It was his story. And in a way, because I worked so long with him on this, maybe it's mine.

I understand how you feel. Mentally Annja crossed her fingers as she typed. I'd be protective, too. But that's not the story I'm after.

The problem is, I'm not going to be able to do anything with the information I've got. The funding for Dr. Krieger's research was cut almost the day he died. With what I'm getting paid, I can't continue.

Annja assured her contact she'd give him full credit in her research.

The artist's name was Jannis Thomopoulos. He was born and raised in Venice, but he traveled extensively. Some of those travels were to Constantinople.

What did he do there? Annja typed.

Found clients and did portrait sittings. He did several

watercolors and sketched a lot. Pretty much lived a hand-to-mouth existence till the end of his days.

Okay, that's great. Annja felt her cell phone vibrate. She glanced at the caller ID and saw that it was Bart. Can I get in touch with you again if I need more information? she typed.

Definitely. And if you find anything out, please let me know.

Annja assured him that she would. Then she took Bart's phone call.

"Nobody got hurt," Bart said.

Annja heard the sounds of traffic passing over the telephone connection and knew that Bart was probably on his way to pick her up. Still, the news was good. She let out a sigh of relief and started packing her computer into her backpack.

"Luigi's all right?" Annja stood and stretched.

"Once you bolted," Bart said, "the guys chasing you vanished."

"Luigi has cameras inside the restaurant."

"We got the storage drives from the cameras. I looked at the images myself. That's one of the reasons I'm calling back so late. We've got a chance at identifying the men who came after you. If they've got records."

"What about Charlie?" Annja asked.

That was clearly a sore subject with Bart. "There was no sign of him. I tell you, Annja, you may feel softhearted toward that old man, but the possibility that he set you up has to have entered your mind."

It had, but for whatever reason Annja couldn't believe that was really what had happened. She slung her backpack over her shoulder, then took another glance at the street below the cybercafé. A few pedestrians moved along the sidewalk. New York never ground to a complete halt in any of the five boroughs. None of the pedestrians appeared to be Saladin's men.

"Where are you headed?" she asked.

"I'm coming to pick you up," Bart growled. "I'm thinking that may be the only way I'm going to get any sleep tonight."

"You don't have to do that," Annja said, meaning that she didn't want him to do that.

"Hey, we're talking about *my* peace of mind here." And that meant that Bart wasn't going to take no for an answer. "You're at the cybercafé a few blocks down, right?"

Annja thought about lying. She had her own life and her own agenda. She really didn't need her friends butting into it. Except that what was going on these past few days had left her owing those people.

"Yes," she replied. "I'll be out front."

"Not out front," Bart said quickly. "Stay hidden. I take it you've looked around."

"Two of them passed by right after I got here, but I haven't seen them again."

"Doesn't mean they're not there hanging around to see if you're going to show."

"I know."

"I don't get the impression that these guys are going to go away easily. Not if they've followed you from Prague."

Annja waved at Graham and Helen, who were in the process of turning the evening shift over to the night manager and night cook. They waved back. A few of the gamers called out halfhearted goodbyes, still wrapped up in the imaginary worlds on their screens.

She told Bart she'd see him in a few minutes, then folded the phone and put it away. She went down the steps quickly and waited just inside the doorway. Her mind spun as she tried to process the new information.

Okay, the news about the other artist is good, she told herself. That gives you an avenue no one else who's been looking for this thing has explored. Maybe Roux and Garin don't even know about Thomopoulos. Just focus on that for the moment.

As she stood in the foyer, she felt the night's chill soak into her bones. Her eyes burned with fatigue. She hadn't slept well in two nights and it was catching up with her.

A moment later Bart's unmarked car slid to a stop at the curb. She pushed through the door as Bart got out of the vehicle and looked around. His hand rested on the pistol holstered at his hip.

Sliding into the car was almost anticlimactic. Annja sat back in the seat and cranked the heater as Bart slipped back into the car.

"Did you just offer to take the homeless guy out for dinner?" Bart asked irritably. He pulled the transmission into Drive and pulled away from the curb.

"Yes."

"He didn't even have to give you a sob story about being hungry."

"I could see that he was hungry. He looked like he hadn't eaten well in days," Annja said.

"Terrific. You and I need to compare notes on your idea of keeping a low profile."

"I didn't expect those men to show up here."

"You also said you thought they were after this guy, Garin Braden."

"I think they were."

"Well, where's he?"

Annja refused to look in Bart's direction, but she watched his reflection in the windshield. He clearly wasn't happy.

"I don't know," she answered. "How did those men find me?"

"I told you, the old man—"

"He didn't have anything to do with those men showing up at Luigi's," Annja protested.

"Do you have some special mutant ability for detecting lies that I don't know about?" Bart asked.

"It's the same one you have."

"That guy, he was burying the needle on my radar."

"You never talked to him."

"I didn't have to," Bart said.

"There's something decent about him."

Bart shot her a perplexed glance. "Decent?"

"Yes."

"He's covered in street muck—"

"He's relatively clean."

"He doesn't have a pot to—"

"There are public bathrooms."

"Yeah. Normally anywhere those guys are standing."

Annja didn't bother to respond.

Bart sighed. "Look, I don't want to hurt your feelings or get into an argument here. I hear what you're saying, but I don't believe it. You want my opinion—and yeah, I get that you don't, but here it is anyway—that old man sold you out."

"If he was hooked up with the men who came to Luigi's, don't you think he'd be better dressed? Better able to take care of himself?" Annja asked.

"Maybe he's disguised."

Annja turned to him. "Are you listening to yourself?"

Bart held up a hand in defense. "Okay, maybe that's a little far-fetched. But I'm tired. And I've been worried about you."

"I appreciate that."

"You could act a little more appreciative."

"And you could be a better listener."

Bart growled in frustration. His jaws clenched and he readjusted in the seat. "Maybe I could," he said.

"There had to be another way those men found me at Luigi's."

"The easiest way is for the old man to tell them."

"He was with me at the museum all afternoon. Why didn't he call those men then?"

"I don't know. Maybe he couldn't get hold of them."

"Think, Bart. There has to be a reason. You're the trained investigator. You tell me."

After a moment of tense silence, Bart answered, "You used a debit card when you paid for the meal. I checked the receipts."

Annja remembered that. She'd given her cash to Charlie. "They can track my debit card?" she asked.

"It's possible. If you want to factor the old man out of the equation, that's what you're left with. It plays." Bart scratched his chin with his thumb. "The easiest way is to figure the homeless guy for it."

"No," Annja insisted.

"Then those guys could have tracked you through computer databases. You used your card while you were in Prague, didn't you?" Bart asked.

Annja took only a moment to remember that she had used her card while shopping. "Yes."

"They came at you in Prague. If these guys are as well equipped as they seem to be—and getting fully automatic weapons in this city, while not impossible, is still difficult, not to mention expensive—then imagining they have a geek squad able to do something like that isn't a big stretch."

Annja didn't think so, either. Suddenly she felt incredibly vulnerable.

"Hey," Bart said softly. "You okay?"

Not trusting herself to speak, Annja just nodded and kept her eyes locked straight ahead of her. She walled all the feelings out and concentrated on herself. That was what she'd always done in the orphanage when things turned against her.

More than anything, she wanted to talk to Roux at that moment. She wanted to know what was going on. But for the first time she was afraid to talk to him because she knew he'd turn down her attempts to question him.

He's not your father, she told herself angrily. He doesn't owe you anything. Despite the fact that he helped you find the sword—and that hasn't always gone well, has it?—he's never promised you anything. And he hasn't gone out of his way to give you anything, either, has he?

And how many times has he nearly gotten you killed?

Still, she remembered the way he'd talked to her when they were together on occasion. And she remembered the conversation she'd had with him when she'd gone out with Garin that night in Prague. He'd been angry at her, but part of that anger stemmed from the fact that she'd hurt him.

"Hey, Annja. Are you okay?" Bart asked softly.

Annja tried to speak, but couldn't. She just nodded.

"It's going to be all right," Bart said. "I promise."

It sounded good to hear Bart say that, but he didn't know about swords with strange powers or men who could live for hundreds of years. Annja had the distinct feeling that if he had, Bart wouldn't feel so sure of himself at the moment.

He touched her shoulder hesitantly. Then, when she didn't push his hand away, he put his arm around her.

"It's going to be all right," Bart said softly. "We'll figure this out."

"I know," Annja answered, but she said it because she knew he expected her to say that. She didn't believe it. For the moment she just simply shared in the illusion.

But when they pulled up to her building, Charlie was sitting on the steps with Wally.

28

Garin was late getting back to the house Roux had arranged outside the Hague. As he'd seen to the care of the men who'd been wounded, and to the disposal of the bodies of those who had been lost, his anger had become well stoked. By the time he parked his Mercedes in the large driveway, he was seething.

The encounter at the Danseker estate was hours in the past. News stories about the break-in and subsequent murders filled the news channels. CNN and Fox News had picked up the story because of the macabre nature of the painting.

Images of the painting had already flooded the Internet. So had vicious theories about devil worshiping and ritual sacrifice gone wrong.

Dressed in a suit, Garin left the armored luxury sedan and crossed the flagstone walk to the big house's front door. The structure was three stories tall and felt empty. Garin wondered if Roux owned it or had leased it for the effort to get the painting.

To the east, the sun had started to streak the sky in purple and gold. Garin didn't plan to be in the Netherlands by the time it reached its zenith.

Inside the house, Garin could smell frying sausages and potatoes. He followed his nose to the immaculate kitchen at the back of the big house. He kept his hand on the gun holstered at his hip. The next unpleasant surprise that met him was going to receive a bullet between the eyes.

Jennifer stood at the stove, bathed in the soft glow of a small television mounted on the counter. The channel displayed the scenes of the violence at the Danseker estate.

She'd put on slacks and a sleeveless blouse. With the short heels she wore, she looked like an elegant wife making a quiet and private breakfast.

Garin stared at her. The woman was beautiful; there was no doubt about that. He could see what Roux had seen in her.

She moved smoothly and reached toward a ladle, but her hand instead sought out a small flat black autopistol hidden in a dish towel. In the space of a single breath, she came around in profile with the pistol leveled before her.

"What are you doing here?" she demanded.

Garin left his hand on his holstered pistol, just in case. "I came to see the old man."

"Why?" Jennifer didn't lower her weapon.

Garin frowned. Now he had to entertain the possibility that she'd feel threatened enough to pull the trigger. Garin planned on living, so he'd be forced to kill her. It seemed like such a waste.

"To talk to him," Garin answered.

"About what?"

"To let him know I'm out."

"You're quitting?" She didn't lower the pistol.

"Unless he comes clean with me, I'm done with this thing."

Jennifer held the pistol steady. "He told me, on more than one occasion, that I wasn't to trust you. He also told me that you had a rather nasty habit of killing people who got in your way. And that you were vengeful to the nth degree."

"Really?" Garin grinned. It was all true, and a savage part of him took pride in the fact that Roux had recognized those capacities in him. Of course, the old man was no pushover, either. Maybe not as vengeful in the long run, Roux still didn't suffer enemies who were determined to return again and again.

"Yes. So you can appreciate that we're at something of an impasse here."

"Well," Garin said affably, "you're going to have to trust me a little, unless you plan on shooting me. If you're prepared to do that, then go ahead." Even though he said it in an off-handed manner, he still tensed in expectation of a bullet striking home.

Her eyes narrowed, but Garin paid attention to the nail on her forefinger as it rested on the trigger. So far the nail hadn't whitened with pressure.

"After what happened back there, I didn't expect you to come here," she said.

"Actually, I hadn't planned to come. I left. Twice, in fact. Both times I ended up retracing my tracks. Finally, I gave up and came here." He shrugged. "I didn't expect a party on my arrival, but I hadn't foreseen this."

"You lie. You know Roux doesn't have a lot of faith in you."

"No," Garin said. "That's where you're wrong. That old man has every bit of faith in my ability, and in my nature. I sometimes think he knows what I'll do before I do. I think that's why I haven't been able to kill him when I tried."

"He said you hadn't tried as hard as you could have."

Garin shrugged. Maybe that was the truth, too. The world would certainly have been a different place without Roux in it.

"But he sent for you to help him in this," Jennifer said.

"He did."

"And you came."

"I did."

"Both of you are bloody buggy—you know that, don't you?" Jennifer lowered her weapon and put it back on the counter within reach.

"He tends to make people that way." Garin took his hand off his pistol and took a seat at the breakfast bar behind her.

"I know he's had that effect on me."

"It's not just you," Garin said. "Did you burn the sausages?"

"No." Jennifer seemed frustrated. Her hands shook with restrained emotion.

Garin abandoned his seat and went to the stove. "May I?"

When Jennifer looked up at him, there were tears in her eyes. "Sure." She took a cup of coffee from the stove and slid away to rest a hip against the counter. "Do you know how to cook?"

"I'm a fabulous cook," Garin assured her. He set the sausages aside to steep in their juices.

"I'm afraid the eggs are ruined," Jennifer said.

Garin scraped at the blackened husks. "So they are."

"We've more in the fridge."

Concentrating on making a meal, giving his hands something to do, Garin relaxed.

"He seems to prepare for everything, doesn't he?" Jennifer asked.

"Except for failure," Garin agreed. "When it comes to that,

when it's something he actually cares about, he doesn't do so well. Is he here?"

"Out back. In the garden."

"He's brooding," Garin said.

"He claims to be thinking."

"He can call it whatever he likes. He's brooding."

"I know. I've seen it before. Not often."

"Do you like crepes?" Garin asked.

"Yes, but you needn't go to all the bother."

"I'm having crepes. It won't be any trouble to make you some."

Jennifer wiped her tears away. "Thank you."

Garin looked at her. "For what?"

"Breakfast." Jennifer shrugged. "For not making me kill you."

"You wouldn't have killed me. And you haven't had breakfast yet. You may want that pistol back."

Despite her sadness, Jennifer laughed.

SALOME, DRESSED tourist casual, walked through Schiphol Airport. Her short skirt and one-size-too-small blouse drew attention away from her face. She wasn't wanted anywhere, but it still helped blunt identification by onlookers if something should happen. The papers Drake had secured came through his private security corporation, but sometimes complications arose.

Last night happened, didn't it? she asked herself again. She hadn't slept yet. After barely escaping, she and Drake had fled. She stopped at the gate and checked her watch. It was twenty minutes until boarding time.

Less than three minutes later, Drake joined her. He was dressed in jeans, good shoes and a pullover shirt. He looked as if he'd just stepped from the pages of a fashion magazine.

"Hello, pet," he greeted her.

Salome tilted her head up and presented her cheek for a chaste kiss. Drake's stubble grazed her flesh. He smelled of cologne and male musk.

"Did you get the luggage dealt with, dear?" she asked.

Drake took her by the elbow and guided her from the gate and toward the nearest wall where they could have a little privacy.

"I did," he said. "There was some argument about weight allowances. I told you not to pack so much. I had to pay a little extra for your bags."

Salome smiled at him. "But you know I'm worth it."

"I do." Drake grinned back at her, and the ease and expression—even the answer—weren't all due to playacting.

When they reached the wall, they were all business.

"Did you find Annja Creed?" Salome asked.

"I did." Drake shrugged. "I have to admit that the feat was a lot easier than I was expecting. You would think that anyone involved in the television industry would be more protective of her address."

"Where does she live?"

"In New York City. One of the boroughs. Brooklyn."

Salome hadn't been there, but she knew that Drake had. His American contracts—especially assassination—often took him to the largest metropolises.

"Is she there?"

"Yes. I've got a team posted at her address. Are you sure this is the avenue you wish to pursue, love?" Drake asked.

"It's all we have left to us. Roux—"

"Only got a look at a forged painting the same way we did," Drake said.

Although she knew he was trying to allay her fears, his efforts weren't successful. She didn't have the heart to tell him that. He worked very hard to please her, and she almost loved him for that.

But she loved the power of the objects Roux knew about even more. If she could get her hands on even one of those, she would have everything she had ever imagined.

"You don't know what Roux is like," she said. "He knows so much."

"Not enough for him to keep from chasing the same painting we were after."

"I've never seen him pursue the painting this hard before. Even though the painting was counterfeit, I'm certain he's holding something back that we haven't yet thought of."

Drake's face hardened. "I think you've turned that old man into your own personal boogeyman."

"I haven't." Salome captured Drake's chin in her palm and gazed into his eyes. "I haven't done that. I just know what he's capable of. And this thing he's after, it's important."

"How do you know that? You've never said."

Salome knew she was going to have to come forward with something. "While I was with Roux—"

"While you were his assistant, you mean."

Salome nodded. "Exactly. While I was helping him with his studies, I discovered his secret." There was more, of course, and Drake refused to hear that. An assistant would never have been able to find the things she'd found. It had taken the betrayal of a lover to do that. And she'd betrayed Roux's trust in her with her youth and beauty that bewitched so many men.

Drake took her hand and kissed her palm. "And what was the old man's secret, love?"

"He has a secret journal. It's a catalog of artifacts, talismans of power, that have been lost through the ages. I copied the journal." Salome shook her head in frustration. "I haven't managed to translate the whole book. There are too many languages that are unknown to me. And to every expert I've been to."

She'd been careful about that. Any one of those linguists could do the same thing to her that she'd done to Roux. As a general rule, she didn't even trust the knowledge they locked away in their heads, much less committed to paper. She'd left all of them dead in her wake.

As she told this to Drake, she wondered if it wouldn't be better to kill him, as well. If things didn't work out, she knew she'd have to. She couldn't afford anyone else knowing what she knew. Roux, she was certain, felt the same way about her.

"The painting is a map," Salome told Drake. Even as she told him that, she knew she was passing a death sentence on to him. She wondered if he knew. She suspected that he did, but from Roux's hand, not hers. He'd never expect her to harm him. That was the power she had over him.

"A map," he repeated. "To what?"

"Power," Salome said. "Possibly the greatest power known to this world."

"I don't know what that means." He showed her a troubled smile.

Salome shook her head, frustrated. "Nor do I. But I know that Roux cares about Annja Creed. You've had men watching them. They've seen them together." She took a deep breath. "If we kidnap her, we can force Roux to tell us everything we want to know."

"What will you do," Drake asked softly, "if that old man doesn't care about Annja Creed as much as you think he does?"

Salome looked into his eyes. "Why, I'll kill her, of course. I want Roux to know that I'm not going to be trifled with."

Drake grinned. "Have I ever told you how very attractive I find your bloodthirsty side?"

Salome touched his lips. "Many times." She kissed him just as the preflight boarding for their plane was called. Excitement thrilled through her. It wouldn't be long before they were in New York.

Then she would find out exactly how much Roux cared about his newest darling.

29

As Annja got out of Bart's unmarked police car in front of her building, Charlie stood and waved from the steps where he'd been seated. His smile was big and generous, as innocent as a child's.

"Hey, Annja," he called. "I'm glad to see those men didn't get you. I was pretty sure they wouldn't, but you never know."

Annja wanted to ask Charlie how he'd gotten away, but there wasn't time. Agitation rolled off Bart in waves as he threw the car in Park and opened the door.

Wally pushed himself to his feet self-consciously and dusted his thighs off with his palms. He wasn't one to drink outside and usually confined his beers to watching ball games in his own apartment. He bent down and gathered the empty bottles. There was a considerable number of them and he quickly realized he was going to have to make more than one trip.

Annja also knew the meeting wasn't going to go well. Bart was out of the car in a heartbeat. His left hand slid around under his trench coat to the back of his belt. When it reappeared, he was holding a set of handcuffs that he kept mostly hidden.

If Charlie saw the cuffs or suspected what was coming, he gave no indication. He just stood on the steps and looked at Annja.

"Bart," Annja said softly.

"No, Annja." Bart's voice was hard and resolute.

"What are you going to do?"

"Arrest him."

"Isn't he supposed to do something wrong first?"

Bart ignored her, which was something Annja hadn't experienced before. Normally Bart was attentive and willing to listen to her.

Annja managed four quick steps and cut him off. She gazed into his eyes. "This is so wrong," she said softly.

"Annja, please don't do this." Bart stared back at her, but his eyes were also on Charlie. "You're interfering with a police officer in the pursuit of his duty."

"He's an old man."

"He's a danger," Bart replied. "To you. And to himself." His eyes softened a little. "Please let me do my job. There are agencies out there who can help him. For all you know, he walked away from his family to track you down and tell you the world was coming to an end. He could have sons and daughters who are worried out of their minds right now. Grandkids."

He's right, Annja admitted to herself. And that was the awful truth of the matter. She didn't think for a moment that Charlie had set her up with Saladin's men. But the scenario Bart described was entirely possible.

"Annja," Bart said quietly.

Reluctantly, she stepped aside and folded her arms across her chest.

Bart went forward. "Turn around. Put your hands behind your back." His voice was hard, totally cop tone.

"What?" Charlie asked. He stood wavering slightly on the steps. He must have been feeling the beers.

"Sir," Bart barked, "put your hands behind your back, please."

"But why? I haven't done anything."

Bart moved quickly to step in behind the old man and grab his left arm. He slipped the cuff around Charlie's left wrist with practiced ease. The metal clicked as it closed.

Annja watched, bereft.

"Let me go," Charlie cried. "I haven't done anything."

Bart put a knee behind the old man's leg and snapped it forward, buckling Charlie's leg until he rested awkwardly against the short wrought-iron railing that lined the steps.

"I'm taking you into custody for your own good," Bart said. "You need to relax. I'm not going to hurt you." He captured Charlie's other arm and pulled it behind his back, as well.

"No!" Charlie bellowed. "This isn't right! I haven't done anything!"

"Sir," Bart said. "Please stop. You're going to hurt yourself."

Charlie fought, but it didn't do any good. Bart had size and strength and youth on his side. He kicked the old man's feet out from under him as gently as he could and forced him to sit on the steps.

"Annja," Charlie pleaded, staring at her as if he'd been betrayed.

"I'm sorry," Annja said. She felt the tears burning in her eyes again, but she didn't let them fall. How had everything gotten so screwed up?

"Annja," Charlie pleaded again. He struggled against Bart, but Bart sat behind him and kept one hand on the short chain linking the cuffs.

"It's for your own good," Annja said, hoping she could make the old man understand.

"No," Charlie said. "No, it's not. You can't let him do this. You *need* me. Annja, you need me! Without me, the world is going to end!"

"No, it's not," Annja said. "Everything's going to be all right."

Bart talked on his cell phone, and Annja heard enough of the conversation to know that he was calling in someone from psychiatric care.

Wally left the bottles in a stack and came over to stand with Annja.

"I didn't know anything was wrong," Wally apologized. "He just came by. Said he wanted to see you. I told him you weren't here, but he said he'd wait. I figured I'd wait with him. Then I figured we'd wait better with a beer." He shrugged. "I guess maybe the beers got outta hand a little."

"Yeah," Annja said hoarsely. "I guess they did." As she stood there listening to Wally and watching the heaviness in Bart's face, she realized that none of them were happy.

AFTER FIFTEEN MINUTES of protesting his innocence and telling Annja that she needed him to stop the world from ending, Charlie fell quiet. He leaned against the railing and stared at her.

It took almost an hour for the psychiatric team to get there. When the ambulance pulled to a stop out in the street, the whirling lights flashed across the neighborhood and drew a few more of the neighbors out of their homes.

Bart used his badge to force most of them to stay back. He'd also suggested that Annja go inside and not hang around.

"I can't," Annja said. She stayed outside and waited and watched, and finally got cold enough to shiver.

Wally retreated to his apartment and returned with one of his baseball jackets. It was too big and the sleeves hung past Annja's fingertips, but it blocked the wind.

The psychiatric team wore heavy jackets over pale blue scrubs. They talked to Charlie calmly and tried to get him onto the gurney by himself. When that didn't work, they manhandled him. Charlie fought them with all his strength, but in the end he couldn't prevail. Still, he'd fought them fiercely enough they'd had to medicate him.

When the drugs filled his system and sapped his senses, Charlie became a loose bag of bones. The attendants loaded him onto the gurney with ease, then belted him on across his forehead, chest, hips and knees.

All through the humiliating event, Charlie stared at Annja.

"Could I have a minute?" she asked as they were about to load him into the back of the ambulance.

"We really gotta get going," a guy with dirty-blond hair and a heavy five-o'clock shadow said.

"Hey, man," a big black attendant said. "Cut the lady some slack. Her grandpa ain't doing so good here. This wasn't any fun for anybody. Give her a minute."

Annja put her hand over one of Charlie's. "I want you to get better," she said.

"I am better," he croaked in the drug-induced slur. "I'm not supposed to be here. You and I are supposed to stop the sleeping king from destroying the world."

"The sleeping king," Annja said confidently, "isn't here in this world to destroy it. He's here to save it."

"Not when he's lost," Charlie said. "And he's lost."

With a supreme effort, Charlie focused on Annja. "You've got to save him."

"Who?" Annja asked.

"The sleeping king."

"Who's the sleeping king?"

The two attendants hefted the gurney, collapsed the legs and shoved it into the back of the waiting ambulance.

"Save the sleeping king," Charlie said. "He's been hurt too much for too long to know what he's doing."

"Who?" Annja asked. She started to pull herself into the ambulance with the gurney.

The black attendant blocked the way. "Sorry, miss," he rumbled. "Grandpa's gotta go. The docs will get him better in no time. You'll see. We got great docs at Peaceful Meadows."

Bart stepped behind Annja and wrapped his arms around her. "Annja, come on. Back off. Let them do their jobs."

"Just give me a minute," Annja said.

"No. This isn't going to get any easier." Bart held tight enough that she knew she'd have had to hurt him to get free.

"Annja," Charlie called from inside the ambulance.

"I'm here."

"You've got to save the sleeping king."

The black attendant shut and locked the ambulance doors. He turned to Annja and gave her one final reassuring smile. "He's gonna be better the next time you see him. You'll see."

Stunned, her mind whirling from everything that had been going on, Annja stood helplessly and watched the ambulance drive away.

Bart released her and stepped back. He kept his hands in front of him in case he had to defend himself.

"You gonna be okay?" he asked.

"I'm fine," Annja answered. She didn't look at him, and she knew she didn't sound fine. She didn't know how she sounded.

She took a deep breath and let it out. More than ever, she wished she had some way of getting hold of Roux and Garin.

"Annja," Bart said.

She acknowledged him with a brief glance, then quickly looked away. "I don't really feel like talking right now."

"Sure." Bart stuck his hands in his pockets and shrugged. "I get that. I just had to do what I did, you know."

"I know."

"He needs help."

He needs *my* help, Annja thought. She didn't understand the whole "sleeping king" reference, but she understood that someone was in some kind of trouble.

"They'll give him help," Bart was saying. "This clinic is really good. I've run street people through there before. They care about them."

Annja didn't believe that. When she glanced at Bart, he ducked away from her gaze. He didn't believe it, either.

He'd acted to protect her. She knew that. But it didn't make her feel any better.

"I can come up," Bart offered. "Those guys that came after you are still out there."

"I know. And no, you can't come up. I don't want to deal with that right now." If Bart came up, Annja knew he'd spend hours justifying his actions to her. He wouldn't understand that she'd already accepted what he'd done. She just didn't like it, and that wasn't going to change anytime soon.

In a day or two—or three—everything would be back to normal between them. She just needed to know that Charlie was being cared for.

"You shouldn't stay here," Bart said. "If they found you by your debit card, they can find your address."

"I know." Annja turned and headed up the steps.

"You should get a hotel room and get out of here," Bart said.

"If I check into a hotel, I've got to show ID," Annja said. "They'll log that."

"Annja, you can't stay here."

"I know. I know. Just give me some space here, okay?" Annja walked away from him and didn't look back.

30

"How long have you known him?" Jennifer asked, meaning Roux.

"A long time," Garin answered. They sat at the small breakfast table where they both watched over Roux.

The old man sat in the garden. Colorful blossoms covered bushes and plants. Garin couldn't identify them but he liked them and he knew why Roux sat there in the muted sunlight under the sighing boughs of the trees.

The old man had always seemed closely aligned with nature, always more at home there and able to make use of it—whether as camouflage or in making herbal remedies—than he'd ever been able to demonstrate to Garin.

Garin hadn't ever seen Roux looking so old. The realization was startling, and for a moment he considered going out to check on the old man. But he knew from past experience that would only make Roux angry. Roux would only talk when he was ready to talk.

"The way he talks about the two of you," Jennifer said, "it sounds as though you've known each other forever."

"We have."

"He left me thirteen years ago without explanation." Jennifer pinned Garin with her gaze. "You look almost young enough to be my son."

Garin smiled at her. "That's very flattering, but—if I may be so bold—you don't show your age."

"I don't hide it as well as you do."

"I owe it all to good genes."

Jennifer looked doubtful. "He doesn't trust you."

Garin sipped his coffee. "He told you he has reason not to."

"Yes."

"He does."

Jennifer studied him, and wistfulness touched her dark eyes. "That's the way it is in families sometimes. You always hurt the ones you love."

"We're not family."

"The way you fight and bicker? The way you dropped everything when he asked? The way he—and I know how pigheaded and stubborn he can be about asking for help—decided to ask you for help?" Jennifer shook her head. "You could have fooled me."

"I was just a poor bastard child when Roux found me. He's fond of saying that I've changed two of the three. I'm rich and I'm grown, but he says my breeding shows through."

"That sounds like something he would say when he's ranting."

They watched Roux in silence for a while.

"You honestly don't know why he wants the painting?" Jennifer asked.

"No. I wish I did. It might make it easier to figure out what I'm going to do."

"I thought you were going to leave."

Garin sipped his coffee. "I am. I just don't know if I'm going to regret it later."

"You mean, if he needs you."

"Or I missed out on discovering some of those big secrets he's been hiding all these years," Garin said.

Out in the garden, a cloud passed overhead and blunted the sunlight falling on Roux. The old man gazed up at the sky in annoyance. Then he shook himself and stood. He stamped his feet to restore circulation, then headed for the house. He opened the door and let himself inside. He sniffed, then looked at the stove.

"Who made breakfast?" Roux demanded.

"Garin did," Jennifer said.

Roux harrumphed. "Didn't anyone think to invite me?"

For a moment, Garin thought about arguing and pointing out Roux's own quarrelsome nature when he got in a snit. Then he realized that it would only be a waste of breath. Roux would never admit he was at fault.

Instead, Garin caught Jennifer's arm when she started to get up from the table. "I'll fix his breakfast," he said.

Roux eyed him with bright challenge. "Can you resist the urge to poison it?"

"That'll be hard." Garin reached into the refrigerator and took out the batter he'd set aside. He'd known Roux would want breakfast.

"I'll be watching you carefully," Roux admonished.

"I wouldn't expect any less."

As he went about his preparations, Garin remembered how many times he'd fixed the old man's breakfast while they'd ridden together on horses, then in trains and in cars as they'd explored the world and searched for the talismans for which Roux claimed to be a caretaker.

For most of those years Garin had resented the obligation of making breakfast and taking care of the baggage, even when Roux had been the only thing that had stood between him and certain death at the hands of bandits, wild animals or simply starvation.

They'd been through a lot together when they'd been together. Even now their lives weren't totally separate. Since Annja had claimed Joan's sword, they'd been drawn together on several occasions.

But as he fixed breakfast, he couldn't help thinking that this might be the last time. What surprised him most was how sad that might be, and how much relief was involved.

"What are you going to do?" Garin asked.

"I'm going to pursue the painting."

"The painting wasn't real."

"Not that one. You have to look beyond what we've discovered so far, Garin. I've told you that since you were a boy. You have to think beyond what you believe you know, because you don't truly know even that."

Maybe poison would have been good, Garin thought. He refused to be baited by Roux's mysterious comment.

Jennifer, however, wasn't so inured. "What are you talking about?" she asked.

"I'm talking about the painting that sold at the auction." Roux poured himself a cup of fresh-brewed tea Garin had prepared and sat at the table with Jennifer. "Someone brokered the sale. Someone painted the painting. I want to know who that was."

"You think whoever made the copy knows something about the original," Jennifer said.

"Yes," Roux replied.

"Unless," Garin stated pointedly, "it was merely someone who had enough knowledge of the painting to take advantage of old fools looking for it for reasons they don't care to share with anyone else."

Roux glared at Garin. "As you know, I keep my own counsel in many matters. I always have. This is one of those matters."

As he looked at Roux, Garin knew he didn't want anything to happen to the old man. At least, he didn't want anything to happen to him today.

Tomorrow might be another matter.

And he also knew what he was going to do. Without another question or even another word, he finished making Roux's breakfast. Then he rinsed the dishes and put them in the dishwasher.

When he was finished he rolled down his sleeves, got his coat from the back of the chair where he'd left it and made himself presentable once more.

"I'm going to Istanbul," Roux said. "I was thinking that you might get some of your mercenaries and have them—"

"No," Garin said.

Roux regarded him with an owlish expression.

"I'm done working in the dark," Garin said. "I'm done being treated like a child, and I'm tired of paying men to die for you for something I don't understand. If you want me to help you, then you tell me why we're doing it and what that painting means."

Anger ignited in Roux's eyes. "Then I don't need your help."

"That's fine." Garin forced himself to turn to face Jennifer. "My advice to you is to run. Whatever it is that you think you feel for this old man, whatever you think you owe him, you don't. It's too costly. He's mean-spirited and thinks everyone but him is stupid and a dullard." He paused. "If you remain foolish or beholden to him and he lets you, I wish you only the best. It's been a pleasure meeting you."

Without another word, Garin left the house. He didn't look back. It was a struggle not to do that. Even worse, the silence that followed him out of the big house was crushing in its emptiness.

But he knew what he was doing. He had a plan. It wasn't necessarily a good one, but it was the best that he could do.

31

In the end, not having anyone else she could call, Annja called Stanley Younts, the bestselling writer she'd met while searching for a friend's murderers. He was able to arrange a well-secured hotel room at a moment's notice.

The hotel staff was in awe, though many of them were disappointed when they found out the author himself wouldn't be there. Stanley had a lot of fans.

"I'll reimburse you for the hotel room," Annja had offered. "When I get the final bill, I'll cut a check. After this confusion has been cleared up. I don't want these people trying to find me through you." She had worried that they might track her bank-account activity.

"It's no sweat," Stanley had said. "Stay at the hotel as long as you like. It's on me."

Judging from the ornate lobby and the attentiveness of the staff, Annja knew the hotel stay was going to be expensive. "I can't let you pay for this."

"Sure, you can," Stanley said, and she could hear the broad

smile in his voice. "Did I ever tell you how much I made off that book I loosely based on our little adventures chasing that relic?"

"No."

"Well, between you and me and the wall, it's an obscene amount. And it's still rolling in. You just kick back and enjoy yourself. If you want, I can recommend some good body-guards. I can send you one of my guys."

"No. That's all right. I just need a place where I can stay incognito. I can handle this." If she couldn't, Annja didn't know what she was going to do. But she knew she couldn't depend on other people. That had never been her way.

"It's your call," Stanley said. "But if you need anything, you know the number. Don't hesitate."

"I won't. And thanks, Stanley."

"My pleasure. Just make sure you take care of yourself. This sounds like a story I want to hear someday."

Annja just hoped that the story had a good ending.

AFTER ARRIVING at the hotel, Annja had started with the phone. She called art galleries in Istanbul first, asking about Thomopoulos, the man who had touched up the painting of the Nephilim, rather than Tsoklis, the man who had painted it originally.

If Roux had been tracking the painting for years, Annja felt certain he would have found any information that might be had there. She had to take a different route.

By seven o'clock that morning, after nearly five hours nonstop on the phone and on the computer, she had one of the first connections she needed.

"What did you say your interest in Thomopoulos is?" the woman at one of the Istanbul art brokerages asked. She sounded older and British. Her name was Liz Sharpe-Withers.

A busybody, Annja thought. That was a problem when dealing with people instead of a dig. An archaeologist sifting through the earth worked to satisfy her own curiosity, not assuage that of others. Ultimately, in the archaeologist's point of view, they would all be served if her questions were answered.

But not answering could offend those whose help was necessary.

"I'm doing research into Thomopoulos's influence on other artists," Annja said.

"Who's this for?"

Annja thought for just a moment, then seized on what she figured would be the most exciting and the hardest to confirm. "Steven Spielberg is putting together a new movie. Kind of a follow-up to *Schindler's List*."

"Well, that's exciting."

"It is," Annja agreed. People loved being involved with movies. While she'd been in Prague with the special-effects crew, she'd heard a lot of the younger members of the crew pitching movie ideas to each other.

"But what does that have to do with Thomopoulos's artwork?" Sharpe-Withers asked.

"The film centers around all the art Hitler's soldiers 'liberated' from various families during the war," Annja said.

"That's a hot topic."

Annja knew that it was, and it was the perfect cover for what she was doing.

"In my research I discovered that Thomopoulos had worked on a painting Hitler's troops had hunted for during the Second World War."

"There was such a painting. It was originally painted by— let me think—"

"I've got it here in my notes," Annja said, and she paused as if she were checking her notes instead of simply knowing the name. "Tsoklis."

"Yes, that's right." Sharpe-Withers paused. "It's also very strange."

"It is?"

"That painting was supposedly sold in the Hague yesterday. It's been in the news. I'm surprised you haven't seen it."

"Really?" Annja checked some international news sites. She found a headline that promised details about a "bloody break-in and art theft" in the Hague. Photos of the victims, Mrs. Ilse Danseker and an unidentified man, were featured prominently.

"Yes, it's—"

"I have it here on the Internet," Annja said. She scanned the information quickly, searching for Roux's or Garin's name or description. Neither of them was mentioned.

"The police there appear to be quite stymied," Sharpe-Withers said. "Also, the painting that the unfortunate woman—"

"Ilse Danseker," Annja supplied.

"Yes. Her. Anyway, that painting appears to have been the catalyst for the break-in."

"But it was fake?"

"Yes."

"I thought the painting was lost," Annja said.

"Apparently it was in a private collection for some time. That's what usually happens with art pieces. Something as old as this, families will sometimes hold on to it for generations."

Annja's pulse quickened and she felt some of her fatigue evaporate. "Do you know the seller?" she asked.

Sharpe-Withers hesitated. "I could probably find out, now that this has all come to light. Of course, no one may be talking. It's possible that the owners fell on hard times and had a forgery created of the original so they could sell the forgery and keep the original."

Annja knew enough about the art world to know that was a frequent scam. But with all the verification possible these days, such things were harder to pull off. To complicate matters even further, several paintings believed to be originals were either copies by the original artist or knockoffs by others equally gifted and from the same time. Even museums had forged art hanging, sometimes with the knowledge of the curators.

"If you could do that," Annja said, "I'd be very grateful."

THREE AND A HALF HOURS later, Annja scored again on an e-mail from a small museum. An assistant curator was familiar with Thomopoulos and his work, including the painting of the Nephilim.

The man, Anil Patel, had left a phone number. Annja called at once, hoping to catch him before he left for the day.

"Until the murders at the Hague yesterday," Patel told Annja in a clipped Indian accent, "I'd thought the Nephilim painting was merely a legend. Or a rumor."

"I wasn't sure." Annja paced the large hotel room. She wanted to go out, get away from the room and simply be in the wind. Usually she could take days and weeks of being alone, but now she wanted to see, hear and feel other people around her. "It would have been a shame if it were, of course. But for the purpose of the movie, it doesn't really matter."

"The murders were a very strange thing," Patel said.

Annja massaged a shoulder. Her eyes burned and she felt the stiffness in her legs and back. She missed being physical. She needed a session at the gym, some time with the heavy bag and the speed bag.

She also needed to know how Charlie was. The homeless man hadn't been far from her thoughts.

"It was a waste of life," Patel said. "And it was made even more wasteful when the painting turned out to be a forgery."

"I know." Annja turned away from the window. A glance at the time in the lower right corner of her computer revealed that it was eight minutes to ten—almost five o'clock in Istanbul. Patel would be going home soon. "Do you know if any of Thomopoulos's journals of sketches or his personal life remain?"

"One of the other museums has a small collection of his works," Patel said.

"Collected or original?" Annja asked.

"Does it matter?"

"The closer to original, the better. The director on the film is insisting on as much authenticity as we can fake." Annja was sticking with the movie cover story. "Authenticity, especially in a film like this, is everything to the director." She'd heard that a lot in Prague.

"I understand. I believe one of the smaller museums, the Holy Constantinople Museum of the Apostles, has a collection of Thomopoulos's journals."

Annja could barely contain her excitement.

"You won't find much in the way of helpful research in Thomopoulos's journals, though. Primarily they're just sketchbooks. Thomopoulos was largely illiterate. He was self-taught in art, but he never learned to read or write."

"He was a craftsman," Annja said.

"I'm afraid so. However, there are several other artists from the same time period that I could recommend. If you'd like."

"I would," Annja replied.

32

The Peaceful Meadows Mental Health Clinic was located in Brooklyn not far from where Annja lived. She'd been surprised at how close it was, and she'd wondered if Bart had chosen to send Charlie there for that very reason.

The clinic consisted of six buildings, all of them constructed of ancient gray stone. Annja stared at the squat structures. They looked like stunted gargoyles heaped on the green grass that surrounded them.

Annja decided that she wouldn't ever want to be in a place like Peaceful Meadows. The landscaping inside the high fence was lovely, but she noted that few of the residents were out in the sunshine and the breeze.

She waited in the main office for over an hour before a young man came out to speak with her. He quickly explained that Charlie—they still hadn't identified him, but the young man seemed certain that would happen at any moment—didn't need company.

"We're still adjusting his meds to get him to calm down,"

Dr. Paul Davis said. He was young enough to have just finished med school. He also didn't seem to have any particular affinity for his patients. "Outside stimulus is going to be
a problem for him."

"When do you think I could see him?" Annja asked.

Davis steepled his fingers in a manner that he wouldn't be
able to properly pull off for another fifteen years. Annja
almost laughed at him but stopped only because she knew it
would only cause problems.

"Are you family, Miss Creed?" the doctor asked offi-
ciously.

"No."

"Then I'm afraid you really don't have any rights where
Charlie is concerned."

"I'm his friend."

The doctor grinned smugly. "Trust me, Miss Creed, in the
state that old man's in, he doesn't know what world he's in, much
less who else might inhabit it. Friends aren't much help there."

"He wasn't that bad," Annja said. "When I spoke with
him, he was coherent."

"Really?" Davis flipped through a thin file folder in front
of him. "Since he's been here, all he's done is ramble about
saving the world." He took out a ballpoint pen, clicked it open,
made a few notations on the papers and closed the folder.

Annja sat quietly in the straight-backed chair even though
she wanted to scream in frustration. She hated administrative
apathy.

"He's even built you into the architecture of his fantasy.
So you see, your visit to him would only be detrimental to
what we're trying to accomplish with him." Davis pushed
Charlie's folder to one side and reached for another. "Now,
if you'll allow me, I've got a ton of work to sign off on."

Summarily dismissed, Annja left.

A few minutes later, she stood out by the curb and searched for a cab. She felt agitated and frustrated. It was never a good combination. Then she felt a presence beside her.

Automatically, she dropped into a self-defense stance on the balls of her feet as she spun around. Her hands came up to frame her face and head.

Charlie looked down at her and smiled. "Hello, Annja."

Stunned, Annja could only stare at the man. He wore a hospital gown and looked clean and happy.

"What are you doing out here?" Annja asked.

"You came for me, didn't you?" Charlie nodded and waved to passing pedestrians. Most of them just ignored him, or they glared at Annja as if she was somehow responsible for his presence.

Annja lowered her hands and smiled, feeling better almost instantly. "Yes. I did come for you."

"And they didn't allow you to see me."

"No."

"That being the case, since you weren't going to be able to work within the system to free me, I decided it was best to free myself."

"How did you do that?"

With a grin, Charlie leaned down and whispered conspiratorially, "I waited till no one was looking, then I sneaked out."

Despite the gravity of the situation, Annja couldn't help laughing in delight. She couldn't believe it had been that easy.

Charlie laughed, too, but his voice was slightly off, a little too loud and a little too forced.

"You're drugged," Annja said, understanding then.

Grinning, Charlie said, "I have to admit, the medicines are

quite entertaining." He looked around. "I seem to see brighter colors. And if I stare just right, it seems as though I can see things from the corner of my eye that I couldn't normally see."

"What things?"

"Strange things, I assure you. I'm pretty sure they're not real. You don't see that, do you?" Charlie pointed across the street.

Annja looked but didn't see anything out of the ordinary. Pedestrians walked in front of small businesses and shops. "What?"

"The griffin."

Annja looked again, searching for a statue or an image painted on a window for a creature with head and wings of an eagle and the body of a lion. It wasn't there.

"No," she said.

"Ah, well, it's probably better that it's not real." Charlie looked back at the entrance to the hospital grounds.

At that moment two burly men in hospital scrubs bounded out of the gate. They looked around, then one of them pointed in Charlie's direction.

"Oops," Charlie said. "We'd better make haste. My escape attempt no longer possesses stealth, I'm afraid." He threw up a hand.

Annja stepped between Charlie and the approaching men. She knew it wasn't going to do her relationship with Bart much good for her to help Charlie escape, but she couldn't just leave him again.

Brakes squealed at the curb.

When Annja looked back over her shoulder, she saw that a cab had braked to a halt.

"Your carriage awaits, my lady." Charlie opened the cab door and bowed.

Despite the desperate nature of their circumstances, Annja

grinned and slid into the backseat of the cab. Charlie followed her with alacrity and managed to slam and lock the door before the two orderlies reached the vehicle.

One of the orderlies beat on the top of the cab and demanded that the driver unlock the door.

"Sheesh," the driver said as he pulled away from the curb and merged with traffic. "What's the problem with those guys?"

Annja couldn't believe it. They were in front of a mental-health facility, in front of a sign that even offered a traffic advisory about mental patients, and Charlie wore a hospital gown. Maybe it was just New York and maybe it was the jaded nature of the city's cabbies.

"Where are we going?" the driver asked.

Annja gave the name of her hotel.

"Sure thing. Have you there in a couple shakes."

"Well," Charlie said, relaxing in the back of the cab, "that was certainly exhilarating. Do you think we can get something to eat when we get to the hotel? I'm famished."

"Yes."

Charlie eyed her speculatively. "And you need to get some rest if you're going to save the world."

Annja started to ask him if he really believed she was going to do that. Then she stopped herself. Of course he did. But she didn't. All she was trying to do was find a painting, and maybe the secrets it held.

"There's going to be a lot of danger," Charlie said thoughtfully. His rheumy eyes glanced around the cityscape. "So many things are different these days. And we have a number of powerful enemies arrayed against us."

Annja silently agreed with that.

Charlie looked at her. "You're a very special young woman, Annja Creed."

"Because of the sword?" Annja whispered.

Charlie laughed and shook his head. "No. Of course not. The sword was drawn to you because *you* are special. You were marked for your destiny the day you were born."

What he said sounded crazy, but so had several of the conversations Annja had had with Roux and Garin. Yet at the same time his words held the timbre of truth.

ANNJA WOKE thinking that her travel alarm went off. Her hand shot out and silenced it only to discover it was 10:37 p.m. She'd set the alarm for midnight, hoping to get an early start tracking down the museum curator in Istanbul.

Then she became aware of voices in the outer room of the hotel suite.

She'd left Charlie there watching movies after they'd had room service delivered. That had been the first time either of them had eaten since dinner the previous night. Once the meal had been finished, she hadn't been able to keep her eyes open.

Charlie had told her to go to bed, that he'd slept enough the previous night, thanks to the drugs. He'd settled into the plush couch with a banana split, and Annja went to bed.

But someone was with Charlie now.

Annja didn't know who it was, but she couldn't imagine anyone who would be there who would have their well-being in mind. She listened for a moment, but she only heard Charlie speaking.

"The battle at Roncevaux Pass was the worst of it," Charlie was saying. "I fought at Roland's side at that one. But as much as we wanted to triumph, the Basques wanted it more. I'd never seen Roland so crushed in defeat. It took him a long time to get over that."

"I brought the army in across Vasconia," Charlie went on.

Charlemagne, Annja remembered, the king of the Franks, had been in charge of that army. Charlie, whoever he truly was, knew his history.

Quietly, without making a sound, Annja rose from the bed. She wore only a football jersey and had her hair pulled back out of her face. She reached into the otherwhere and pulled the sword to her as she walked to the door. Her senses fired to full life and her blood sang in her veins.

33

Garin caught sight of Annja as she edged up to the door. Her eyes met his, then recognition—and maybe a little irritation—flared. She regarded him with undisguised wariness. Then, as she stepped into the room with the sword in her fist, he also noted the football jersey was short and her legs were long and supple.

Although he didn't think it was going to work, Garin tried a smile. "Hello, Annja."

"How did you find me?" she demanded. She kept her distance with her sword at the ready. Her stance was automatic, bladed so the sword could easily come between them.

Garin remained seated on the couch with the old man who had introduced himself as Charlie. The old man's presence had been a complete surprise. When he'd knocked, Garin hadn't expected to find Annja. The man wore baggy gray pants, a dark blue golf shirt and loafers. He looked like someone's great uncle. Except for the hint of insanity in his eyes and the hospital band still around one wrist.

She referred to the fact that she wasn't signed in at the hotel under her name.

"I tried your loft first," Garin answered. "I let myself in and saw that you'd packed. I also noticed that someone had broken in, by the way. It was a professional job. Very good."

"Burglars? Is my loft—"

"Everything is fine," Garin told her. "This was a professional job. Nothing was out of place. But I could tell someone had been there."

Annja didn't look relieved.

"I had one of my people check to see if your passport had been used. It hadn't. So I checked around your neighborhood—you're quite popular, you know—and found out about the attack in the restaurant. I knew you'd go into hiding. Since you haven't used your credit cards or hit any kind of financial records, I knew you probably hadn't left the city."

Annja held up her hand. "Enough with the Veronica Mars summary."

"Who?" The name was lost on Garin.

"Never mind. You checked around and figured that I hadn't left the city. How did you know I was here?"

Garin smiled. "You don't have a whole lot of friends capable of hiding you, Annja. I knew you wouldn't stay with friends for fear of endangering them. Especially after the attack at the restaurant. So you had to have money, and someone's ID, to vanish. Whoever it was had to have money and be able to protect himself." He held up three fingers. "That left three people that I know of that you would know and would—perhaps—ask a favor of. Roux. Myself. And Stanley Younts. It took me only a few minutes to find out Younts was registered in the city, but when I called him, he was at home."

"I could have left the city for a job," Annja said.

Garin's grin grew larger. "With so many questions unresolved?" He shook his head. "No. Especially not after the attack on you here."

"Okay." Annja shifted her attention to Charlie. "And you—why did you let him in?"

"Because you weren't awake," Charlie said.

A dumbfounded expression filled Annja's face. "You let him in because I wasn't awake?"

"Yes. He wanted to wake you up, but I told him you needed your sleep and that you'd be up soon enough."

"You shouldn't have let him in," Annja said.

"I had to," Charlie said. "He's part of this. You need him."

"I don't need him."

"Of course you do. And he needs you."

"I wouldn't say that I—" Garin began. Then he shut his mouth because his denial was entirely hollow and everyone in the room knew it because he was there. He tried to escape from it as gracefully as he could. "Roux needs you."

"The sleeping king," the old man said, then nodded. "He's lost at the moment. Caught up in his own guilt and despair. The two of you have to rescue him before he does irreparable harm to the world."

Garin had heard a little of that while he'd talked with the old man. He didn't understand it, so he'd ignored it. The only thing that had kept him from waking Annja had been the knowledge that he'd have to injure Charlie to do it, and that Annja probably wouldn't like that. Waiting hadn't been such a hardship. The old man told wonderful stories.

"Where's Roux?" Annja demanded.

"In Istanbul," Garin answered.

"What's he doing there?"

"He thought he'd found the Nephilim painting in the Hague, but—"

"It turned out to be a fake." Annja fixed him with her beautiful eyes. "Did you kill that woman?"

"No." Garin acted offended. He wasn't, though, and he could tell Annja didn't buy into the act in the least. "Salome did."

"Salome?"

"She's another problem. An old problem. She's after the painting, too, and she's currently employing a man who is extremely capable and cold-blooded."

"It's funny that you should show up here so soon after I was attacked," Annja said.

"I was busy in the Hague not killing that woman over the painting."

"Why did Roux go to Istanbul?" Annja asked.

"To track down the man who brokered the sale of the painting. He thought the man might know more than he was telling."

"We need to get to Istanbul," Annja said. "Can you arrange it?"

"Of course. Do you know where the painting is?"

"No, but I may know where the next-best thing to the painting is." Annja looked at him. "Why did you leave Roux?"

Garin reflected on that for a moment and tried to figure out what he was willing to tell her. Finally, knowing that she would recognize a lie, he decided to tell her the truth.

"Because I'm afraid for him. And *of* him."

Annja's eyebrows rose. "Why?"

"You've never seen him like this," Garin said. "I rarely have."

"Like what?"

"When he finds something like this, he gets consumed."

"An artifact, you mean?"

"Yes."

"Like the sword?"

Garin nodded.

"What's so special about the painting?" Annja asked.

"It contains a map."

"To what?" Annja asked.

Garin shook his head. "I don't know. Roux has never told me." He paused. "That alone tells me how powerful whatever he's looking for is."

"It has the power to change the world," Charlie said. "He mustn't be allowed to possess it. It's going to provide a temptation like he's never before dealt with. Not even in his long years."

Annja looked at the old man for a moment, and Garin could see that she was troubled by what Charlie said. She was still new to the oddness in the world that Roux drew to him. And he realized the sword probably attracted it, as well.

"If I get dressed," Annja asked, "can you get us a plane to Istanbul?"

Garin nodded. "I've got one standing by."

"How soon can we leave?"

"Let me make a phone call and we can be cleared for takeoff as soon as we arrive there," Garin said.

The sword faded from Annja's hand, and she turned back to the bedroom. "Let's do that."

SALOME SAT in the bar across the street from the hotel where Drake's private security team had trailed Annja Creed when she'd abandoned her loft the previous night. Frustration chafed at her, and she hated the fact that she was trapped and unable to act.

Drake, however, sat like a statue and looked as though he could sit there for days.

It was a skill, Salome knew. She'd learned it, as well, but

it had been a reluctant skill and she still didn't enjoy employing it. However, breaking into the hotel wasn't an option because the security was too good. Drake had assured her they could work something out in less than twenty-four hours. If they had to. That was one of the last plans Drake wanted to put into action.

But sitting there was hard. Especially after they'd seen Garin Braden arrive almost an hour ago. Something was going on.

Drake's head turned toward Salome. "Annja Creed and Garin Braden are leaving the hotel."

Excitement flared within Salome. It was early in the morning, too early for movement to be a casual thing. She reached up and turned her earpiece back on. Listening to monosyllabic chatter among Drake's troops was in no way entertaining, and it got on her nerves.

She listened to the men work through the containment structure Drake had established. Annja and Garin were in the hotel lobby. When the men inside the hotel announced their departure from the hotel's interior, Salome saw the three of them emerge from the hotel.

She still couldn't figure out what the old man had to do with anything. Drake's team had taken the old man's picture, but none of their research had thus far indicated any possibilities of identification. Their sources within the NYPD indicated that the police were coming up against the same thing.

"What do you want to do?" Drake asked.

Salome was torn. She was tempted to allow Garin Braden and Annja Creed to go wherever they were going and follow them. But the city was large and there were too many variables. If Drake hadn't been able to put someone on Annja Creed as soon as she got off the flight from Prague, they might not have her now. The hotel security would have protected her.

A valet brought around a luxury car.

"The car's armored, love," Drake said.

Salome had suspected that. The car sat lower than it should have due to the extra weight, and she knew Garin wasn't one to drive around unprotected.

"If we don't take them now," Drake said in an almost conversational tone, "it will be harder once they're under way."

Salome stood up from the table and reached into her handbag for the pistol that she carried. Getting armament was no problem for Drake. All of them had weapons permits.

"All right," she said as she headed for the door. "Take them."

34

"Annja, get in the car."

Even before Garin's growled command reached her ears, Annja knew something was wrong. Too many people, too many vehicles, converged on the front of the hotel at one time.

Garin shoved Charlie into the backseat, then slid behind the steering wheel himself.

Annja stood at the passenger's side with the door open. She held her backpack by the straps in one hand. A van bore down on the front of Garin's car.

"Annja," Garin called urgently.

Immediately, Annja dropped the backpack on the floorboard in front of her seat and slid into the car. The van grew closer.

A man with an assault rifle leaned out of the van's passenger's window.

The hotel valet staff scattered and ran back inside the building.

"Are the windows bulletproof?" Annja asked.

"Yes. Why?" Garin asked.

"Because they need to be."

The assault rifle suddenly danced in the man's hands as muzzle-flashes lit up the man's dark features. The bullets turned out to be a decent grouping over Garin's side of the windshield. The glass spiderwebbed, but it held.

Annja let out a tense breath.

"Hold on," Garin ordered. "He's going to ram us." Smoothly, he shifted the gear selector into Reverse and the transmission bucked.

Then the van met the luxury car head-on. Annja braced herself, one hand gripping the handle above her head and the other on the dashboard in front of her. The impact rocked the luxury car, but Garin maintained his grip on the steering wheel and kept backing up. The van's momentum added to the car's velocity.

The air bags deployed with thunderous booms and filled the interior of the car with the scent of gunpowder. Incredible force slammed into Annja's chest and knocked the breath from her lungs. The air bag shoved her against the seat, but she fought against it.

Almost immediately, Garin had a knife in his fist. He thrust once into his air bag, then the one holding Annja. Both deflated.

Gratefully, Annja sucked in a deep breath.

Garin cursed as a delivery truck rocketed along the street at the rear of the car. Annja understood immediately that the second car was supposed to strike the rear of their vehicle and pin them against the raised wall in front of the hotel.

Garin stomped the brakes and shifted gears again. The car jumped as the tires fought for traction on the pavement. Shrieks of tortured rubber filled Annja's ears, and the acrid burning stench stabbed her nose.

The delivery truck clipped the back end of Garin's car and sped behind. Even though it missed smashing them into the raised embankment, the van tore across the back bumper and effectively boxed them in.

Garin cursed again, shifted gears to try to go backward but couldn't. The tires whined against the movement as they spun without gripping.

Calmly, though she knew she had to hurry, Annja twisted and pulled up the door lock. She yanked on the lever and shoved the door open with her shoulder. By the time she slid out of the car, she had the sword in her hand.

"Annja!" Garin cried. "No!"

Ignoring the call, Annja ran to the back of the Mercedes while staying low. A man thrust an assault rifle through the window and fired at her. Bullets skipped across the Mercedes's trunk.

In three quick strides, Annja was behind the delivery truck. When she glanced back at the side of the truck, she noticed the shadow of a man coming toward her position from the vehicle's side. The man was unmindful of the streetlight behind him.

At the same time, a strong arm reached from under the canvas covering the rear deck section of the delivery truck. The arm closed around Annja's neck before she knew it and lifted her off the ground. Annja acted out of instinct, curling her body around and planting both knees into where she judged the man's face was.

The man crumpled and went down. He dropped Annja unceremoniously as he staggered back.

Annja twisted and landed on her outstretched left hand and both feet. She dropped the sword. Movement sounded above her. When she looked up, she spotted a rifle barrel poking through the canvas.

She reached for the sword without looking. Even though she didn't know where she'd lost it, it materialized in her hand. With a quick push, she gained her feet and brought the sword around in a vicious arc that sliced through the rifle barrel at the time the man fired his weapon.

The rifle blew apart in the man's hands, and he fell back screaming. Three other men bailed from the back of the truck.

At full speed Annja swept the sword around and knocked rifles from two of the men's hands. Still in motion, she pivoted on her left foot and drove her right foot into the face of the third man as he tried to aim his weapon. He flew from his feet and thudded against the truck.

The man on the passenger's side of the truck arrived faster than Annja was prepared to deal with. He had his rifle up and grinned, knowing she was aware she was done.

Then two quick cracks sounded and the man's head exploded. As the man dropped, Annja glanced back at Garin and saw him leaning from the open door.

"Hurry!" he yelled.

One of the men reached for his weapon. Annja caught him by the collar of his coat and rammed him into the truck's bumper. Unconscious, he dropped at her feet. She backhanded the remaining man hard enough to dislocate his jaw and whip his head around. He toppled without a sound.

She ran to the front of the truck, caught the pistol the driver thrust through the window and wrenched. The pistol dropped away as the man screamed in pain.

Still holding on to the man, Annja popped the door open, then released her hold on her opponent's arm and yanked him out of the truck cab. With a leap, she pulled herself into the vehicle. The controls were familiar to her. She'd driven big trucks while at various digs.

After cranking the engine over and listening to it catch, she put the transmission in Reverse, shoved down on the accelerator and released the clutch. The truck bucked and rolled backward. She stopped it as soon as it cleared Garin's car.

Garin raced the luxury sedan out from the hotel driveway. He slid to a tire-eating halt in the middle of the street. Traffic going both ways had halted.

The van tried to follow Garin. Annja shoved the transmission into first and powered forward. She hit the van and muscled it into the raised flower bed.

Other men raced on foot across the street. Garin pulled a machine pistol from under the car seat and sprayed the advancing troop. The line broke as the attackers took cover.

Another group of men fired at Annja. The truck's windshield vanished in a deluge of broken glass. Chunks of the square-cut safety glass peppered her back as she slid out the door. She ran for the sedan.

The front passenger's door was on the other side. She threw herself across the hood in a baseball slide and dropped to the street. Her hiking books thudded against the pavement. Headlights from the stalled cars played over her.

I hope there aren't any photographers out there, she thought as she pushed herself up and toward the open door. Denying participation in a running gun battle in Brooklyn was hard to do. Especially if there were pictures or video footage. She'd learned that from experience.

She slid into the seat and closed the door. Bullets hammered the glass, spiderwebbing it, and beat a tattoo on the metal door.

Garin didn't wait for her to fasten the seat belt. He applied his foot heavily to the accelerator and shot through the stalled traffic.

Annja looked over her shoulder and spotted a car racing after them. "There's a car."

"I see it." Garin was calm. "It'll be taken care of. I have to admit, the attack at the hotel was unexpected. Since no one had bothered you, I thought we might get out of there uninterrupted."

"You brought them there," Annja accused.

"No, I didn't."

At that moment a man with a rocket launcher settled over one shoulder stepped forward and took aim. The rocket leaped from the tube and struck the car, turning it into a roiling ball of flame that slammed into the side of an office building.

"If we got lucky," Garin said, "Salome was in that car."

"Do you think she was?"

Garin shook his head. "She's too good to take chances out on the battlefield." He sped through traffic.

Annja kept watch as Garin sped through the Brooklyn streets. There were no more signs of pursuit.

"How do you know you didn't bring them with you?" she asked. "You said she was over in the Netherlands with you and Roux."

"She was. They didn't have time to arrange an elaborate setup like this since I arrived." Garin took a hard left and reduced speed. "Remember, your loft had been burgled."

"You said they didn't take anything."

"They were looking for you." Garin looked at her. "They knew where you were. I'd say they had someone on you as soon as you got back from Prague."

"And Salome isn't linked to Saladin?"

"They're bitter enemies."

"So we have two groups after us?" Annja asked.

Garin nodded.

Annja sighed. "The more the merrier, I guess."

"In your endeavors," Charlie said, "you're going to find that you have any number of enemies. You'll certainly have many more enemies than friends who will be drawn to your calling."

Annja settled in her seat. "Have you and Charlie met before?" she asked Garin.

"No. I thought he was your friend."

"Not until recently."

Charlie sat happily in the backseat. "Other than the ambulance the other night, it's been a long time since I've ridden in an automobile. It's much more exciting than I remembered it being."

Garin looked at Annja. "You make strange friends."

"Personally, I think it all started when I met you and Roux," she said.

35

Annja carried her backpack to the spacious cabin area in the private jet. She took her computer out and hooked it into the aircraft's communications array.

Charlie appeared utterly thrilled to be on the private jet. Questions flowed out of him, and they were all directed at Garin. Annja was pleased to see how much that annoyed him.

When Charlie mentioned that he was hungry, Garin took him forward to the kitchen and placed the old man in the capable hands of the young female chef he'd hired to cater for the flight.

Garin dropped into a seat beside Annja. "Why are we going to Istanbul?"

"Because Tsoklis wasn't the only artist who worked on the Nephilim painting."

"When I left Roux in the Hague, he told me he intended to pursue the forger who made the painting we were chasing," Garin said.

"Why?"

"Roux said that the forger had to have a source he worked from."

Annja agreed with that logic. "If the painting was good enough to fool Roux for a time—"

"It was. You should have seen his face when he thought it had been destroyed." Garin grinned, but Annja knew his heart wasn't in it. Worry showed in his face.

"Roux never explained the painting to you?"

"No." Pain flickered in Garin's black eyes. "He raised me, Annja. He was a father to me in so many ways. But even fathers don't always tell their sons everything."

"No parent does," Charlie agreed. He strode back into the cabin area carrying a large platter filled with food.

Where does he put all that? Annja wondered. Eating that much just doesn't seem humanly possible.

"Now that we've heard from Dr. Charlie," Garin said disdainfully, "perhaps you'd like to finish what you were saying."

"If the painting was good enough to fool Roux with all that he knows about it," Annja said, "then someone else has to know a lot about it."

"The forger."

Annja nodded. "Was it an old forgery or a new one?"

"Roux believed it was recent."

"Why?"

"He didn't say. I have to assume it was because of the materials involved."

Annja tried to shrug off the frustration that scratched at her nerves.

"You said there was another artist who worked on the Nephilim painting," Garin said. "Could he have been the forger?"

"No. His name was Jannis Thomopoulos. He lived about two hundred years after Tsoklis."

"So?"

"At one point Thomopoulos touched up the Nephilim painting for the man who owned it in Constantinople."

"Before the city fell?"

"Yes."

Garin sat back. "Two hundred years later."

"Two hundred sixteen, to be exact," Annja said.

"Why did he touch up the painting?"

"Some older paintings required touching up because the materials the artists used didn't last. A lot of pieces in private collections and museums have been restored. If the original is found, I'd be surprised if it hasn't been touched up since."

"So why is it we're trailing Thomopoulos?" Garin asked.

"He had to have had reference to work from," Annja said. "I'm hoping that reference might still be in some of his materials."

"What kind of reference?"

"Sketches."

"You think Thomopoulos may have made sketches of the original painting?"

"It's how it's usually done." Annja had studied quite a bit about art during her university days, as well as after. Too many archaeological records resided in artwork to ignore it.

"And you know where Thomopoulos's materials are?"

"I do."

Garin smiled. "Now, wouldn't that be interesting?"

"What?"

"If we—not having the original painting—are able to figure out the map before Roux does. And if the answer to the puzzle he's worried about for hundreds of years was actually there in front of him the whole time."

Annja frowned and bristled a little. "It wasn't exactly in front of him. He may not know Thomopoulos was involved—"

"He doesn't or he would have mentioned him before now," Garin stated confidently.

"It's possible that Thomopoulos's work hadn't been gathered up in a collection."

"However it goes," Charlie said, "you can't allow what Roux seeks to fall into his hands."

Garin looked at the old man. "You know what it is?"

"Of course." Charlie wiped his hands on a napkin.

"Then tell us."

"No."

Anger, hard and frightening, flared to life within Garin. It was a part of him that Annja knew she would always have to be wary of, and she knew it would always be a part of him. Whatever had marked Garin in his early years had marked him forever.

"I could make you tell us," Garin threatened.

"No," Charlie stated, "you can't." He smiled. "And even if you tried, Annja would stop you." He picked up a chocolate chip cookie.

Garin looked at Annja. "My way would be easier and faster."

"We're not going to torture him."

"He's old. It won't take much. He may talk tough, but he's not going to be hard to break."

"No." Annja tried to rationalize the way Garin had been in Prague when he'd taken her out and how he was now. It was impossible. Garin had two sides to his personality, and both were equally strong and passionate. She had to wonder which he would choose to be when they took up the trail on the map.

Garin cursed in disgust.

"You need to have open minds when you find it," Charlie said. "Otherwise your expectations will affect how you treat it. Roux already has his expectations, and his needs, and that's why it's so dangerous for him to be near it."

"Can you tell us anything about it?" Annja asked.

"I've told you, Annja," the old man said patiently. "It has tremendous power. With it, the sleeping king can destroy the world."

"THE DOOR'S LOCKED."

Roux glanced at the ornate doorknob in front of him. "Is it?"

"Yes." Hamid stood in the hallway outside the large condominium they'd come to burgle. Roux had known the man for over twenty years, and their business together had never been legal. He was small and dark, and his eyes moved restively and fearfully at all times. "And there will be alarms."

"I thought you took care of the alarms," Roux said.

Hamid shrugged. "I took care of *some* of the alarms. The men you can buy these days, they aren't all trustworthy."

Roux grinned at the little thief. "Not like you, eh, old friend?"

Hamid smiled. "Exactly."

"Then it's a good thing for you that I didn't just count on your skills." Roux turned and nodded at Jennifer.

With a quick look around the luxurious hallway, Jennifer reached into her coat and brought out an electronic device. She attached it to the electronic lock and activated a sequence.

"If we're caught out here with that," Hamid said, "they'll put us in prison forever. They don't suffer thieves over here."

Roux knew that. "It's fascinating, though," he said as Jennifer worked with the device, "don't you think? We'd be viewed as thieves for breaking into Vilen Bogosian's residence. Yet, in certain circles, he's known as quite the artiste of forged paintings."

"He's accepted here," Hamid explained. "He hasn't run afoul of anyone in Istanbul."

"I'm sure that's only because no one has yet discovered his crimes. I hardly think he's living the life of an angel here."

Jennifer straightened up with a frown. "I can't get the combination. It's not going to open."

Anger seethed through Roux. He'd spent two days trolling the seamier side of the Hague to find out who was responsible for the forgery that had been sold at the art auction. Getting that information had taken time, money and many favors he'd called in.

Jennifer had accompanied him, but she'd remained tense. They didn't talk about Garin's decision to leave or the fact that they hadn't been able to replace what Garin would have brought in the form of men and matériel.

Just go slowly, Roux thought. You've almost found the prize you seek.

Unless it was lost and gone forever. Part of him would have been relieved, he knew. But part of him would have gone ballistic.

"Try it again," Roux said.

Jennifer hesitated only a moment, but she applied the device once more.

Roux hated trusting such things, but it was the way of the world these days.

This time the lock clicked and sounded like a pistol shot in the quietness of the hallway.

"Very good," Roux said.

"I don't understand," Jennifer said. "It should have worked the first time."

"You're too edgy. Just be glad that it worked this time." Roux pulled the door open and slid a pistol out from under his jacket. He stepped inside as Jennifer put the device back into her jacket and took out a pistol of her own.

Despite her misgivings, Jennifer had thrown her lot in with him. He still didn't know if it was because she cared about him, in spite of what he'd done, or because she was curious about what secrets the painting held.

"This could be a very bad mistake," Hamid said.

"Quiet," Roux ordered in a raspy whisper. He entered the room. Even though it was cloaked in darkness, he knew his way around.

Hamid had arranged to get the blueprints of the condominium. For all of Hamid's lack of a spine, he was quite the ferret when it came to getting necessary things.

Voices came from a room on the other side of the large and elegantly furnishing living space. Roux identified the room as Bogosian's work space. Quietly, he crossed the room. His heart pounded in anticipation. There were other things he'd chased over centuries, but nothing like what he was after now. He calmed himself with effort.

Bogosian was in his early thirties, a bull of a man with a broad chest and curly black hair. Black leather pants encased his legs and hips. The black shirt was open to midchest and tailored to reveal his biceps and musculature. He laughed and joked with a model on the small stage in the workroom.

Lights flashed as Bogosian snapped pictures.

Roux vaguely recognized the woman. She was an American actress whose career had started to accelerate her to the A-lists. Roux couldn't remember her name.

She held her long brown hair back off her naked shoulders as she flirted with Bogosian and his camera. Roux knew that the painter supplemented his forgeries with legitimate work. But even painting American actresses in the nude didn't pay as well as forged masterpieces.

"Don't worry about the tattoos," Bogosian said in accented English. "I can airbrush those out. Just relax and have fun."

The actress saw Roux as he stepped into the room. Her eyes rounded in surprise and she reached for the dark blue robe on the floor.

Even so, Bogosian kept shooting pictures and took a moment to turn around. "What are you—"

Unable to stop himself, Roux crossed the distance and grabbed the man around the throat with his free hand. Bogosian struggled and tried to get free. Roux's anger and desperation gave him incredible strength. He lifted the man to his tiptoes with one hand and shook him.

"Quiet," Roux advised. He showed the painter the pistol. "Quiet, and you may yet live in spite of all that you've done."

Bogosian nodded.

Arm trembling from the effort of holding the man, Roux released Bogosian. "Now," he said in a voice clotted with rage and need, "we're going to talk, you and I. And if you lie to me, you'll never paint or look at beautiful women again. Understand?"

"Yes."

"Tell me about the Nephilim," Roux ordered. "How can I find it?"

36

"Ms. Creed," Elton McPhee greeted as Annja entered the Holy Constantinople Museum of the Apostles. From the way he'd rushed up to her, he'd been waiting for her arrival. "It's so good to meet you. I never miss an episode of your show. Fascinating. Simply fascinating."

"Sure," Annja said. Even after many similar encounters, she still wasn't quite certain how to respond when dealing with the attention *Chasing History's Monsters* brought her.

McPhee was a heavyset man with thinning blond hair and round-lensed glasses that matched his round face. He looked pale enough that Annja assumed he rarely went outside.

The museum was a simple affair and had a modest selection of exhibits. A large mosaic of Constantinople as it had been before the Ottoman invasion filled one wall behind the counter.

"And who are your companions?" the museum curator asked.

Charlie stepped up before Annja could say anything.

"I'm Charlie," the old man announced, and took McPhee's

hand, though the curator seemed somewhat loath to let him have it.

"It's very nice to meet you, Professor Charlie," McPhee said.

"He's not a—" Garin started to say, but Annja quieted him with a look. Garin sighed in displeasure, then turned and walked away.

"Thank you," Charlie said. "It's a pleasure to meet you, too. We're here to save the world."

For a moment McPhee stood frozen. Then he noted the medical bracelet on Charlie's arm.

"Of course you are," McPhee said quickly after his discovery.

Annja ignored all of it. As long as they got to see Thomopoulos's sketchbooks, nothing mattered.

Charlie folded his arms behind his back. He walked away and began inspecting the exhibits out in the main hall.

"Is he all right?" McPhee asked in a quiet voice.

"He's fine," Annja assured the curator.

McPhee tapped his wrist. "Because he, uh…"

"A private joke," Annja said. "He can be a little eccentric."

McPhee nodded. "Sure. Sure. I understand. Many people in the field tend to get that way after a while. Can I get you anything?"

"I'd really love to see the Jannis Thomopoulos collection."

"Of course. I've already moved everything we have to a viewing room." McPhee swept an arm forward. "This way, please."

McPhee was organized. Annja saw that at a glance. The workroom was small, but the curator had made the best of it. Books and statues shared table space. Paintings, the few the museum had, hung carefully on the walls.

Annja walked through it all to get a sense of it and to see

if anything leaped out at her. The paintings seemed to be generic, as did the statues.

"Our collection of paintings and statues is modest, of course," McPhee apologized. "But we're fortunate in some respects. Thomopoulos's real worth hadn't been discovered before the museum had most of these pieces. Later, they became harder to acquire."

Garin picked up a statue of an archer.

"Please," McPhee said tensely as he rushed over to take the statue and place it once more on the table. "Please, don't touch anything."

For a moment Annja thought Garin was going to strike McPhee. She stepped forward to block any attempt, but Garin blew out an impatient breath and nodded.

Annja settled into one of the chairs and donned a pair of gloves McPhee provided. There were at least fifty sketchbooks, all hand bound with paper that had survived hundreds of years without yellowing. That particular secret of making paper seemed to have vanished somewhere in time.

She turned the pages reverently. She knew she held history, unique and important, in her hands. The thoughts and ideas that were passed on from one generation to another were as important as a piece of pottery or armor. No artifacts told history and the lives of people like a book.

She had to focus on what she was there to find because each turn of the page threatened to lose her in history.

NEARLY THREE HOURS LATER, her back stiff and hunger gnawing at her stomach, Annja found the journal that contained the sketches of the Nephilim. She'd almost missed it because there wasn't a fully drawn sketch on the pages. Rather, it held pieces of the finished painting. If Annja hadn't seen the representation of the one that Ilse Danseker had been murdered for, she wouldn't have found it.

Breathing shallowly, her head about to explode from excitement, her eyes burning from strain, Annja leaned forward, placed the book on the table and took her digital camera from her backpack.

"You found something?" Garin asked. He sat at the head of the table, a position he'd automatically assumed.

"Yes."

Garin came to join her. Charlie did the same.

"Where?" Garin demanded.

"Here." Annja took pictures with her camera.

"There's no painting there."

The page only held bits and pieces of drawings.

"You're trying to see the whole painting," Annja said. "Thomopoulos didn't render his sketches that way."

"He drew separate images of them." Charlie grinned. "You did very well, Annja."

"Thank you."

"This is stupid," Garin growled. "I still don't see what either of you are talking about."

Charlie leaned forward. "May I?"

Annja nodded and handed him the book. She dug her computer out and attached the camera to it through a USB cable. Then she brought the computer on-line.

"Here," Charlie said. "This is the face of the Nephilim." He pointed at the coldly handsome face that sat disembodied on the page.

"All right," Garin said grudgingly, "I'll admit there is some resemblance."

"There's more than a resemblance," Annja said. "It looks drawn to scale."

"How do you know that?" Garin asked.

"The thumbprint beside the face." Annja brought up the pictures she'd taken and quickly saved them.

Garin had to lean close to see it. But it was there. Annja had noted the ghostly image and Charlie had seen it, as well. Finally, so did Garin.

"All right, there's a thumbprint," Garin admitted. "That doesn't mean it was drawn to scale."

"But it does," Charlie said. "Artists often use their thumbs or a brush as a measuring tool to calculate sizes. There's no other reason for the thumbprint to be there."

"Is that important?"

"It tells us these other drawings are drawn to scale, as well," Annja said. "And that is *very* important. If you're going to draw a map, as you said Roux believes this picture holds, then scale is everything."

"I saw that painting," Garin said. "There was no map." He looked over her shoulder at the image she was using.

Annja had captured the image from a CNN headline broadcast that had covered the Ilse Danseker murder. She'd lifted it from a repeat broadcast online that had been saved in high definition.

After she captured the Nephilim's face from the photo she'd taken, Annja superimposed it over the image of the Nephilim she'd taken from the television broadcast. She had to shrink the image down to get it to fit properly. She paid attention to the percentage of shrinkage she'd had to employ.

Then she grabbed one of the pieces that had been around the face at the center of the page.

"What are you doing?" Garin asked.

"I think this belongs on the painting." Annja shifted the piece around on the painting image.

"Why?"

"Because it was on that page."

"That doesn't mean anything," Garin said.

"I think it does. I think all of those images were drawn to scale for a reason."

Garin looked at the painting image. "It's not part of that painting."

"Not now," Annja agreed. "But I think it once was."

"You're wasting time and—"

"There," Charlie interrupted quietly. He pointed to a corner of the screen. Part of a design in the stone floor matched part of the image on the piece Annja was trying to manipulate.

Annja moved the piece into position, shrank it down and grabbed the next piece. It held a matching design in the painting, as well.

Garin became silent.

"I'm very good at puzzles." Charlie smiled.

There were nine pieces in all scattered around the painting. It only took Annja a few moments to blend them into the digital capture of the forged painting Ilse Danseker had purchased.

"Whoever created the forgery saw the original painting," Garin said.

"I think so, too," Annja agreed. "However, the original painting is no longer original." She nodded at the adjusted image she'd created. "Thomopoulos, for whatever reason, painted over the original and hid these pieces."

"He did it to hide the legacy that was contained in the painting," Charlie suggested.

"What legacy is that?" Garin demanded.

"One of the most powerful objects in the world," Charlie said.

"What?"

"It's not for me to say," the old man replied.

"Gabriel's Horn," Annja said, remembering Dr. Krieger's research.

Charlie looked at her. Then he smiled. "Yes."

"What does Roux want with it?" Garin asked.

"The horn," Charlie said softly, "has the power to unmake the world."

37

"Roux," Jennifer said, "you need to slow down and think things through."

Roux regarded the woman. He remembered all of their years together, and some of the happiness they'd had. It had been hard to leave Jennifer. She was fiercely proud and extremely confident.

But the time had come those years ago, and it was either move on or reveal more about himself to her than he was comfortable doing. If he'd looked younger, he might have been able to give her more years.

In the end, though, Roux knew from experience, it would only have gotten harder to leave her.

"I *am* thinking things through," he told her as he shoved another pistol into the pocket of the coat he wore. "I know where the painting is, Jennifer. I can't leave it out there."

"This could be a trap." Jennifer folded her arms and regarded him defiantly.

"I don't think it is." Roux believed the story Bogosian had

told about the location of the Nephilim. The painter had been given no room to lie, and Roux had put him in considerable pain.

"Then you're a fool if you think you can just walk in there and buy it." Her voice sounded ragged.

"The man who has the Nephilim doesn't have any idea what he truly has," Roux said. "He's an art collector. He has an interesting piece. I have more than enough money to acquire it from him."

"What if he doesn't want to sell it?"

Roux knew wealth meant more to most people than simply owning something. "He'll sell it to me," he said confidently.

"What if he doesn't?"

Roux smiled. "Then getting it will be a little harder. Not impossible."

"Let me go with you."

"You've done enough."

"You shouldn't be alone."

"What I shouldn't do," Roux said patiently, "is allow you to risk your life any more than you have."

Tears welled in Jennifer's eyes. "You're being bullheaded."

"I am." Roux gently stroked her face with his forefinger. "But I care about you."

"This isn't dangerous. You said it's not dangerous."

"I know. But I need to do this myself." Roux drew his hand back. "Wait here. I'll call when I have the painting. Then we'll go celebrate." He leaned forward and kissed her forehead. "Be well until I return." He left without a backward glance.

"HOW DOES the map work?"

Annja felt pressured by Garin's question, but she knew that came more from herself than from him. After saving the reconstructed image, she lifted the pieces off again, put them into a new file and started manipulating them.

"I don't know. Yet."

Garin leaned in closer to her. She was aware of his cologne and the heat coming off his body. She didn't know if those things were attractive or threatening.

"If it's a puzzle once," Garin said, "maybe it's a puzzle twice."

"Now you're an expert?" Annja mocked.

"I'm just saying." He sounded as irritable as a bear awakened from hibernation.

Anxiety coursed through Annja. She pushed the pieces together. She realized there was no way all the pieces fit as one thing. She studied them and saw other ways they fit together.

Five of the pieces lay together in an interlocked design.

They're complete, she told herself. Accept that. Now what do you do with the other four pieces?

Slowly she began putting them together. It was harder. She could get any three of them together but she couldn't get the fourth to drop into place. The fourth piece had a section of design that fit over the other three pieces, and also allowed it to fit with any of the other two.

"It doesn't go there," Garin said. "It has to be something by itself."

His words triggered a sudden understanding. Working smoothly, Annja fit three of the pieces together, then placed them over the last piece.

All the designs fit exactly.

"A hidden room," Annja whispered, understanding. "Wherever this is, it has a room below."

"But where is this?" Garin asked.

Annja looked at the grouping of the first five pieces. "This looks like a cross."

Another memory clicked into place.

Annja walked out into the main museum lobby and looked at the mosaic of Constantinople on the wall. She searched the buildings represented there.

McPhee hurried over from one of the exhibits he was working on. "Is there something I can assist you with, Ms. Creed?"

Annja pointed at the cross-shaped building near the center of the city. "What church is that?" she asked.

"That's the Church of the Holy Apostles," McPhee answered immediately. "It was built in 330 by Constantine the Great. It was supposed to be a repository of the twelve apostles of Jesus. Unfortunately, at least this is what legend tells us, only the relics of Saints Andrew, Luke and Timothy were ever housed there."

"Is that shape unique in the city?" Annja asked.

"Yes. Why?"

"The church fell, didn't it?" Annja said. Bits and pieces of the story came back to her.

"It did. After the invasion of the Ottoman Turks the church was destroyed and a mosque was built on the site. It was called Fatih Carmi, the Mosque of the Conqueror. Most people know it simply as Fatih Mosque."

"There was another structure in that area," Annja said.

"Not to my knowledge."

"Something was there. Probably underground."

The curator stared at the mosaic and thought for a long moment. Then the doubt cleared from his face, and he turned to look at her.

"There were catacombs in that area," he said. "Burial facilities for the clergy and their servants. I'd just assumed the bodies were relocated and the catacombs were filled in."

"But the catacombs might still exist?"

"I don't know."

"I need to talk to someone who does know," Annja declared.

ROUX SAT at a table in a bar across the street from the large brown building on Bagdat Avenue. He sipped wine and tried to keep the urge to do something at bay.

Over the past few days, since Jennifer had come to him and told him about the Nephilim painting, he hadn't been able to rest. His sleep had consisted of brief minutes of pure blackness that he'd been able to seize.

For the first time in a long time, he wished that Garin were with him.

It's your fault that he's not here, he told himself angrily. Why would he stay for something he doesn't understand? You wouldn't.

Roux rubbed his burning eyes. He clung to the thought that the artifact was close to hand. Once he had it in his possession, he could fix the mistake he'd made all those years ago.

He would finally have some peace.

Roux knew he'd pushed himself too hard when he only then noticed that the two men who had been sitting at the table next to his hadn't been talking. They'd been mostly noncommittal, like men waiting for something together.

His senses flared to life. The server hadn't gone near them to check on them, either. That suggested they'd arranged for her to stay away.

Without a word, he dropped money on the table and started for the door. But it was too late. The men got up to follow him.

Then another man stepped through the door. He looked to be in his thirties, lean and muscular. He looked enough like his ancestors that Roux recognized him at once even without the green-scimitar tattoo on his neck.

"Roux," Saladin said.

"You've got the wrong man," Roux said automatically. But he knew he'd played it wrong the instant he'd come to a complete stop. A stranger would have kept walking.

"I don't think so," Saladin said. He smiled. "You see, I found the Nephilim painting only days ago. I haven't been able to decipher its secret."

"That's because there is no secret," Roux stated flatly. "It's a fool's errand."

"Yet you've looked for it for a large chunk of your life."

"Merely the vanity of an old fool."

Saladin smiled, but the effort was cold and distant.

Knowing he had no real choice and no real chance of success, Roux reached under his jacket for the pistol in his shoulder holster.

But Saladin lifted a device and fired. Instantly two darts sped out and sank into Roux's chest. They trailed microthin wires behind them. In the next instant they pulsed fifty thousand volts.

Roux felt his body convulse as every muscle screamed in protest and clenched. Then his mind slid into blackness.

38

Trying to get information from the mosque proved fruitless. Annja wasted nearly three hours waiting for someone to tell her that the old catacombs area wasn't accessible from the mosque. The underground tunnel that led to the crypt area had been sealed centuries earlier.

Garin had been ready to give up but Annja was determined. She walked along the crowded street in the direction the crypts had lain. She'd discovered two buildings that might be above the catacombs. When she'd talked with the first building manager, the man had claimed no knowledge of the crypts.

A woman in her fifties managed the second structure. That building was renting out office space to small businesses.

"I don't know anything about crypts," the Armenian woman said in heavily accented English. She wore a long dress, a scarf, dramatic makeup and large hoop earrings. An unfiltered cigarette dripped ash from her mouth. "But there is storage space below."

Annja's spirits rose. "Could I see it?"

The woman looked from Annja to Charlie and then to Garin. His suit obviously inspired her.

"This job is a good one," she said. "I don't want to get into any trouble."

"You won't get into any trouble," Annja assured her.

"If I send you on your way," the woman replied, "I won't get into any trouble."

"We just need to—"

"How much do you want?" Garin's voice overrode Annja's. He reached into his jacket and pulled out a wallet thick with currency.

They haggled briefly, then a price was agreed upon.

"I always thought that place was creepy," the woman said. "I told my boss that I felt something down there wasn't right. He told me that it used to be part of the piracy network that filled the city. I believed him. At least, I thought I did. But I've never been at ease when I had to go down there for supplies. Is that what you're looking for? Ghosts?"

"No," Annja replied. "I'm not much of a believer in supernatural things." She knew that was ludicrous to say, especially in light of the fact that she carried a sword that had reforged itself.

The woman introduced herself as Naz as she reached for a huge ring with many door keys on it.

In the storage room, Naz slid one of the many wire racks to the side and revealed a heavy trapdoor in the floor.

"It's down here. My employer told me it was used a lot in the old days by pirates and black marketers. The building next door has access to the tunnel, too. They store things down there, as well." She kicked the door's iron ring. "But you're not going to find anything. Only extra supplies are down there."

"We're paying you to take a look," Garin said. "We'll be back quick enough."

Annja reached into her backpack and took out a flashlight. She switched it on. Then she leaned down and caught hold of the iron ring. As she pulled on the ring, she leaned back to put as much weight into her effort as she could.

Garin, a flashlight from his own pack in hand, caught the iron ring in his other hand and pulled. Together they lifted the trapdoor from the floor. There were no hinges. It came straight up. They placed it on the floor a short distance away.

Annja shone the flashlight into the opening. Irregularly spaced bricks jutted out to form hand- and footholds. The tunnel floor was at least ten feet down. It was made of brick, as well.

The thick stench of trapped, damp air filled Annja's nose. She took a final deep breath and climbed down.

"WE COULD GO IN after them," Drake suggested.

Salome took a deep breath, then focused on *not* exercising that option. "Is that how you'd handle it?"

Seated in the luxury car beside her, Drake shook his head. His gaze seemed centered on the mosque down the street.

"No," he said. "I'd be patient. We've got the building surrounded. They can't get back out of there without us knowing about it. It's better if we wait."

"Then why are you suggesting we go after them?" Salome tried not to let her anger show. They'd only just arrived in Istanbul after trailing Garin's plane around the world. Drake had a team on the ground in the city that had tailed Garin and Annja Creed from the airport. So far keeping watch over the woman had been easy.

"I'm not," Drake replied smoothly. "That course of action would be a mistake. If we flush them, try to catch them inside the building, we could lose them. There are too many hiding places and things will become hectic very quickly." He glanced over at the computer screen that showed the video surveillance they had on the building. "It's better if we're patient." He looked at her. "Better if you're patient."

"I know." Salome made herself breathe. It was hard.

"Besides, we don't know if Annja Creed has even found anything," Annja said.

"She does have a remarkable knack for finding things."

"Then let's hope she finds this thing for us." Drake took Salome's hand in his and kissed her fingers. "If she does, we're only a moment away from having it. It will be like we found it ourselves."

"I know." Salome made herself wait, but her eyes never left the computer screen. One way or the other, it wouldn't be long.

THE PASSAGE RAN a hundred feet and dipped slightly as it progressed.

Annja played her flashlight beam from side to side across the tunnel. It was almost ten feet tall and almost twelve feet wide. As Naz had informed her, there were a lot of boxes and crates in the tunnel that held supplies and equipment. There were also rats. Several of them squeaked and fled from the flashlight beams.

Concern tightened Charlie's features. Maybe there was even a little fear there. "We're very close now. You have to be very careful. The horn has been hidden away for a long time." He frowned. "It would have been better safely forgotten about."

The tunnel ended as it widened out into a room twenty-five feet across. Annja thought she could see where the stone had been chipped away for the crypts that had once honeycombed the walls. The dead had been laid in that place to wither away to dust. The thought chilled Annja for just a moment, then she concentrated on finding the entrance to the lower room.

If it existed.

She played her beam over the floor, searching for any kind of discrepancy that might reveal a hidden door. Nothing immediately met her eye. Whoever had put the room together had gone to considerable trouble to disguise the hidden level.

Charlie had dropped to his haunches against the wall in the entryway and simply watched. Annja didn't ask him why he wasn't helping. She just accepted that he wasn't going to.

Despite her thorough search, it was Garin who found the concealed access.

"Here," he called.

Annja got up from her hands and knees and went to him.

Garin aimed his flashlight beam at a section of the floor near one wall. That section looked like the rest of the ground except the symbol that had joined the three images from Thomopoulos's sketchbook showed on the floor. Garin wiped away layers of dust and spiderwebs to reveal it.

"I can't believe you found this," Annja said.

"Me neither." Garin shook his head. His eyes never left the spot on the floor.

"How did you find it?" Annja blew dust away in an effort to reveal an outline of the door she felt must be there.

"I *felt* it," Garin said. "I passed over this section of the ground, and I felt something under the floor."

"It's his nature," Charlie said. "He's been around artifacts like this before. He's sensitive to them."

Annja kept blowing dust until a crevice finally revealed

itself. As she blew, dust sifted through the crack and left behind a thin, empty line in the stone.

Satisfied that she'd found the secret of the floor, she reached into her backpack and took out a small pry bar that she'd packed for the excursion. She worked the bar around the floor section.

"There should be a release," Garin said.

"I know." Annja tried to keep the irritation out of her voice, but she knew she failed. "Sorry."

"It's all right. I feel the same way."

"Can you move the light over here?"

Garin did.

A moment later Annja found the locking mechanism. It was a simple pin construction that she easily negotiated. The mechanism slid a couple of inches, then clicked open. She pushed the pry bar under the edge and levered it up enough to wedge her fingers under.

When she lifted it, she stared down into the hidden chamber.

39

The chamber was thirty feet across and seven feet high. The low ceiling made Annja feel slightly claustrophobic after she dropped down inside and stood. She shone her flashlight around the space, and her breath froze in her lungs.

The room was filled with paintings, statues and books.

"I guess the church was better off than everyone thought," Garin said drily. He shone his flashlight around, as well, then followed it to stacks of goods.

"Many churches had wealth," Annja said automatically. "The Church of the Holy Apostles was ransacked by European forces in 1204 during the Fourth Crusade. They took everything they could find."

"Nothing's sacred when gold is involved," Garin said. "I've certainly taken my share of it when opportunity presented."

Annja politely refrained from saying anything.

"Why hasn't the old man come down?" Garin asked as he rummaged through the hidden treasure.

"I don't know."

"He acts like he's scared."

"Maybe he has good reason to be. Maybe we should be." Annja tried not to think like that too much.

"That's nonsense. All we had to do was beat Roux here. If you believe what that old man has been saying."

"Do you?" Annja asked.

Garin was silent for a moment. "I don't know."

"Some of the artifacts you and Roux have searched for have had incredible powers." That was the part that Annja kept trying to wrap her mind around. Her sword was proof of that.

"They have." Garin shifted a stack of crates one by one.

"What's the most powerful thing you've ever seen?"

"Other than your sword?"

"The sword can't be the most powerful thing," Annja said.

Garin looked at her. "You don't completely know what that sword is capable of. Or you wouldn't say that."

Annja conceded that.

"There are things you're not ready to deal with," Garin said.

"Yet I'm here looking for Gabriel's Horn."

"That's just one of the names the artifact we're searching for is called."

"I thought you didn't know anything about what we were looking for." Suspicion darkened Annja's thoughts.

"I didn't know what the painting hid," Garin corrected. "I know about the horn." He paused. "At least, I know part of the story."

"Can it destroy the world?" Annja asked.

Garin hesitated. "It's possible. What we're dealing with here, Annja, are very powerful things. Your sword alone caused me to live five hundred years. Think about that. And that isn't even what it was created for."

"What was it created for?"

"I don't know."

"Does Roux?"

"Maybe. You'd have to ask him."

"I have." Annja grimaced. "He's not exactly forthcoming."

Garin smiled. "He never has been. His business has always been his business."

"Do you know what the horn looks like?"

"I've never seen it," Garin said.

They began searching.

Annja spotted a battered wooden box tucked under bolts of rotting purple-colored silk. Nervously, she reached for the box. It was almost two feet square and a foot deep. A leather carrying strap had been affixed to either end. She somehow felt drawn to it.

"What's that?" Garin crossed over to her, feeling it, too.

"I don't know." Annja steeled herself and reached for the box. When she lifted it from the shelf, it was lighter than she expected. Cautiously, she slipped the simple latch and opened the box.

Inside, on what felt like a feather pillow, rested a horn. It was constructed of conical brass tubing bent into five complete circles. The tubing ran through its own center, as well, to provide handholds. There were no keys to change the pitch of the notes.

"This is it," Annja said quietly.

"Doesn't look like it's worth much," Garin observed.

Annja turned around and found Charlie standing there.

"Decided to join us, did you?" Garin asked.

"After you found the horn." Charlie nodded. "I wondered if you'd be foolish enough to try to blow it."

"It doesn't look overly complicated," Garin said.

Annja knew Garin was only taunting. She'd seen the respect—and maybe a little fear—in his eyes.

"You won't be able to touch it," Charlie said. "Only she can. She doesn't harbor the darkness in her heart that you do."

Garin cursed. Bah," he snarled. "Now that we've got it, what do we do with it. Destroy it?"

Charlie smiled. "You can't destroy that horn any more than you can Annja's sword."

"The English destroyed the sword," Garin said. "I saw that happen."

"The sword was destroyed, yet Annja carries it still." The old man's smile mocked Garin. "It would be the same with this horn."

Annja put the horn back inside the box and closed the lid. She set the latch, then slung the leather strap over her shoulder. "Maybe we should think about getting out of here before anyone else finds us."

She led the way.

SOMEONE SLAPPED Roux back to wakefulness. The pain stung sharply enough to get his attention even through the fogged recesses of his mind. A big man squatted before him. He struggled to remember where he was, then finally remembered he'd been shot with a Taser. His chest muscles still ached from the painful contractions triggered by the voltage.

"So you're still alive, are you, old man?" the big man taunted.

For a moment, because his vision hadn't yet returned to normal, Roux believed the man in front of him was Garin. The big man backhanded him across the face again. This time Roux tasted blood while his cheek and temple felt as though they had been set aflame.

Roux struggled to stand, but discovered that his hands were cuffed behind him. He lacked the balance. Fearlessly, he locked eyes with the man. "I promise you that you will die for that," he said.

The big man laughed, and his casual disregard only stoked the fires of Roux's rage. "You're in no position to be making threats, old man. And you're not going to live long enough to have any hope of making good on any of them."

Roux sat silent and proud. He and death were old friends. It did not scare him.

As he looked around, he discovered he was in the back of a large cargo truck. He tried to peer through the windows to figure out where he was.

He felt certain he was still in Istanbul. Surely he hadn't been unconscious long enough to be taken out of the country. There were no drugs in his system that he could tell.

Someone opened the back of the truck. Twilight had settled over the city. He also believed he was still downtown. Farther down the street, pools of neon light fought the encroaching darkness.

Saladin stood at the back of the truck. He glanced at the big man. "Get him out of there." He spoke in Arabic, either not knowing that Roux spoke the language, as well, or so convinced of his triumph that he didn't care.

40

The big man yanked Roux from the seat bolted to the truck wall and tossed him out. Roux tried to keep his feet under him, but it was impossible given the fact that his hands were bound behind him. His forward momentum was too great for him to handle.

Off balance, he smacked into the rough ground hard enough to knock the wind from his lungs. He was only able to keep his face from getting smashed by turning it to the side. A cut opened up over his right eye and oozed blood that blurred his vision.

Roux didn't try to get up. Instead, he looked around to get his bearings. The city was behind him. The Golden Horn stretched before him. The harbor and bay were filled with ships and freights. No one was close enough to see what was happening. Or perhaps no one cared. Istanbul was a dangerous city.

"Get him up," Saladin ordered.

The thug grabbed Roux roughly and yanked him to his

feet. Stubborn and defiant to the last, Roux stomped the man's instep hard. When the man howled in pain and bent down toward his foot, Roux head-butted him in the face and broke his nose with an audible crack.

Dazed, the man rocked back and collapsed onto his backside. His nose drained blood. Before anyone could move, Roux kicked the man in the mouth and broke several of his teeth. This time he fell back totally unconscious.

Saladin drew a pistol and pointed it squarely between Roux's eyes. "Keep it up and you'll die now."

Roux was tempted to push the fates. That was the way he'd done things when he was a young man. But that had been so long ago, and so much had changed.

Breathing raggedly, he stood straight and stared down the pistol barrel. He tested the cuffs binding his wrists but there was no give.

"Who knows?" Saladin asked. "If this goes right, maybe you'll even get to live."

Roux didn't respond.

"Annja Creed is here in Istanbul," Saladin said.

That surprised Roux.

"So is your friend Garin," Saladin continued.

He ran straight to her, Roux thought.

"I believe she's figured out how to decipher the Nephilim painting," Saladin said. "Salome believes so, too."

Roux grinned. "You've been following Salome."

Saladin smiled back. "Of course. In fact, I've got someone within her ranks. After all, we're all players in this little game. At the moment, Annja seems intent on following up an abandoned tunnel orphaned from the Church of the Holy Apostles. Do you know why?"

"No." Roux's mind raced. Had Annja truly found the horn?

Despite his predicament, excitement flowed through Roux's veins.

"Salome has managed to follow her," Saladin said. "She and those killers she employs are waiting outside the building they entered."

Fear for Annja replaced some of the excitement, but not all of it.

Saladin held out a cell phone. "I want you to call them."

"Why? So you can ransom me?" Roux shook his head.

"If you don't tell them," Saladin said, "they're going to walk into Salome's trap. I can assure you she won't show them any mercy." His dark eyes focused on Roux. "I give you my word, on the names of my ancestors, that Annja Creed will not die by my hand."

Roux knew that Saladin would honor his word. But he had no doubts that the man would also kill him as soon as it benefited him to do so.

"What do you want to do?" Saladin demanded.

Roux took a deep breath. There was no choice.

GARIN'S PHONE VIBRATED in his pocket as he and Annja replaced the trapdoor that led to the first tunnel.

The number was unknown to him. But the caller ID indicated it was Roux.

Garin frowned.

"What's wrong?" Annja asked.

"I've got a call from Roux."

"Answer it."

"The caller ID shows Roux's name," Garin said. "He wouldn't have a phone number in his name."

"What do you think it means?" Annja asked.

"It can't be anything good," Garin assured her.

"Answer it," Annja said.

The phone stopped ringing and the number faded.

"Too late," Garin said softly.

THE ANSWERING SERVICE picked up the call.

Roux smiled and pulled his head back from the phone. "Evidently he's busy."

"I'll call again." Saladin punched the redial key.

Idly, Roux glanced at the water in the harbor. It was only twenty feet away. He might be able to get there before Saladin's men gunned him down. He was quick. And he'd rather drown than be killed by his enemies.

The phone rang but this time Garin answered. "Hello."

Saladin pushed the phone toward Roux's face.

Roux spoke calmly and quickly. "You're surrounded in that building. Salome has people all around it."

"Where are you?"

"Saladin has me. He intends to trade me for whatever object you recovered."

Saladin grinned in anticipation.

"Personally," Roux said, continuing on in Latin, "I don't trust him. Get Annja and yourself out of there. Run and don't look—"

"Old fool!" Saladin snarled. He struck Roux in the face with his gun barrel and drove him to his knees.

Roux got his feet under him and tried to rush Saladin, but a man tripped him and another put his foot in the middle of Roux's back to pin him to the ground. Roux struggled, but he couldn't get up.

"Are you there?" Saladin demanded.

"I am." Garin's voice sounded cold and efficient. "Don't hurt him."

"I am sorely tempted. He is a most vexing man."

"I know, but you're not going to get what you want if he's killed."

Saladin let out a breath. "Do you have the treasure that the painting led you to?"

"Yes."

"You could be lying to me."

"I'm going to have to trust you not to put a bullet through Roux's head. You're going to have to trust me regarding the artifact."

"Very well."

"Is what Roux said about Salome true?"

"Yes."

"Are you coming here?"

"No. You will meet me at the harbor." Saladin gave directions.

"Getting out of here will be difficult," Garin said.

"I will be praying for your safety."

Garin's voice dripped sarcasm. "Great. And I'll tell you something else, Saladin. If you harm that old man, I will track you down if it's the last thing I do. You'll die a slow, horrible death."

Saladin grinned. "I look forward to meeting you. I'm told your ancestor killed my ancestor."

"It runs in the family," Garin agreed. "You keep that in mind. I'll see you as soon as I can."

The phone clicked dead.

Amused, Saladin put the phone in his pocket and gazed down at Roux. "Your son seems quite full of himself."

"You might be better off killing me," Roux said. The side of his face had swollen badly. "No matter how this turns out, Garin is going to kill you."

"He won't live long enough to do that," Saladin promised.

"And I'm not going to kill you until I get the treasure. In case your son decides to get cute while we're trading and wants to verify that you're still alive."

Garin would, Roux knew. And if he was dead, then maybe Garin and Annja would live. Calmly, Roux started voicing a litany of insults about Saladin, his parentage and everything else he could think of.

As he stood in the fourth-floor office of the building and surveyed the team waiting out in the street, Garin felt scared. It was the first time the emotion had touched him so hard in years.

"Are you going to be all right?" Annja asked. She stood at his side.

"We're trapped," Garin said.

"We can get out of the building unnoticed," Annja said. "There's another trapdoor in the next building."

They'd found it while searching for the hidden chamber. They'd also spotted another security team around the building and figured they belonged to Salome. Garin and Annja had caught sight of them at roughly the same time. Neither of them had taken their departure for granted.

"If we escape Salome, we're only going to meet Saladin's people and they'll kill us." Garin paused, then made himself voice the alternative because they both needed it said. "Or we escape and let Saladin kill Roux."

Annja frowned.

"Escape isn't an answer. Not if we're going to save Roux. And I'm not going to leave him in their hands," Garin stated.

"Neither am I. What about the men you have at the airport?"

"If they come in the helicopters, they're going to be seen. If they try to drive, it'll take too long." Garin nodded. "There's an army waiting out there. We just need to mobilize it." He grinned. "Do you feel lucky?"

"Do I have a choice?"

"No."

"What do you have in mind?"

"I'm going to go after Roux. You wait till you get my signal, then let Salome's people see you escaping from the building. The harbor is half a mile to the west. If you run fast and use the terrain, you can get there in a few minutes. Salome and her people will follow. If we get a break, Saladin and his warriors will come this way hoping to get their hands on the horn. If we get really lucky, they'll fight each other and we can escape in the confusion."

"How fast can you run?" Annja asked.

Garin looked at her. "I'm not going to—"

"Yes, you are. I'm smaller than you are. I should be able to get in closer. And if they see me, there's a chance they won't know who I am. For a while, anyway. You're too distinctive."

Garin started to argue.

"Garin," Annja said softly, "you know what I'm saying is true."

Garin cursed. He did know that.

"However you want to do this," Annja said, not challenging him, "we'll do it that way."

She knew not to try to argue with him. By leaving the decision totally in his hands, he had to take everything into consideration. He was a master strategist.

"All right," he said. "Just find Roux and take care of him. I don't want—"

"I know," Annja said. She turned to Charlie, who watched them both in silence. "Maybe it would be better if you sat this one out."

"I can't," Charlie said. "If the sleeping king gets his hands on the horn—"

"That's not going to happen," Annja said. She'd taken her computer and other devices from her backpack and stored the horn there. "It's not going to leave my sight."

"Okay," Charlie said. He didn't look happy, either.

"You've got your phone?" Garin asked.

Annja slipped the phone from her pocket, showed it to him and replaced it.

"Try not to get killed," he said.

"You, too," she replied. Then she stepped from the office they'd broken into and disappeared.

Careful of the window, Garin waited and tried to remain patient. But he wondered if they were all going to be dead before morning.

41

Escaping proved to be relatively simple. Annja accomplished it in minutes. If Roux hadn't been in Saladin's clutches, she thought, they all could have gotten out of the building easily. But there were just too many people involved in the pursuit of the Nephilim painting and its hidden treasure.

Of course, Annja reminded herself, that overabundance of enemies was going to work for them in just a few moments.

The plan was daring, but anything less wouldn't work. They had all agreed on that. Annja had been surprised at how quickly they had come to that agreement and that Garin wanted Roux to live.

Free in the alleys, Annja skirted Salome's guards and started to run. It was only half a mile to the bay. At least no one was shooting at her. Garin wouldn't have that luxury.

CHEST HEAVING and lungs burning, Annja stood in the shadows of the docks. She'd had to ask a fisherman repairing nets for directions to the berth where Saladin held Roux.

She took cover in the huge bulk of a freighter that was moored only a short distance from the truck Saladin had told Garin about. The proximity to the water was an unexpected bonus.

Heart rate and breathing once more at ease, Annja took out her phone and speed-dialed Garin.

"I'm here," Annja said. "Roux's alive. Give me two minutes to get into position, then get Salome's attention."

"Two minutes," Garin agreed. "Don't get yourself killed."

"You, either." Annja closed the phone and stored it in a waterproof section of her backpack. Then, keeping the freighter between her and Saladin's men, she lowered herself into the dark water and started swimming.

BY THE TIME the two agreed-upon minutes had expired, Garin and Charlie had taken up positions inside the adjacent building after coming up through the trapdoor.

Garin had pistols in both fists. He looked at the old man. "If you falter, I'm not going to stay behind to help you."

Charlie nodded. "You won't have to wait for me. You just need to concentrate on getting those people down to the harbor. And getting your people here in their helicopters." He paused. "I know you don't think so, but the real danger here isn't Salome and Saladin. It's—"

"The sleeping king. That's what you keep saying."

"The horn can't be allowed to fall into Roux's hands."

"That's not exactly the problem here, now, is it?" Garin didn't bother to hide his flaring temper. He turned his attention back to Salome's guards.

When he stepped from the shelter of the building, Garin felt as if a sniper's crosshairs fell over him. He was quite surprised when a bullet didn't crash through his skull.

He walked straight for the nearest guard. The man was stationed there with a small sedan. Another guard lounged behind the steering wheel.

Be patient, Garin reminded himself. Make sure of the kills. You don't want a bullet in the back.

The guard didn't pay any attention to Garin until he was within twenty feet of him. By that time, it was already too late.

Garin kept moving. He managed two more long strides before the guard reached for the weapon under his jacket. Garin recognized the Ingram MAC-10 submachine pistol as it came around on a sling.

Calmly, as if he had all day, Garin lifted his pistol and fired almost point-blank into the man's face. The shots sounded incredibly loud even against the backdrop of city noises.

As the man fell, Garin stepped to the sedan's door and hoped the glass wasn't bulletproof. He fired three times, centering on the driver's face.

The guard slumped against the door. Garin opened the passenger's door and slid across. Shouts from other guards reached his ears as he opened the driver's door and shoved the body out.

Charlie slid into the passenger's seat as Garin keyed the ignition and started the engine. Garin put his hand over the old man's head to push him down below the dashboard.

"Stay down," Garin growled. He pressed the accelerator and pulled out into the street as bullets peppered the sedan. Heart racing almost as quickly as the sedan's engine, he glanced in the mirrors and saw that Salome's gunmen had sprung into action.

Garin pulled up onto the sidewalk to avoid a line of cars waiting for the light to change. He crashed through an empty sidewalk café. Tables and chairs went to pieces and flew by the wayside. Something smashed into his windshield and shattered it. Crooked lines snaked across the glass.

He roared through the intersection and clipped the front end of a car when he went against the red light. But he made it. He just hoped that Annja and Roux were still alive.

ANNJA SWAM UNDERWATER to the harbor's edge where Saladin held Roux captive.

Roux lay face-first on the ground. A man stood nearby and kept one foot lodged firmly between his shoulder blades. Amazingly, Roux somehow knew she was there. His head turned in her direction and his eyes found her in the darkness.

His lips moved but no sound came forth. He said, "No."

Then gunfire broke out and Saladin's warriors braced for attack.

One of the men said something in Arabic. He pointed up the street at the building near where the mosque sat. His men relaxed a little, understanding that the threat wasn't to them.

The man spoke again, his tone indicating that he was giving orders this time. Most of the men crawled into nearby vehicles and quickly roared up the street. Evidently Saladin didn't want to lose out on his chance to get the treasure that the Nephilim painting promised.

The man in charge returned to Roux. "You keep the company of fools, do you know that, old man?" He kicked Roux hard.

Annja had to force herself to stay in the water. Finally, the man turned his attention toward the street. Police sirens had started to mix into the sounds of battle.

Quietly, Annja eased from the water. Her clothes felt like lead. She reached for the sword and drew it to her, preferring that weapon instead of the pistol sheathed on her hip. She eased her backpack off and left it on the ground.

None of the five men looked in her direction. Only Roux watched her.

Coldly, Annja focused on the sword and the way she planned to take the attack to them. She kicked the back of the leg of the man who held Roux trapped on the ground. With his support gone, the man started to fall. He yelled in warning as he twisted and caught a brief glance of Annja.

Holding the sword blade, Annja rammed the hilt into the man's forehead between his eyes. She knew these men were killers, but she would only kill if necessary. She had enough blood on her hands and wasn't eager to add more.

The hilt met the man's forehead with a dull thunk. His eyes went wide, then rolled back as he fell.

The next man turned around and swung his machine pistol toward her. She met the threat with steel, blocking the pistol, then driving an elbow into the bridge of the man's nose. Knowing the other men were trying to track her, Annja spun and lashed out with a foot. She swept one man's legs out from under him, and he flew backward.

The remaining two men opened fire. Annja stayed low. Their bullets chopped into the guard as he fell to the ground. By that time Annja had taken brief respite behind the truck. She flicked the sword out and cut the disposable plastic cuffs that bound Roux's wrists behind his back.

Without a word, Roux hurled himself forward for the fallen weapon of the first man Annja had downed. A shadow drifted around the corner of the truck.

Annja stood with the sword raised in both hands.

When the man came into sight, Roux opened fire with the MAC-10. The bullets drove the man backward in short stutter steps. Then he looked down at the bright blood staining his chest in disbelief. After that he didn't see anything at all.

Roux pointed along the side of the truck, urging Annja to get moving.

Annja gave Roux a quick nod, then went forward. There were at least two men left in the confusion of vehicles in the parking area. She'd lost track of both of them.

42

Garin dug his cell phone from his pocket, used the speed-dial function and held the instrument to his ear. "Where are you?"

"On our way, sir," his man responded. "Our ETA is less than two minutes." The sound of helicopter rotors provided a thundering backdrop to his words.

"Have you got GPS locks on myself and the two people with me?"

"Yes, sir."

"Then make sure you don't shoot us in the confusion." Garin closed the phone before the man had time to reassure him that that wouldn't happen.

A sports car shot up next to Garin. He didn't recognize it, but he recognized Salome sitting in the passenger's seat. He also recognized the assault rifle she held in her deadly hands.

God, how he hated her, he thought. He'd never been able to get along with her when she'd worked with Roux. Now he wanted nothing less than her death.

Knowing he couldn't outrun her, he stomped on the brakes

just as she opened fire. The bullets beat a savage rhythm along the front end of the car, then started chipping the street.

For a moment Garin felt pleased that his surprise maneuver caught the man driving the sports car off guard. Then the left front tire, obviously punctured one or more times, unraveled and dropped the bare metal rim on the asphalt. The rim chewed into the asphalt, then dug in.

Garin knew that he'd lost control. The steering wheel jerked and shivered in his grip. The wheels locked and the car turned sideways, then flipped.

Desperate, Garin threw himself toward the passenger's side. He put a hand over Charlie to hold the old man in place because he wasn't wearing a seat belt. The car rolled over and over.

Finally it skidded to a stop. Garin hung upside down, trapped by the seat belt. The succession of impacts left him dazed and disoriented.

The sports car braked to a halt only a few feet away. The lights shone inside the overturned car and nearly blinded Garin. He watched helplessly as Salome and a man he didn't know got out. The smell of gasoline filled the air.

A BULLET RICOCHETED from the asphalt parking area less than an inch from Annja's left foot. She knew immediately that one of the gunners had dropped to his knees on the other side of the truck and tried to take her out by shooting her feet. She'd gotten lucky.

Annja scrambled to the top of the truck's hood and climbed to her feet. The fast move caught the gunner off guard. Still on the ground, his gun hand thrust under the truck, the man looked up in surprise and tried to bring his weapon to bear.

Annja dropped down beside him. One kick cleared the

pistol from his hands. The follow-up kick, delivered to his temple, rendered him unconscious.

She sensed the movement behind her, rather than her side. She tried to move, but what felt like a sledgehammer slammed into the side of her head. Her knees turned to rubber and nearly gave way beneath her. The sword disappeared from her lax grip.

Blood trickled down the side of her neck. She knew from the spreading warmth that she had been shot. Fear screamed through her because she wanted to know how bad the wound was. If the bullet entered her brain, could she still function?

She didn't know the answer to that. For all she knew, she was dying. But she also knew that she could move—just not very well. She slid sideways, tried to bring the sword to her but failed. Her concentration had to be sharper. She lifted her hands before her and wondered where Roux was. He should have been in a perfect position to shoot the man advancing on her.

"You think you're clever, don't you?" the man demanded. Anger pulled his face into a ruthless mask. "Now you've gone and gotten yourself killed."

"You were going to kill us anyway," Annja said.

Farther up the street, the sounds of battle—gunfire and the screams of wounded people—continued.

Annja concentrated on Saladin, for she was sure that's who he was. He was smart with the pistol. He stayed just out of reach of a punch or kick.

"I was," Saladin said agreeably. "That old man owes me blood. No negotiations or treasures would've gotten him out of that. Or anyone who claimed him as a friend. All of your lives were forfeit."

Annja struggled to clear her head and get her balance back, but the pounding pain inside her head didn't ease. Blood continued to spill down her neck and chest. Why doesn't Roux shoot him? Then a bad thought entered her head as she remembered that she'd left the backpack and the horn near the water's edge.

Saladin extended his arm and took deliberate aim. Annja knew he wasn't going to wait any longer. Risking everything, she raced at Saladin. The closer to him she got, the more he'd have to move to compensate. If she'd tried to run away, the adjustment would have been small.

She ducked and rolled, landing on her shoulder and then shoving herself up on her hands. Her left foot caught Saladin in the chest and knocked him to the ground.

The pain in Annja's head increased. Nausea spun through her stomach. She thought she was going to be sick. Instead of neatly recovering, she rolled awkwardly and managed to get to a seated position.

Saladin had maintained his hold on his pistol. He pointed the weapon at her while he shoved himself to his feet. He didn't try to make any last-minute death threats or promises. He was just going to shoot her until she was dead.

Annja focused on the sword, imagined it in her hand and felt it there. As soon as the familiar weight was at the end of her arm, she reversed her grip on the hilt and threw the sword like a spear.

The sword flashed across the distance and thudded home in Saladin's chest. He staggered back, staring down at the sword in surprise.

Annja called the sword back to her. Immediately blood poured from Saladin's body once the wound was undammed.

The pistol tumbled from Saladin's fingers and he fell.

On her feet, sword in hand, Annja jogged to the back of the truck. But everything she'd feared was true.

Roux was gone. So was her backpack.

"GARIN, ARE YOU still alive?"

Hanging upside down in the car, Garin didn't answer. He tried to break the seat belt lock, but it held stubbornly. Then he noticed one of the pistols he'd thrown onto the seat when he'd taken the car.

Salome knelt down and folded one arm around her knees. She held a pistol in her other hand. Her smile seemed joyful and insane at the same time.

"Good," she said. "You're still alive. I was worried that the crash had killed you."

A man came to stand beside her. He held a pistol in his fist.

The sound of helicopter rotors suddenly blasted across the street. There were four of them and they made a lot of noise.

Salome and the man looked up.

Garin didn't blame them. If he hadn't been the cause of the helicopters being there, he probably would have looked up, too. But only after he'd killed the man he'd gone there to kill.

With a twist, Garin freed his shoulder and scooped the pistol up from the roof of the car. He hoped the safety was off as he shoved it toward Salome. She had to die first. Even if the man killed him, Garin was determined the woman wasn't going to live another moment. Not after the way she'd betrayed Roux and nearly killed him.

His movement must have caught her attention. She looked down just as he leveled the pistol. She tried to bring her own weapon into play, but Garin squeezed off a shot that caught her in the throat.

Knocked backward by the bullet, as well as her own frightened reaction, Salome tried to scream and couldn't. Her lifeblood poured between her fingers.

The unexpected sight froze the man in his tracks. Instead of shooting Garin, the man dived for Salome.

Mercilessly, Garin empted the clip into the man. He sprawled across Salome and held her in his numb embrace as she breathed out her last time.

Charlie popped up and Garin pointed the pistol at the old man and pulled the trigger three times. Only then did he realize the pistol was empty.

"It's all right," Charlie said. He slashed the seat belt with a pocketknife. "We've got to get out of here. We have to stop the sleeping king."

We've got to get out of here before this gasoline catches fire, Garin thought. He scrambled through the smashed window, but the top had crushed slightly and the fit was tight. His efforts ripped his clothes.

When he was on his feet, he reached back for Charlie and pulled the old man through.

"Are you all right?" Garin asked as he led the old man away from the overturned car.

Without warning, the vehicle exploded and became wrapped by flames.

"I'm fine. But we need to find Annja and the sleeping king."

All around them, door gunners mounted in the helicopters marked Salome's men and shot them down. They did the same for Saladin's fighters. The street became a battle zone littered with bodies.

Garin's phone rang and he answered it. "Annja?"

"It's Roux," Annja gasped.

Sickness swirled inside Garin's head. He couldn't believe the old man was dead.

"He's got the horn," Annja went on.

"The sleeping king has the horn," Charlie echoed. "We have to stop him. We have to save the world."

"Where did he go?" Garin asked.

"He stole a boat. I couldn't get to him in time."

Garin looked up at the helicopters hovering overhead. "We'll get him. Stay where you are."

Annja stared helplessly as the boat chugged away from the dock. The distance was already too far for her to catch up.

Police sirens screamed. When she looked back at the city, she spotted the flaming car at the center of it. Several police cars were already on the scene. She knew others would crowd the harbor once they realized the battle had stretched that far.

Then one of the helicopters retreating from the downtown area descended overhead. It hung only ten feet above her.

Garin waved to her from the cargo area.

Annja jumped and caught the rope ladder, then she pulled herself up. She got herself secure and pointed at the motorboat.

Garin nodded and talked briefly over the headset he wore. The helicopter streaked after the boat and overtook it within seconds. Carefully, the pilot held his craft only a few feet above the boat.

Roux tried evasive techniques, but the craft he'd stolen was too ponderous to do much. He angrily waved them off.

Annja leaned forward into the wind, judged the distance and

jumped. She landed on the boat's deck and felt as if she'd driven her legs up into her hips. She caught herself on her hands.

A heartbeat later, Garin landed beside her. Together, they walked toward Roux.

He looks different, Annja couldn't help but think. He was bloodied and worn. Madness danced in his eyes.

"You shouldn't have come," he shouted over the roar of the engine and the helicopter's rotor wash. "You should have stayed away."

"What are you doing, Roux?" Annja asked.

"I'm going to fix what never should have happened," Roux declared.

Annja focused on her backpack sitting at Roux's feet. All she had to do was get it. Not that she believed any of the nonsense about saving the world.

As if reading her thoughts, Roux revealed the MAC-10 he was holding. "If you come any closer, if you try to take the horn from me, I'll kill you, Annja. I swear that I will."

Annja stopped moving and spread her hands. She couldn't believe what was happening.

Beside her, Garin froze, as well. "Are you going to shoot us, Roux?" he challenged.

"I will," Roux said. "I've searched for this for over four hundred years. Ever since she died tied to that stake." Pain pulled at his face. "It's my fault that she died there. She wasn't supposed to die. She was supposed to live. She was supposed to do great things. I destroyed that."

"Joan's death wasn't your fault," Annja said.

"It was," Roux said. "I was supposed to be with her. I let my own interests deflect me. I lost her and I cursed us."

"This isn't what you've stood for, Roux. All those years I followed you around, all those people we fought for, all those lost causes. You were always the good one. You've always been on the side of the angels," Garin said.

Roux shook his head. "It wasn't always that way. In my day, in my time, I've been every bit as black hearted as you are, Garin. Maybe more so. I had people who showed me how to live my life. You had no one."

Garin took another step. "I had you."

"Capricious fates," Roux argued. "I wasn't prepared to be either a father or a mentor. I took you because I didn't want to prepare my own meals anymore."

"No," Garin said. "You cared for me. I know that you did. You took in a small boy whose own father had turned away from him."

"Why are you doing this?" Annja demanded.

Roux pointed the pistol at her. "Stay out of this, Annja."

Roux took a fresh grip on his pistol and shifted his aim back to Garin. "This needs to be done, Garin. Our lives— mine, yours and Annja's—don't matter in the long run."

Without warning, Charlie jumped from the helicopter.

Roux was momentarily distracted.

"Annja," Charlie said, "draw your sword." There was steel in the old man's voice. "Do it now!"

Annja reached for the sword, and it was in her hand. She held it up before her, wondering whether she could truly attack Roux if it came down to that.

Roux stared at the blade.

"Remember the sword," Charlie said. "You searched for the pieces. You found them. You found the woman who is yet to face the evil that is let loose in this world."

Roux wavered.

"Joan's sacrifice wasn't just for that time and that world," Charlie said. "It was for you and for Annja and for this world, too. This world also needs protection. You know that. You've felt the evil loose here. Without that sacrifice in the past, there would be no one now to combat that."

Roux lowered his pistol. "What am I supposed to do?"

"You know what you're supposed to do," Charlie said. "You've always known. The horn wasn't meant to stay in this world."

Roux looked at Annja's bag. Then, without warning, he flung it far out into the sea.

epilogue

Annja woke later than she'd intended to. The alarm by her bed showed that it was after 3:00 p.m. She realized she must have slept through her automated wake-up call.

And neither Roux nor Garin had come to interrupt her. That was surprising.

She showered quickly and dressed in some of the clothes Garin had ordered delivered to their rooms. It was good to be rich, she'd decided. Maybe someday she'd work on that.

After she was dressed, she tried calling Garin and Roux. Neither of them answered, but that wasn't surprising, either.

Famished, Annja decided to find something to eat. If the others were sleeping, she could grab something by herself.

She found Charlie sitting outside her room in the hallway. He was reading Stanley Younts's latest thriller novel.

"Good morning," he said. He turned down a page to mark his spot.

Annja hated to see anyone do that to a book, but she smiled. "Good afternoon. Have you been out here long?"

Charlie shrugged and smiled. "A little while." He nodded at the large window at the end of the hallway. "It's a nice place to get indirect sunlight. I thought I'd take advantage."

Annja settled her backpack over her shoulders. Garin had seen to having one of his security people recover her personal belongings and replace her knapsack. They had arrived with the new clothes.

"Have you seen Roux and Garin?" she asked.

"They're gone," Charlie said.

"Where did they go?"

Charlie shook his head. "I don't know. They had things to take care of."

"Of course they did," Annja grumbled.

"I'd like to take you to eat. If you'd allow me," Charlie said.

Annja sighed. "Okay."

Charlie offered his arm in a gallant manner. She took it and he led her to the elevator bank.

"Did you sleep well?" he asked.

"I did. Too well. I should have been up before now."

"Nonsense. You've had quite an adventure."

Annja grinned wryly at him.

"What do you think would have happened if Roux had tried to use the horn?" she asked.

"Perhaps nothing." Charlie sighed. "Maybe he would have gotten hurt. That wouldn't have been a good thing. Or he'd have had to realize that he'd chased something that didn't exist for hundreds of years."

"That could have been disturbing."

"I know. But it didn't work out that way."

They left the elevator and crossed the spacious lobby to the restaurant Annja had spotted on her arrival last night. The food smells put a razor edge on her hunger.

Within a few minutes, they were seated at a table. Both of them ordered from the breakfast menu.

"You're a complicated man," Annja observed.

"Thank you." Charlie smiled. "I wasn't always homeless. I've had a rather eventful life." He sipped the glass of orange juice the server brought to him. "In the meantime, you need to realize that time in this world has been forever altered."

"Oh?" Annja raised an eyebrow.

"The sword," Charlie said. "You won't believe how many lives have been saved since the day that you picked it up. Or how many have yet to be saved."

"This is all a little over my head."

"Perhaps for now," Charlie agreed. "But there will come a time when all of this is plain to you."

"What about you?" Annja asked.

"What about me?"

"Am I going to see you again?"

"Perhaps, but I also hope it won't be under such dire circumstances."

"Am I ever going to know who you truly are?"

"A friend, Annja. I'm just a friend. You, Roux and Garin are all inextricably linked in events that are going to be important to the world. Danger will come at you from all quarters. Every now and again, you're going to need a friend."

Annja silently agreed with that. "Okay," she said. "I can always use a friend. Especially when I'm spending time with those two."

Charlie laughed. "Make no mistake. They love and hate each other at times, but that's how it is between fathers and sons in every family."

"Most of them don't try to kill each other, though."

"No. They don't. What you've got, Annja, is a very special

family." Charlie regarded her. "And that's what they are to you. Never forget that."

"I'm beginning to understand that," Annja replied. And, despite the danger and duplicity—and the fact that she always seemed to be the last one to know Roux and Garin's secrets—that thought warmed her heart.

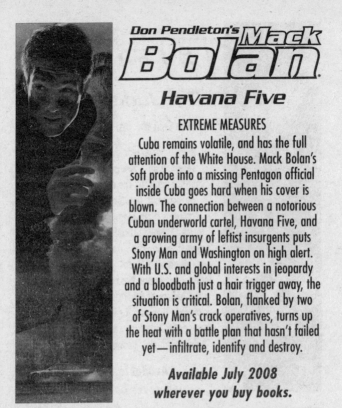

ROOM 59

THE HARDEST CHOICES
ARE THE MOST PERSONAL....

New recruit Jason Siku is ex-CIA, a cold, calculating agent with black ops skills and a brilliant mind—a loner perfect for deep espionage work. Using his Inuit heritage and a search for his lost family as cover, he tracks intelligence reports of a new Russian Oscar-class submarine capable of reigniting the Cold War. But when Jason discovers weapons smugglers and an idealistic yet dangerous brother he never knew existed, his mission and a secret hope collide with deadly consequences.

Look for

THE ties THAT BIND

by

cliff RYDER

GOLD EAGLE ®

Available October 2008
wherever books are sold.

www.readgoldeagle.blogspot.com

GRM594

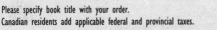

JAMES AXLER

DEATH LANDS®

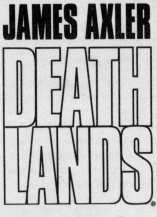

Thunder Road

Fight or die in the raw and deadly frontier of tomorrow…

Thunder Rider is a self-styled superhero, prowling the Deathlands and serving up mass murder in a haze of napalm and nerve gas. Ryan Cawdor accepts a bounty from a ravaged ville to eliminate this crazed vigilante. But this twisted coldheart has designs on a new sidekick, Krysty Wroth, and her abduction harnesses the unforgiving fury of Ryan and his warrior companions. At his secret fortress, Thunder Rider waits—armed with enough ordnance to give his madness free rein….

In the Deathlands, justice is in the eyes of those who seek it…

Available September wherever you buy books.